ALICE
IN
FAELAND

A.L. KESSLER

ALICE IN FAELAND

Histria SciFi & Fantasy

Las Vegas ◊ Chicago ◊ Palm Beach

Published in the United States of America by
Histria Books
7181 N. Hualapai Way, Ste. 130-86
Las Vegas, NV 89166 USA
HistriaBooks.com

Histria SciFi & Fantasy is an imprint of Histria Books encompassing outstanding, innovative works in the genres of science fiction and fantasy. Titles published under the imprints of Histria Books are distributed worldwide.

Library of Congress Control Number: 2025930141

ISBN 978-1-961511-95-8 (softbound)
ISBN 978-1-961511-94-1 (eBook)

"I'm having that dream again." Allie looked out the large glass window, studying how the cars lined up in nice neat rows in the parking lot below. "The one where I'm playing checkers with strange-looking seeds as the pieces. Sitting under a giant mushroom, across from the girl in the red dress."

"Those are just dreams, Allie. We've had this discussion."

Just dreams. A constant reminder that she'd never met that girl. She'd never played checkers with the black and red seeds, under the purple mushroom...but she *had* done all that. Only, no one believed her. "Then why does it feel so real?"

The reflection of her therapist in the window shifted her crossed legs as she wrote something on her clipboard. Her face held the calm fake smile in place, giving Allie no hint of what she was thinking. "When you first had these dreams, it was after extreme trauma. It was a way for your mind to deal with the tragedy of losing your brother in that accident."

That accident. Her parents never seemed to have recovered from Brendyn not coming home. They'd found Allie covered in dirt, terrified because her brother had fallen.

Allie's heartbeat picked up at the mention of her brother not returning with her. That seemed so long ago now.

She swallowed as she forced herself to focus on the now. Allie took a deep breath to calm the pounding of her heart. "Dr. Black, this feels like more. It feels real."

"Vivid dreams are like that. You need to find a way to ground yourself in reality. What about taking some classes?" Dr. Black flipped a page, looking back at past notes. "I know you don't want to commit to college right now, but a casual class would help you focus on something else."

Allie rolled her eyes and watched as a car parked unusually crooked in the row of straight cars. "I'm looking into an art class," she said honestly. Dr. Black had always encouraged her to find something just for her.

"Art would be good for you. If you want, we can start some art therapy. Maybe it'll help pull those images from your dreams."

That didn't sound like a bad idea. Allie was about to speak when the buzzer went off, signaling that they needed to wrap up the session.

Allie turned around and faced her therapist.

Dr. Black's glasses were perched on top of her blond hair as she made a note. She looked up at Allie, the crinkles at the corner of her blue eyes grew as she smiled. "I have you scheduled for the same time next week; is that correct?"

Like her parents would let her get out of it. "Yes."

"I want you to keep a notebook of the dreams and think of some of the images you might want to bring to the page for art therapy."

"Okay." She had nothing else to say. It wasn't anxiety, or trauma, or anything else in her head. That world was real, as real as Dr. Black was, with her bright blue eyes and curly blond hair. If Dr. Black wanted her to bring those images to the page, she would. It'd be the only proof that world existed.

The girl in the red dress was real.

Cerise was real.

Allie walked out of the office and found her mom playing some game on her phone. "Ready?" Allie asked, and her mom looked up.

Her brown eyes were a shade darker than Allie's, and her hair matched. She smiled. "Of course. How was your session?"

"It was okay."

She kissed Allie on the forehead even though they were the same height, and Allie cringed a little, but in her heart she loved that her mom still showed her affection like that. "Okay, let me know if you want to talk about anything."

Allie knew how that would go over. It'd be the same thing that the therapist would say. None of those dreams are real. "Can we get coffee?"

"Of course. It wouldn't be therapy day without a cup of coffee after."

They walked to the car as clouds rolled over the sky, blocking out the sun. A shiver crawled over Allie's back, and out of the corner of her eye something moved. She turned to catch a better look and paused. Nothing there.

Her mom put a hand on her shoulder and urged Allie forward. "Just a rabbit, Allie. Come on, let's get in the car before the rain lets loose."

Just a rabbit.

Allie looked around the parking lot to see if she could spot it. Rabbits weren't unusual around here, with their little fluffy tails and their floppy ears, but the white one staring back at her from across the spaces felt different.

Familiar almost. Like the one that Brendyn and she had chased.

"Allie?" her mom called, with her car door open.

Allie got into the car and looked away from the rabbit as she buckled up.

White rabbits were common. There was nothing different about how this one looked.

No, she felt different. Like she was waiting for Allie to do something.

Allie sat on the floor of her room with her sketchpad on her lap. Her pencil moved across the pages almost of its own accord. The lines overtook her thoughts and she let them guide her hand. The shapes became clear and the image in her head transposed itself onto the paper.

The white rabbit.

But not as the creature she'd seen today, no. This was a teenager, her back leaned against the stalk of a giant mushroom, her face tilted down as she examined the clock in her hands. Her long white hair fell from down her back. She wore a vest that the pocket watch chain trailed from, dress pants and black shoes. This was the white rabbit Allie was familiar with.

She pulled out her colored pencils and markers to finish the drawing when a knock interrupted her flow.

She let out a frustrated growl. "Yes?"

Her mom looked in. "Hey, dinner's just about done. Get to a stopping point?"

Allie glanced down at the picture that she'd poured her time into for the majority of the night. "Um, yeah, I can stop now." Or she wouldn't stop at all, and she'd never hear the end of it. She put her sketchbook down on the ground and gave the White Rabbit one last look before she went downstairs.

Her dad placed the plates down on the table as Allie sat down.

The light shined off the curve of his bald head. Allie couldn't remember a time when he had hair. Occasionally he'd grow a beard, but now he was clean shaved, which made him look younger. "What are your plans for tomorrow?" he asked as he sat down.

Allie shrugged one shoulder. "I was thinking about stopping by the community college to see what art classes they have to offer. Maybe go for a walk in the park across the street."

"I think that's a great idea. Maybe peek your head into some places to see if they are hiring?" Mom asked.

Allie was about to answer that she would, when her dad cut her off.

"An art class? That would be good for you, and don't worry about looking for a job. If you're looking into classes, I'd rather you focus on that." He'd been pushing off her looking for a job any time she expressed interest. He preferred Allie to be close to home. Sometimes she thought he was worried she'd just disappear, like Brendyn did.

"Yeah, okay. I drew another picture tonight." She pushed her broccoli around the plate, surrounding her mashed potatoes with it.

"I can't wait to see it." Her mom smiled. "Digital or traditional media?" She always encouraged Allie, despite what the subject was, which was helpful. Her dad tried, but his praise came across as forced. He'd expressed once that he just didn't understand what she created.

It was like mom got her and dad lived in a whole other world.

"The white rabbit."

Her mom's smile faded a little around the edges and worry crossed her eyes. "From your dreams?"

"Yeah."

"You haven't drawn any of those characters for a while. Not since we moved." Her dad put his fork down and glanced at mom. Three years ago, we'd moved into the city, out of the mountains where the accident had happened.

Her mom recovered her thoughts and her smile was back in place. "I can't wait to see how the character design has improved."

"Thanks, I like it." Allie busied herself with eating and not bringing up any more thoughts or comments about her dreams. The air seemed heavy with tension while her parents also ate silently. There was no chatter about how work was, or how their day went. They just sat there in silence.

And it was weird.

She went straight to do dishes as soon as she finished her dinner. Her drawing kept calling her back and it would give her a chance to avoid the awkward silence between her parents. The sooner she finished the dishes, the sooner she could lose herself in the art again.

She started the dishwasher and ran up the stairs to go back to her drawing.

Except, it wasn't there.

She looked around the normal places she would have stashed it. Dug in the drawers where she hid all the drawings and notes she didn't want her parents to see.

Nowhere.

She flipped through the sketchbook that she knew she was working in, but the page was gone. The page under it was clean and smooth, like she hadn't been drawing on top of it.

Where was it?

A strange sinking feeling filled her stomach, and she sat on the floor where she'd been working. The mirror across the room gleamed like a light hit it, catching her attention. Allie stood and walked over to it and found her image taped to it. Where it hadn't been before.

Her heart pounded. Who was in her room? What could move so fast to put it on the frame of the mirror without her noticing? Without making a sound?

She pulled the image off and turned the drawing over.

"The Red Princess formally invites The Alice back to her land for a tea party." -Oriana

Allie stared at the note and sat down in front of the mirror. This was impossible. Or was it? Just a few hours ago, hadn't she been convinced that what she'd seen in her dreams was real? Oriana, the white rabbit, Cerise, the Red Princess, they were real. And now they were asking Allie to come back.

The only problem was, she didn't know how to get back to the fae world. The first time Allie and Brendyn fell through a hole trying to catch Oriana. After that, Cerise had always pulled Allie through with magic. But Cerise had once said something about how Allie could return to Fairy on her own.

The memories of the words wouldn't come to her. She let out a frustrated growl and shoved her sketchbook and the drawing away from her. Maybe she'd remember in her sleep tonight, maybe the dreams would tell her.

Oriana reappeared through the portal and adjusted her white hair behind her pointed ears. She'd been cutting it close in Alice's room when she'd written the note and hung the picture. The human couldn't see her, not yet, but it was important that Alice get that note.

"Did you do it?" Devlin pushed off the stem of a mushroom. His red hair curled out from under his green hat, covering most of his pointed fae ears, and his matching tailcoat flared out around him as he stepped forward, his boots making no sound on the ground.

"Yes, let's hope that Cerise doesn't find out or she'll be furious."

"Alice is the only hope that Cerise has right now. The woman has gone mad, and bringing back Alice is the only way to stop Cerise's rampage." Devlin shook his head. "So it's worth the risk. Hopefully, Alice remembers how to get back here."

"And if she can't?"

"Then we give her another clue. Lead her to the answer again."

Oriana snorted. "I am not turning into a rabbit to lure her again."

"First off, that was by accident, second off, I think she's too old for that trick." He laughed.

Oriana crossed her arms. "You'd be surprised what humans chase after."

"Hmm." Devlin shoved his hands into his pockets. "So now we wait for Alice?"

"Now we wait for Alice." Oriana turned toward the black castle on the hill. Red and black storm clouds gathered around it, and she swallowed. "And we hope she comes soon."

The storm crashed against Allie's window as she turned on her side, trying to sleep through the thunder and the clacking of tree branches against glass. Turning over didn't help much—now the shadows danced on the wall, giving her illusions of people walking through a forest.

Lightning flashed, followed by house-shaking thunder. She grumbled and got out of bed, wrapping her blue blanket around herself. She draped part of it over her head. Allie pulled the blanket tight around her as she went to the kitchen.

Maybe some tea would help her get to sleep and stay asleep. This storm was ridiculous. She paused at another silhouette in the kitchen already leaning over the tea kettle. "Dad?"

He turned around with a mug in his hand and steam rising from it. "Oh, hey sweetie. Weather keeping you up?"

"Yeah, will you make me a mug too?"

"Of course." He turned back around and grabbed a mug from the shelf above his head.

Allie sat at the table and waited while her dad fixed the mug and he sat with her.

Another crack of thunder had her flinching and her dad reaching across the table for her hand.

"Remember when we used to watch the storms roll in together? We'd sit on the porch?"

She let the warmth of the memory wash over her. They'd sit on the step of the porch and watch the clouds roll from one area to another. With each flash of lightning, they'd count together until the sound of thunder crossed the sky. "Yeah, it was the coolest thing because we could see the sheet of rain coming towards us."

He smiled. "The storms are a bit different here, aren't they?"

"Louder," she offered. "Stronger."

Her dad squeezed her hand. "We'll get used to them here."

He told her that every storm, every year. Like the thunder and lightning hadn't been the same since they left their old house.

She sipped her tea and watched the raindrops race down the window. "How can mom sleep through them?"

Dad laughed. "Your mother has done her time being up late at night; now she sleeps like the dead."

Allie opened her mouth to say something, but the sound of crashing glass echoed through the house. The flash of light and booming thunder came through the house and the fading sound took the lights with it.

Allie swallowed as her dad took her hand.

"It's okay, Alice, take a deep breath."

She gave herself a moment to let her eyes adjust to the darkness. "What was the crashing noise?"

"Maybe a window upstairs." He started walking forward. "Come on, the flashlight's on the fridge."

She held tight to his hand as he led her to the fridge, and a moment later, a steady beam of light shone in front of her.

Instantly, her chest loosened. They made their way to the stairs and her dad motioned for her to go first. If it had been a window, shouldn't the storm be louder? There was no sign of the wind whipping through a room, or louder rain.

With each step her mind raced to the worst-case scenario. Had a tree fallen on the roof? How could her mother sleep through the crashing noise? Had the tree crushed her mother?

No, all of that would have made a louder noise. She pushed her door opened and found that her mirror had fallen over. She glanced at her dad before walking further in.

"Careful, you don't want to cut your feet on any glass." He swept the light over the room and she expected to see it reflecting off the broken mirror pieces, but there was nothing there.

Allie slowly picked up the mirror by the edge and put it back up on its feet. Her dad stepped up next to her and shined the light on it. The glass had spider webbed across the surface, except...

She put her finger against the strange tinted glass pieces to see if it was really pushing out away from the mirror.

"It almost looks like something hit it from the other side," her dad whispered. He glanced at her window when the lightning flashed again, but Allie kept her gaze on the mirror, and when the lightning shone again, she caught a glimpse of another face. One with wide green eyes and a wicked grin that meant trouble.

They were calling for her to come back. And now she remembered how.

CHAPTER 2

"Once upon a time, there was a girl named Alice and she followed a white rabbit down a rabbit hole with her brother and found an entire new world." The girl in the red dress giggled and leaned back on her hands. Allie squatted and contemplated her next checker move, for checkers was a serious game.

"Quiet, I'm trying to think." Allie picked up the black seed and jumped it over two red seeds. "Ha! King me!"

"Queen me." Cerise drew out the word queen. "There are no kings in my court right now. Only a queen." She picked up her red piece and set it back down. "Oriana says you have to go home soon."

Allie wrinkled her nose. "I don't want to go home. I want to stay here with you and Kit and have tea parties and play games." She flung herself backwards and stared at the sky. "Home is boring."

"Yes, but Dor says that your parents miss you and are looking frantically for you." Cerise crossed her arms. "So it's time for you to return, but...if you want to come back and play, the looking glass is where I can be found."

Allie sat up and titled her head to one side. "The looking glass?"

"A mirror silly, if you know the words, any mirror will lead you *here, or back to the human world. You don't have to tumble down a rabbit hole to get here." Cerise grinned.*

"And how will I know the words?"

"I'll write them down for you. Put it in a safe place when you get home. It'll be our secret." Cerise held her fingers over her lips as if saying shush.

"Where did I put it? Where did I put it?" Clothes flew over Allie's head as she yanked each piece out of her drawers and threw it. She knew she had kept the weird paper she'd found in her pocket the night her parents found her.

It was an iridescent green, with lines that reminded her of a leaf. She could see it in her mind, the writing was silver, Cerise had written it with a fancy pen with a bright pink feather. She'd never needed it until now, because Cerise had always pulled her through with her own magic.

"Come on," Allie growled when she got to the bottom of her last drawer.

"Alice, what are you doing?" Her dad's voice came from behind her, and she squealed and spun around.

"I'm looking for something." She looked at the mess around her and then up at the disapproving face of her father. "I'll clean up the mess in a few minutes," she promised. "There's a piece of paper I've had for a long time and I'm afraid I lost it."

"Okay, typically when you're this focused on something you don't make this big of a mess." He motioned to the pile of clothes on the floor.

She ran her hand through her hair and let out a long growl. "It's super important."

"Then you should have put it in a safe place." He crossed his arms. "Allie, you know—"

"Yes yes, I know. Write stuff down, put it in a safe spot. Everything has a home." She started picking up her laundry and shoving it in her drawers until she saw him raise his brow. She let out a frustrated huff and started folding it before putting it back in the drawer.

Her dad echoed her sigh. "Okay, look, when you hide papers, you typically put them in a book. Try looking in your bookshelf. He walked out as she turned to say something smart-assed back, but then she stopped as she considered his comment.

He had a point. The question was, what book would she have deemed worthy enough for that secret?

She sat in front of her the lower shelves of her bookcase and ran her fingers over the titles. Most of the books showed lined spines from being read over and over. She paused at a leather-bound version of *Grimm's Fairy Tales* and pulled it out. She flipped through the pages and sure enough, tucked in the back was the paper she was looking for.

The silver writing caught the light and seemed to shiver over the veins of the paper. The green had darkened from what she remembered, the dark lines protruding more than when Cerise had given it to her.

Allie touched the writing with her fingertips, afraid it would disappear under her touch. She pressed her lips together before standing and shutting her bedroom door.

She stood in front of the full-length mirror and looked at her reflection. She could return to Fairy and see Cerise and the others again.

Her heart pounded as she looked down at the paper in her hands and read the nonsense words. She waited, looking through the cracks in the mirror.

Nothing happened.

"This is stupid." Allie turned and put the paper on her desk. "The delusions of a little girl and her trauma." She shook her head.

"Allie, dinner!" Her mom's voice came from downstairs and Allie gave the paper one last look before she walked away.

"Dad said you haven't taken the broken mirror out yet. How come?" Her mom put her fork on the plate with a little clink.

Allie looked up. "I just haven't gotten around to it, I guess. I spent all day drawing."

"Please take it out tomorrow; there's no need for you to keep a broken mirror. And I don't want any glass to fall into your carpet."

Allie shrugged. "I guess." Though how was she going to get back to Fairy if the mirror was gone?

She pushed the thought out of her head. Fairy wasn't real; the words didn't work. She needed to forget about the dreams and the rabbit.

"Allie?"

"What mom?" She tried to keep the snapping out of her tone, but she wasn't in the mood to talk.

"Do you need to talk about something?"

She looked into her mom's eyes and then shook her head. "No, I'm just tired. I didn't sleep well last night with the storm."

"We were both up pretty late," her dad chimed in. "There was a lot of noise. Maybe head to bed early tonight?"

She pushed a meatball around her plate. "Yeah, I guess that would be a good idea."

"I think that's a great idea." Her mom's phone rang and she glanced at it. "Sorry, you two, excuse me. It's the school." She answered it and walked out of the room.

"Mom's still going to work for that disaster of a school?" Allie dropped her fork on the plate.

Her dad smiled. "She loves it there."

"It sucks all her time. She's always putting out fires there or covering for a teacher or there's an event. Last year she almost missed my graduation because someone couldn't show up for their aftercare shift."

He shrugged. This wasn't a fight worth having. The school meant everything to her mom and it wasn't going to change.

Allie picked up her fork again and then sat it down. "You know, I'm not really hungry right now. I'll put it in the fridge to eat later."

Her dad opened his mouth and then closed it as if he thought better than to say something. She wrapped her plate in plastic wrap and stuck it in the fridge before going back to her room.

She glared at the stupid broken mirror and then at the piece of paper with the nonsense words on it, except instead of the paper on her desk, there was something else.

A pocket watch. She walked over and picked it up, expecting the time to be shown, but instead all the numbers were gathered at the bottom and the watch hands were gone. The words "You're late" were scrawled on the face of the clock.

How could she be late without knowing where she was supposed to be or at what time?

She looked at the mirror again, but this time, when her reflection stared back at her, her overalls and black shirt were a pair of brown pants and a pirate shirt. The clothes that she'd worn in Fairy, because Cerise wanted her to blend in.

"You're late, Alice," she said to herself. "It's time to go back. Something's wrong and they need you."

She put the watch in her pocket and then put her hand against the glass of the mirror. The cracks smoothed out and disappeared under her touch this time. A blue glow came from it and she simply stepped into her wonderland.

"Your spell was activated, your majesty." Ace's voice brought Cerise out of her thoughts.

"Which spell? There are many I've been waiting on." She lifted her head up from her hand and looked up at Ace. His red tunic had an anatomically correct heart stitched into it on the chest, and was tucked into black pants that faded into his boots. His strawberry blond hair was cut short, the ends of it barely brushing the tips of his fae ears. Scars marred his beautiful face, distracting from the green of his eyes.

"One of your firsts, the mirror portal."

She shot up at those words. Her red dress flooded behind her as she pushed away from the black throne. "And who activated it?" Could it be? Had Alice dared to come back after so many years? Alice was the only one who had that spell, the only mortal that Cerise had ever invited back. She hadn't come back in seven years.

"I don't know, your majesty. I will send my guards out to look for them. I just know that the spell had been activated. Do you know where you had that portal lead?"

Did she?

She paced in front of her throne, her brows drawn together as she thought. Her boots clicked with every step, echoing in the nearly empty throne room.

She stopped and spun to face Ace. "No." It would have been somewhere hidden from her mother, from the guards, but for the life of her, she couldn't remember where.

Was it in the giant forest? Or the tea party garden? She threw herself back into the throne. Cerise tapped her long nails against her chair as she tried to remember. "Where's Oriana?"

"I'm not sure. Would you like me to find her?" Ace continued to stand at attention.

"Yes, tell her that we need to have an emergency meeting because we might have a mortal in our world. And as we know, we don't want those pests here."

The Red Queen, her mother, had made it very clear that there were to be no more mortals in Fairy—and if they came here, they would be beheaded, and their head would be put on a stick outside the palace.

Because mortals were wicked creatures. Cerise felt the hate stir in her heart at the thought of Alice sneaking back into Fairy.

"If you see Kit, tell him I'd also like to see him." She smiled and inspected the blood red of her nails. "I have a proposal for him."

Ace bowed and walked out of the room. If Alice had indeed returned, then the prophecies that had been given to her mother had a chance of coming true. Alice would ruin Fairy.

Cerise refused to let that happen.

Allie looked around where she stepped out of. The giant white stem of a mushroom towered over her. The light purple dome blocked the sunlight from her, casting a shadow on the ground.

She'd expected someone to greet her. Cerise, maybe, after the tea party invite, but no one was there.

"Curious," Allie muttered as she walked out from under the shade of the mushroom. "Notes and letters, knocking at the mirror, and yet here I am alone."

"You wretched mortal." A tiny voice came from at her feet. "Did you learn *nothing* last time you were here?"

She looked down and saw a tiny sprite, mouse brown hair swirled around his head, his dirty colored wings beat against his back, and his gray clothes made him almost blend completely into the ground and the grass that surrounded him.

"Good to see you again too, Dor." She put her hands on her hips and stared down at him.

Dor put a tiny finger up to his lips. "Be quiet. Your clothes are around the Tweedle tree, get changed and let's go. Devlin is waiting for us."

She stepped around the tiny fairy and walked to the Tweedle tree. The Tree towered over the mushrooms, the trunk twisting as it rose. The bark alternated between shades of browns and reds. She paused as she saw a note almost completely hidden within the growth of the bark.

Allie could barely make out that silver letters there. Her name.

"Dor, what's this?"

Dor flew over and hovered near it. "Looks like a note to you. Also looks like you're too late to read it. The Tweedle Tree will not let it go easily."

She ran her hand over the note and the tree shuddered under her touch. The paper sank into the bark, disappearing from view.

Dor chuckled. "Come on Alice, we're going to be late."

She walked around the tree and found the clothes waiting for her, black pants and a black shirt with ruffles at the neck and sleeves. She changed quickly and lay her human clothes at the base of the Tweedle Tree. "Please keep these safe. I might need them again."

Roots slithered up from the ground, wrapped around her clothes, and dragged them under. Allie snorted. "That's one way to keep them safe."

A moment later a sword and sheath bubbled to the earth. She stared down at them and Dor buzzed around her head. "Pick them up, don't question a gift from the Tweedle tree."

Allie snagged the sword off the ground and tied it around her waist. "Where is Cesire?"

Dor said nothing as he sped off further into the giant woods. Allie followed, climbing over branches that were the size of tree trunks in the mortal world, brushing through blades of grass that were taller than she was, and trying to keep an eye on Dor as he navigated his way through it all so expertly.

Dang Fae.

He stopped suddenly and she almost ran her head into him. Foot-steps sounded ahead of them. "Hide," Dor hissed.

Allie jumped into the bush to her left, allowing the long leaves of it to hide her from view. Her heart hammered in her chest as the foot-steps became clearer. The sound of boots echoed the beat of her heart. Dor continued to buzz forward, leaving her hidden in the leaves among the giant plants.

Traitor, she thought, until the footsteps stopped and someone spoke.

"There's a possible mortal in our lands, have you seen her?"

Dor's voice was too soft for her to hear, but Allie tucked herself as low as she could so that the giant plants could shadow her.

"You understand that if you're lying, the Red Queen will have your head?" The man barked in more of a demand than a question.

Allie swallowed. Why was the Red Queen after her already? Where was Cerise? She hadn't been back in Fairy for more than twenty minutes and already she was being hunted.

Maybe this had been a bad idea after all. She put her back to the stem of the flower as the footsteps passed her hiding spots. She held her breath waiting for them to fade before she dared move.

Dor came back to find her a few minutes later. "We move, now."

"Why would the queen be looking for me already?"

Dor shook his head. "Devlin can explain that to you. I'm simply to deliver you to him and Oriana. They can explain to you what's been happen in Fairy for the last seven years."

If she could have grabbed his arm and forced him to face her, she would have, however she probably would have accidentally crushed him instead.

"Keep moving, there's bound to be another scouting crew out here somewhere. And we want to keep you hidden as long as we can." He zipped ahead of her faster, forcing her to step up her pace.

Eventually, through their hike the forest started to grow smaller, becoming more proportionate to her human size, though the change did nothing to ease the feeling eating at her stomach. There were fewer places to hide if the footmen came back again, especially as the trees gave way to rolling green hills.

Joy filled her as she recognized the hills painting the landscape. Oriana's house was hidden in one of those hills, the house that Cerise and Allie had played in before they realized that Oriana lived there. They'd only been caught when Oriana came back for something and they had both been lucky when the fae decided to keep their secret instead of turning Allie over to the Queen at that moment.

Allie glanced around before darting into the field of hills and heading toward the middle of one, as she came closer she saw the door and Oriana standing there. Her white hair flowed over her shoulders, her pointed ears peeking out of the strands. Oriana's head was tilted down as she checked her pocket watch and then looked up.

Allie didn't stop running, she threw her arms around Oriana and held tight. "I knew this was all real."

Oriana chuckled and then pulled her inside the house. "It's all real, Alice. And you are late."

The house hadn't changed since the last time Allie had visited. The dark brown walls were decorated with paintings of different landscapes around Fairy. Some with bright colors and some with a darker motif. In the middle of the room sat a round wooden table with two chairs and the wall behind it was lined with a sink with cupboards above it.

"I have no idea what you're talking about. Late for what?" Allie crossed her arms and sat at the wooden table.

"You and Cerise were supposed to meet again a month after you went home." Oriana pressed her lips together. "Cerise was so upset when you didn't show."

Allie's heart sank. "When I went home that last time, I was in a hospital where I spent the next three months being observed and watched for signs of mental illness." She'd only been eleven that last trip. The hospital had been a cold place where she'd continuously been told that she was dealing with signs of trauma. They'd tried different tactics to help her, medicines that didn't work, therapy that couldn't help. "The humans didn't believe you that this place existed. All they saw was a little girl who was obsessed with finding her brother in a world that didn't exist."

Oriana frowned. "So they locked you in a hospital?"

"Until I was willing to admit that Fairy didn't exist and that my brother...that he died in the accident that first brought us here." Allie cringed as she swore she could hear his screams echoing.

"What happened to your brother was...tragic." Oriana paced in front of Allie. "Humans are fickle like that, they don't want to believe in the unusual."

"They don't want to believe that I fell down a rabbit hole and ended up here. They told me that I'd been wandering the forest for a week, and that it was a miracle that I wasn't dead like Brendyn."

"Hey, we took good care of you when you were here," Oriana growled. "So you were a little dirty after playing around in the forest. You were well fed and had water."

Allie nodded, but she didn't want to think about then. She was back now and she wanted to see all her friends again. "I thought Dor said Devlin was going to be here."

"He's supposed to be, but as you know, he runs late as well." Oriana walked past the table and to a row of wooden cupboards, Allie turned to face her. "How about some tea while we're waiting."

"Sure."

Oriana pulled two out tea cups decorated with rabbits. "I'm glad you got my message."

"You were outside my doctor's office the other day. Why didn't you just turn into your fae form and tell me to come back?"

"Because we're not allowed to invite mortals here anymore and if the queen finds you, you'll be executed without question. She's already calling on her scouts and her closest companions to search for you."

Allie hesitated for a moment. "Oriana, where's Cerise? Why did you lure me back here?"

"Because," a male voice came from the door way and Allie spun around to see Devlin standing there. "Cerise is the Red Queen, and you have to stop her plans."

CHAPTER 3

Allie stared at Devlin for a moment. His red curly hair sticking out from under the green hat, his big eyes watched her closely. "Cerise is queen?" Allie confirmed.

"Her mother grew sick and died. Which made Cerise queen of the Court of Hearts. She now controls the Jabberwock."

Allie raised a brow. "I thought the Jabberwock was nonsense."

"So did Cerise, and now she controls it," Oriana added and sat down a cup of tea for Devlin. "The one who controls the Jabberwock is queen of that court."

Allie watched the liquid in her cup swirl as she tried to wrap her head around the idea of Cerise being queen. Such a young queen couldn't bode well for any type of kingdom. "What is the Jabberwock?"

Devlin started sprouting off in a language that Allie didn't know, but he waved his hands around in a way that made her thing of wings and then made a motion as he describe what might have been a mouth.

She stared at him until he was finished. "I'm still human."

He let out a frustrated growl and threw himself in the second chair. "It's like a huge dragon with a long neck and big teeth, it has two bug eyes. It's terrifying."

It sounded like it. Allie sipped her tea. "So I need to stop Cerise from doing what?"

"She's going to ruin Fairy." Oriana let out a long dramatic sigh. "She plans on controlling each court's abilities that keeps Fairy intact. Having different courts keep Fair balanced. She wants to rule all of it, which would bring disaster to Fairy. Even her mother understood that, as crazy as she was, but Cerise, she wants the ultimate power, the ultimate control over Fairy."

Great, a hungry power young adult, and Allie thought life after high school was hard enough. "I don't understand how I'm supposed to stop that. I'm a mortal with a sword."

"But you're not just any mortal. You're Alice, *the* Alice. You broke through Cerise's shields before and you can do it again."

"I was an eight-year-old in a fantasy world, all I wanted to do was play with the pretty girl that was my age, and go exploring and not go back home. How was that breaking through Cerise's shields?" Allie shook her head. "And then every time I returned after that I was looking for my brother. She helped me, but that's still not breaking through shields. Hell, what shields did she have?" She paused for a moment. "I don't think you understand. I'm an outcast, I'm different, and I'm not a Fae like you guys. Isn't this supposed to be like a fairy-tale? Someone will come sweep the queen off her feet and you guys get to live happily ever after?"

Oriana choked on air and walked to the window. Allie looked at Devlin.

"This isn't a fantasy world to us, Alice, this is our home, and we need your help to save it. We're going to the queen's castle and you're going to get through to Cerise."

Allie sat her cup down and crossed her arms. "And how do you expect me to get through to her? Assuming her men don't find us?"

"I don't know, you'll figure it out," Devlin shrugged. "Now, finish your tea because we have a long journey to the castle, and guards to avoid."

Allie picked her tea cup up again.

"Speaking of. Guards are here." Oriana spun around and quickly grabbed Allie's cup and dumped it in the sink. "Into the hole you go, follow the path." She grabbed Allie by the shirt collar and shoved her towards a wall of dirt. "Go go go."

Allie put her hands up to keep from being shoved against the wall, but her hands went right through and put her into a dark tunnel. She gave her eyes a moment to adjust to the darkness before she moved forward with one hand on the wall to help guide her.

She strained to hear anything around her as she walked, but the dirt kept her isolated from any noise.

She glanced back where she'd come from and saw no sign of a door or a light, her only choice was to move forward like Oriana said. One foot in front of the other was the only way she was going to get out of this tunnel and hopefully to safety.

Oriana leaned against her counter cupping her tea cup, trying to look calm. Devlin took his hat and sat it on the table and crossed his legs, just as the guards walked in the door. They filed into a "v" shape, blocking the exit completely. Their black tunics with a red heart stitched on them seemed to suck the light out of the room. The spears they carried almost touched the ceiling of the room, glinting menacingly in the light from the window.

"Have you ever heard of knocking?" Oriana raised a brow and sipped her tea.

"The Queen of Hearts has requested you come to the palace," the guard in front demanded.

Devlin stood and picked his hat up. "That would be my cue to go. Have a wonderful day, Oriana." He gave her a quick kiss on the cheek. "And remember, that the Raven sends his love in the dead of night."

She had no idea what he was talking about, but it wasn't unusual for him to talk about a raven. "Of course."

Devlin bowed his head and walked straight through the "v" shoving between two of the guards. Oriana put her tea cup down on the counter and turned back to look at the guards. "So what does the Queen want?"

"There seems to be a mortal in our world, she wants to have an emergency meeting with each court about it." The guard shrugged. "Commander Ace told us we were to fetch you at once."

A shadow outside caught her eyes. "How many guards did you bring just to fetch me? You know my court would not go against Cerise."

"There are two other guards outside. The Queen wants to speak to each leader of the courts." That explained why no one tried to stop Devlin.

She pushed off the counter. "Okay then, let's go see the queen."

The guards led the way out of her house and she paused when she saw just one guard standing outside. "Where's your friend?" She raised a brow.

"He went to talk to Devlin, we're also searching your area for Kit."

She smirked. "We haven't seen Kit around since Cerise cursed him. For all we know he went to the mortal world to live out his life as a spoiled house cat." Oriana shrugged. "I mean, I don't think I'd stay around if there were creatures who could eat me in one bite."

The guard studied her for a moment. "You're a rabbit in your other form."

"Yes, but I'm not a rabbit one-hundred percent of the time. Kit is currently stuck in his form, remember?"

The guard chuckled. "Cerise threatened to keep him as a pet."

None of the other fae courts found that funny. Especially the kings and queens. Oriana bit her cheek trying to keep her remarks to herself. Kit was her friend, he'd been Cerise's friend too at one point. They all had.

"Come on, let's go." The guard jerked his head. "I don't want to keep the queen waiting."

Neither did she. The longer Cerise was kept waiting, the crueler her thoughts could become.

In Fairy, things were weird and though Allie remembered this from her last visit, she was surprised by how weird.

Eventually her hand went from feeling dense dirt to feeling tree bark, and a light started to peek through what looked like leaves. The ground sloped upwards as her feet shuffled over it, trying not to trip over anything unseen. She had no idea how long she'd been moving through this tunnel, nor where it led. Her mind turned back to Oriana, did the guards take her?

Would she lose her head for hiding Allie?

Allie pushed the thoughts away as the light became bigger. She climbed up the last few steps and pulled herself out of a hole. She took a moment and sat on the edge to try to find her bearings.

Flowers of all colors flowed out around her. The colors formed a spiral outwards, seemingly going on forever into the horizon. She'd never been to this part of Fairy, most likely there was something in the field of flowers that would kill her. Cerise always warned her that the majority of creatures in Fairy could kill a mortal.

And here Allie was with nothing but a sword to protect her.

"Oriana wouldn't send me into danger," Allie muttered, but she stood and drew the sword. The flowers bristled around her with each step that she took away from the tunnel.

If the guards discovered she'd been at Oriana's and gone through the tunnel, they'd come after her and she needed to be far away from there.

The further away she walked from the tunnel the more the flowers seemed to wrap around her feet. Slowing her down with each step.

Singing filled the air and Allie stopped to listen to the sweet melody. Maybe she could figure out what direction she needed to go if she followed the voices. She tried to think of Cerise's map that she'd drawn in the dirt during their meetings.

"If you're ever in trouble, head to the Tea Garden. Devlin and March will be there, and you might even run into Dor if he's not off spying," Allie muttered. "But Devlin is with Oriana, Dor left me there, I've never met March." And she wasn't sure which way the Tea Garden was at this point.

She continued to drag her feet through the flowers, but her legs ached and she fell to her knees. Her limbs felt heavy with exhaustion as she tried to get up. Her eyelids started to sag as flowers brushed against her skin, beckoning her to lie down. "A quick nap won't hurt." She yawned and stretched. Snuggling down in the flowers, she closed her eyes and sleep swallowed her.

"There once was a girl named Alice, and she wandered into a world she didn't know. Once she stepped from the safe embrace of her friends, she found herself alone and facing death."

Allie stood in the field of flowers. The blossoms leaning away from her now instead of trying to draw her down to sleep. A woman appeared in front of her. Long red hair curled around a heart-shaped face and deep brown eyes. A long red dress encased her body, pooling on the ground by her feet and cascading over the flowers near her. "Cerise?"

"Alice, you aren't supposed to be here. Go home." Cerise turned around, the long red dress wrapping around her legs as she did then flowing behind her as she walked away.

"You invited me here." Allie held her hands out.

"Years ago, when I was young and naïve and wanted a friend. You never returned." She spun around, back around. She grabbed the rose necklace at her throat. "You never came back from the mortal world,

and now you're not welcomed here. My mother made me see my mistakes in wanting to trust a mortal. Go. Home. Or I will have your head." In another swirl, red smoke surrounded her and she disappeared.

Allie stood in the fading light, trying to will herself to wake up, but nothing happened. A moment later a wide grin appeared in the dark and dark gray fur with black strips appeared behind the grin, followed by green eyes. Allie's eyes adjusted to the new shape in the dark and saw a large cat crouched in his paws.

There was something familiar about him, the grin, the eyes, but she couldn't place it.

"Only the mad come here, Alice, the dream realm is not for the mortals. Now, wake up, and run."

Allie shot up in the field of flowers. Voices were closing in on her. The voice she heard echoed in her head, "Run." She jumped to her feet and took off. The flowers didn't hold her back this time— the opposite actually; they parted for her as her feet pounded the ground. The flowers faded into a forest. Alice's feet crunched on the underbrush until she found a tree with a lower branch. She jumped and pulled herself up on it and sank into the leaves the best she could to hide.

The voices came closer, shouting and yelling, but when she understood the words, she realized they weren't looking for her. They were looking for...

"Get the pig! We cannot let that beast escape!" A soldier below her yelled and a moment later more voices came. Footsteps thundered under her as they chased whatever pig it was they were running after.

She sat in the tree branch as the voices faded away again, and she let out a breath. Soldier's hunting pigs, guards visiting Oriana, and Cerise demanding she leave.

"The Raven sends his love at night," Devlin's voice came from above her and Allie let out a small squeak.

"Devlin!"

He jumped down onto her branch. "Alice, glad to see you made it this far."

She nudged him. "How did you manage to leave Oriana's with the guards there?"

"I walked out of the house, and then I...disposed of the one who followed me."

Allie looked the direction that the other soldiers had gone. "Does Cerise know I'm here?"

"I think you know the answer to that." Devlin swung his legs. "Cerise is different."

"Of course she is, we were eight when we met and eleven when we last saw each other. A lot changes when you don't see each other for seven years."

Devlin nodded. "That's the thing, she tried to go see you. She waited for you to come back using her spell. And when you didn't... her mother used that disappointment to poison her heart."

Allie glanced at him. "You're telling me, it's my fault that she's... evil?"

"I'm telling you that her mother used that situation against you both." Devlin shrugged. "You were both children, the promises you made to meet again weren't realistic. The mortal realm and Fairy are different. Expectations are different. Humans get a chance to grow up, Fae...we're forced into our roles at early ages."

Allie looked back at the ground. "How old you are, Devlin?"

"Do you know how I was when we met?"

She shook her head.

"Magic." He chuckled. "I was twelve when we last met."

Allie stared at him. "Twelve?"

He nodded.

"You seemed so much older."

Devlin shrugged. "Dor was nine, Oriana is the oldest, she was fifteen when you met her." He shrugged. "We're all teenagers in a messed up world. Your greatest worry right now is what? College? Work? Ours is the fall of our courts, our powers being drained, and stopping the Red Queen from ruining Fairy."

Allie stared at him. "My biggest concern is the same as yours. Trust me, my mind isn't on school or the mortal realm. It's right here in Fairy and with Cerise."

***

Cerise looked up from the parchment in front of her and smiled when Ace marched Oriana into the castle. "Hello Lady Oriana."

"Lady Cerise," Oriana bowed. "I was told you wanted to see me?" She pulled up from her bow and adjusted her waist coat around her. The blues and greens of the threads caught the light and seemed to shift colors like Oriana's eyes.

Cerise rolled up the parchment and sat it on the table next to her throne. "Yes, it seems that we have a mortal in our mist. One who used an old spell of mine to get in."

Oriana tensed and Cerise raised a brow. "Have something to tell me, Oriana? You were in charge of making sure all those spells were destroyed." Cerise curled her fingers around the arms of her throne.

"You put Kit in charge of it since it was his domain." Oriana met Cerise's gaze. "He was in charge of the magic. You had Knave and I chasing down other things at the time."

Cerise stood and walked down to Oriana. She stopped in front of her old friend, studying the calm demeanor she held. "You and I were friends once. You should join me in my quest. We could be the most powerful creatures, move into and take over other courts and then the other realms."

"We aren't meant to do that." Oriana stood still as Cerise started to walk around her.

Cerise studied her. When Cerise became queen the others became distant. Calculating. They had to be plotting against her and now, with a mortal in the land, she knew they were.

The seer had claimed that Alice would come back and defeat the Red Queen. Originally, Cerise thought it was her mother that Alice would bring down, but as the years went on and the Red Queen grew sick, Cerise realized that the seer had been talking about her.

"Where is Alice, Oriana?" Cerise stopped in front of her. "I know she's here. She is the only one I gave that spell to."

Oriana swallowed and Cerise knew she was getting ready to lie. "I don't know."

Except there was truth to her words. "You don't know?" Cerise took a small step back.

Oriana nodded. "I know what you know, she's in Fairy somewhere, but that's all I know."

"She's running around Fairy alone?" Cerise smiled. "This problem may just take care of itself." She turned to walk back to her throne. A mortal in Fairy wouldn't get far without help and if Oriana didn't know where Alice was, maybe the others didn't either. "Now, where are Kit and Knave?"

Oriana laughed and it made Cerise want to smack her. "I haven't seen either of them since you cursed Kit."

"I sensed him here. So he has to be somewhere." Cerise sat back down and dragged her red nails over the arm of her throne. Oriana let out a strangled noise as blood appeared on her arms in the same scratch pattern.

"I honestly don't know. I haven't even seen a footprint from Kit and Knave and I never got along." Oriana's voice was tight.

Cerise had to give her credit. The fae didn't cover the marks on her arms or make any other noises suggesting she was in pain. "That's right, you and Knave had a falling out after Alice's first visit. You wanted to take her back right away. Knave thought it was good for me to meet a mortal." Cerise smirked. "And look how well that turned out."

Oriana kept her face blank. "I think the outcome on that is still to be determined. May I go? I have court duties to attend to."

"On the promise that you will bring Alice to me if you come across her."

"Alice is her own being, and I have no doubt that she's making her way toward you. Just on her own terms." Oriana spun around, the tails of her coat swishing around her as she walked out of the hall.

Cerise leaned back in her throne. Alice was here and heading toward her? Should she let the world of the Fae kill the mortal? Or have the guards bring her in?

I want to stay in Fairy forever...but I can't.

Alice's words rang in Cerise's head. They'd been children, but she'd hoped that Alice would stay, or at the very least, keep visiting.

Oriana says my parents are looking for me, and every time I come back they are worried that I ran away.

At least Alice had parents to worry about her, Cerise's mom was always more concerned with the kingdom and how Cerise's actions reflected on the royal family. To be seen dancing around with a mortal, or having lunch with one, doing anything with one was unacceptable.

Even as a child.

And if her mother had ever gotten her hands on Alice...well, they wouldn't be in this situation now would they?

Cerise looked at Ace. "Did your guards find any signs of Alice at Oriana's house?"

"No, your majesty. They said that Devlin was there, but that he left when he heard you summoned Oriana."

"And what about Oriana's palace?"

"We haven't checked there, there was no need to since she was at her house."

Cerise glared at him and swiped her hand across the air. Blood blossomed over Ace's face, adding to the angry scars already there. "Go check her palace. I want all of their places searched and if you find a hint of Oriana or anyone else helping Alice, you will bring them back here for punishment."

"Of course, your majesty." He bowed and walked out and she tapped her fingers on the arm of her chair.

Seven years since she'd seen Alice, seven years since a mortal walked into the Fae realm. And this time she was a threat, not a mere child looking for fun, but someone capable of bringing down the Red Queen.

CHAPTER 4

Allie followed Devlin through the forest in silence. They hadn't spoken much since they'd climbed out of the tree. She didn't dare break the silence in case there were soldiers around following them, and Devlin seemed to have the same idea.

The trees started to thin out and they came into view of a city. Allie's heart jumped at the sight of something that seemed so human in this strange world. Roof tops formed waves of pointed silhouettes against the sinking sun, some had smoke rising from chimneys, while others had lights glowing through the windows. Standing at the back of the village was a castle that looked a bit crooked against the skyline, but somehow it felt right.

It was different from the mortal world where there was the glow of electrical lights faded the sky. Here she could see stars starting to dot the sky and knew that once the sun was down completely they would cover the night sky.

"It's beautiful," Allie breathed, and Devlin nudged her.

"Come on, let's get inside before the night creatures come out." He headed down the hill and into the village.

"The night creatures?" Allie followed him down the hill, sliding a little. "Cerise never mentioned night creatures."

Devlin looked over his shoulder. "That's not true, I know she recited the poem of the Jabberwock to you."

"And I thought it was nonsense. This whole freaking world is nonsense." They came to a halt at the bottom of the hill, just on the edge of the village.

Devlin put his fingers against his lips. "Quiet, Alice, you don't want to fae to realize you don't belong here." His voice was low and there was a strange glint in his eyes. He grabbed her hand and wrapped his fingers with hers before pulling her deeper into the village.

Each house seemed silent as they made their way through the shadows of the houses, warm fires flickered through their windows and Allie tried to catch a glimpse of the people living in them as Devlin dragged them past, but they moved too fast.

Suddenly Devlin stopped at a cabin. The walls of the cabin tilted in like the castle, even the window and door skewed with the angles. Devlin waved a hand and Allie heard a lock click before he opened the door.

"Welcome to my work shop." He glanced over his shoulder. "Please don't touch anything, many of these objects are enchanted, and I'd hate for you to get hurt."

Allie gave a slight nod as she looked over the things on the racks: hats, coats, scarves, ties, dresses, corsets...everything was beautiful and well made, and had Devlin not warned her, she would have run her hands over everything. "You made all these?"

Devlin nodded. "I did, I learned the craft from my mother. She was the Red Queen's tailor."

"Was?" Allie glanced at him and he looked away from her without explaining further.

Devlin walked further back and opened a door. "You can stay in here for the night, I'll take first watch. I'm sure Oriana has talked to

Cerise already, and it won't be long until the soldiers are looking everywhere for you."

Allie walked into the small room. Against the windowless wall stood a cot with blankets folded on the end of it and a door was to her left that she assumed was the bathroom. "This is where you live?"

He chuckled. "No, this is where I come to work when I want to get away from things. Tomorrow, I'll show you where I live, but I have no desire to get caught by the creatures that roam the night."

Allie sat on the cot. "What kind of creatures are they?"

"Ones that will tear you apart with their claws and then bath in your blood."

"Sounds lovely. And here I thought all of you were human-like."

Devlin shook his head. "There are so much about us that you don't know, but I hope you're ready because you're going to be getting a crash course in how cruel the fae really can be."

He shut the door and Allie sat on the cot in the darkness, waiting for her eyes to adjust. Outside the door she heard Devlin moving things around and humming to himself. Probably working on something else that was enchanted and would want to kill her if she touched it. Eventually, her eyes drifted shut to Devlin's humming and she hoped that she wouldn't be woken in the middle of the night and told to run.

Crashing and shouting had Allie jumping up from the cot, her heart beating, and her mind racing. She went to the door and heard shouting, but paused as she heard Devlin's voice.

"I swear she's not here. I've been in my workshop all night. I came here after I left Oriana's."

Allie's heart pounded.

"There is no reason to send ten guards here to look for the mortal."

Allie pressed her lips together. She had no real idea how to fight with the sword she was given and there was no way that she could take on ten guards without Devlin's help.

"Devlin, you are under arrest for conspiring against the Queen Cerise and the slaying of a royal soldier." The voice sounded familiar, but Allie couldn't place it. She wished she could open the door and see who it belonged to, but her instinct told her to stay hidden. Devlin knew the guards would be looking for her. He knew what he was doing when he hid her in that room.

Now she just had to trust him.

Devlin's voice hit her. "The Raven sends his love by night. Look for the window and trust the wind."

"Shut up, Devlin, your nonsense drives me crazy."

The voices faded, but before Allie could wrap her mind around what Devlin had been saying, crashing filled the room again, something hit the door and made her jump. Her hands flew over her mouth to keep her from making a noise.

"She's not here, Ace. We've torn this place apart, we have Devlin, let's go."

A long string of curses came from Ace before the noise settled down again. Allie leaned against the door and put a hand to her chest, waiting for her heart to calm down.

They had Devlin. Maybe they had Oriana. She needed to get out of there and figure out how she was going to change Cerise's mind about whatever her plan was and get her friends back.

Allie leaned her head against the door. No one had told her what it was Cerise was really planning, a hostile takeover of the courts, but Allie had no way of knowing who was in charge of the courts or how to protect them.

Honestly, she wasn't even sure what she was doing here. She closed her eyes and took a deep breath.

Cerise was the same age as Allie, and there was no reason someone that young should be ruling the fae world.

"We're forced to grow up here." Devlin's words crossed her mind again.

Allie could find the portal again, waltz through, and be back home where her greatest fear was what to do the next day. Her gut told her that wasn't the answer.

Once she was sure the guards were gone, she pushed the door.

It didn't budge.

She shoved her hands against it, grunting as she tried to force it open. Once more, nothing happened.

There was no window for her to climb out of, but she doubted that Devlin would have left her trapped in the room. She pounded her fist on the door once and a tingle went through her arm.

She shook it out, cursing her stupidity for hitting the wood so hard, but there, in silver scrawling letters, a message started to appear.

"Read the words, grab the box, and off you go. Head to the palace in the shadow of the night, stay in the village during the day."

More words followed in a language Allie didn't know, but she did her best to read them out loud as they appeared.

A click and a pop sounded just before the door opened. Stepping over the threshold, Allie almost stepped on the box wrapped in brown paper. She swept it up and looked around the destroyed shop.

Mannequins were over turn, garments ripped to shreds, hats everywhere, and patterns on the ground. Allie swallowed and picked up a tipped over chair and sat down to open her box.

She slipped her finger under the fold of brown paper and pulled it away, revealing a white box. She lifted the lid and found a note lying on top of a pair of leather gauntlets.

"To The Alice, wear them with pride, and my magic will protect you. Be safe on your journey and I'll see you at the end. Remember, the Raven sends his love by night. Look for the window and trust the wind. –Devlin"

Allie ran her fingers over the soft leather of the gauntlets and the symbol that was stamped into them. She'd wish she'd taken the time to learn more of the Fae language so she knew what the writing was.

She pulled the gauntlets on. Also in the box lay a small purple pouch and another note. "For your day in the village."

Allie peeked in and saw several silver coins. Well, at least she knew she wasn't going to starve. She tied the pouch to her pants and walked out of the cottage. She had a whole day to explore, and as soon as the sun went down she'd be making her way to the castle, hopefully not to be eaten by the vicious creatures Devlin told her about.

***

Oriana looked over the map on her desk. The tunnel she'd shoved Allie through came out in the Field of Sleep, where Devlin was supposed to meet her. Assuming, they made it, they would have had to travel through the forest to get to Devlin's village.

Where hopefully...

Dor started rapping at the window and Oriana looked up with annoyance at the tiny fae. She walked over and opened it. "What are you doing here? The deal was that we stay apart unless there was an emergency," she hissed.

"There is: Cerise had Devlin arrested." His tiny brown wings buzzed behind him as he darted into the room and fluttered around.

Oriana stared at him for a moment. "For what? And where is Alice?"

"I don't know where the girl is, and for conspiring against Cerise. I got there just as the soldiers were dragging him out of his workshop." His hands flew around in the air as he talked.

She looked down at the map and tapped her finger where the cabin was marked. "And Alice wasn't anywhere?"

"Not that I saw or heard."

Maybe Devlin hadn't gotten Alice. He could get distracted in his workshop, which meant that Alice was missing. "We need to find her."

"Forget about the girl, Oriana. Cerise is arresting members of the courts for treason. If she find Devlin guilty, she's going to behead him, and then his court has no one to take over."

Devlin's dad was still alive, but he was more of a figurehead than the actual ruler of the court at this moment. Oriana let out a string of curses. "Okay, go check on Devlin and stay away from Cerise. Report back to me. I'll prepare my own guards for an attack or an arrest. Dammit."

"And Alice?" Dor asked, his head tilted to the side as he fluttered in front of her face.

"We'll just have to hope she can survive on her own for a while, until we can find her and face Cerise."

Dor made a noise that sounded like a disagreement before he shot out of her house. Oriana looked at the map. If Alice was in the Field of Sleep, she would be safe from the guards, the flowers would hide her in her slumber. Until she died that was, but it was safer than other places she could have ended up.

She pulled a map of her own territory over and put x's on it for where she should move her guards. They were already posted at the palace city's gate, and if needed be, she could cast the spell that would freeze her territory in time, but that also meant freezing herself and she wouldn't be able to fight alongside the others.

She was a leader first and foremost. Her mother always drilled into her head that she needed to think of the greater good, and that meant her people first. But her people needed to be protected from the queen right now as well, because if Cerise was looking for Alice, she would burn the whole world if she had to.

And Oriana couldn't risk so many lives. She tapped the paper. What would her mother do?

The answer was simple, but Oriana didn't want to default to it right way.

Her mother would hand Alice over to the queen in exchange for keeping her people safe.

Cerise would kill Alice in an instant.

Oriana let out a growl. She couldn't send an innocent mortal to her death because Cerise was throwing a tantrum. No, she'd have to find a way to keep her people and Alice safe.

She rolled the map up and stuck it in her bag. It was time to talk to her own soldiers and guards and make a plan, because Fairy was going to go to war, the courts against the queen and it was going to be a bloody mess.

The village square was bustling when Allie finally found it. People brushed past her as they went to the stalls that they were looking for, people shouted while others moseyed through the streets. The amount of hustle and bustle made Allie's heart pound as she tried to get some type of bearings. No one was staring at her, despite her not having pointed ears, or wings, or animal ears, or any other sign of being a fae.

It was almost like they couldn't see her. Or if they did, they didn't find anything different about her.

She stopped at a stall that had cloaks hanging from a bar. Different colors and textures flowed down, almost touching the ground. Allie touched the fabric of one. The silver threads woven through the black fabric glinted in the sunlight.

"It's beautiful, isn't it?" The woman at the stall said without looking up from what she was working on. Her dark hair had gray streaked through it and it fell over the project she was working on. "The thread is from the Valley of the Lost, the spiders down there spin it." She glanced up her silver gaze meeting Allie's "Some say that the threads are unbreakable and will protect you from anything. Even the bite of the Jabberwock." She paused. "You're mortal."

So much for no one noticing. "I am." Alice held her head high.

The woman glanced around them and then grabbed her arm pulling Allie into the stall, behind the cloaks where none of the passersby could see. "What are you doing here?" The woman's words weren't harsh, or a demand, but a simple question.

Allie chewed on the inside of her cheek trying to decide what to say. After a moment the fae in front of her seemed to grow impatient.

"It doesn't matter. If you're in this village than you have Lord Devlin's permission."

Lord Devlin? Allie blinked at her. "Um, yes I have his permission. I'll be out of the village at night fall, but until then he told me to explore."

She looked Allie up and down. "Then he must trust you." She reached up and tucked a piece of Allie's hair behind her ear. "So, do you want the cloak?"

Allie smiled. "How much is it?"

The woman pulled the cloak off the rack and wrapped it around Allie. Allie shivered as magic marched down her spin, but then settled around her as the cloak lay against her skin.

"Three silver pieces."

Allie pulled out the silver and handed it to the woman. "Thank you."

She nodded and tucked the coins away. "There's a lovely cafe down the way, I think you might enjoy. Tell them that Murl sent you." She pulled Allie's hood over her head. "You're too plain to be a fae, but people in Lord Devlin's territory don't mind outsiders. As long as they have Devlin's blessing. Now go, eat, I have a feeling you have a long journey ahead of you."

Allie walked out of the stall and kept her head down. Murl was right, every fae she passed was extraordinary in some way, be it the way the sun caught their hair, the way the magic seemed to shimmer around then, their ears, their eyes...everything about them was stunning.

She walked through the cobblestone streets, passing the other vendors. Keeping her head down, she chose not to stop at any of the other shops, but follow Murl's instructions. She hadn't eaten anything since she'd left the moral world and now that she felt safe, her stomach was grumbling.

At the end of the town square sat a small building, the door held open with a stool and the smell of smoked meats coming from it. Allie walked in, her hands hesitating to remove her hood as she did. Murl said strangers were welcomed, but what if...

"Take your cloak off and come in you silly girl. It took you long enough to get here." A man came out from behind the counter, wiping his hands huge hands on his white apron. He had pointed ears peeking out of his black hair and the color of his eyes switched between different hues of green. "Sit, sit. I'll get you some soup and bread to eat."

Allie pulled off her cloak and folded it over her arms while she sat down at an empty table. The people around her once again didn't seem to notice her, their heads down while they ate, but the man gave her a big grin has he sat a bowl and plate in front of her. Vegetables bobbed in the broth with chunks of meat surrounding them. The steam rising from the bowl brought a delicious smell with it.

"Um, Murl sent me," Allie said, tearing her eyes away from the bowl.

He laughed. "Oh I know, she's my wife. I noticed her handy work on the cloak." He nodded toward the garment in question. "You're also not from around here and she tends to send new comers here for a meal."

Allie smiled at him. "Thank you, honestly I'm overwhelmed by your kindness and your wife's, but I won't be sticking around long."

"No, I think not. There's a big fuss going on about you and these others," he waved his hand around at all the other fae in the room. "They aren't taking notice of you, so I'm willing to bet that you're wearing something made by Lord Devlin himself. Something to protect you from the prying eyes of others."

Allie raised a brow. "If that is the case, why can you and Murl see me?"

"Because we are Devlin's eyes in the village. We tell him what's going on and what disputes have arose. So he trusts us to keep tabs on anything he deems worth. That would include you, blondie."

Allie ran a hand through her short hair and wrinkled her nose.

Blondie was not a nickname she enjoyed. "Why do you call him Lord Devlin?"

"Well because, he's the lord of the court here and he deserves the respect."

And just like that, the truth fell into place. If Devlin was the lord of this court, chances were that Oriana was the lady of her court.

"And what court are we in?"

"You're in the Court of Enchantment," he said. "And it's the most marvelous court of them all."

CHAPTER 5

Cerise walked down the stone stairs to the dungeon, keeping her dress gathered in one hand to keep it from the dirty floor. Rows of cells lined the wall when she reached the bottom of the steps and she walked past the silent prisoners until she reached the one she came to visit. Cerise stepped in front of Devlin's cell. Iron bars wrapped around the cell. The stone ground lay uneven beneath Devlin. A rat scurried across the back of the cell, staying far away from the fae inside.

She kept a step away from the iron to make sure it didn't harm her, but she could see the paleness on Devlin's face as the iron in the cell cut him off from his magic.

"Hello, Devlin," she cooed at him.

He glanced up at her. "Cerise."

"Queen Cerise," she corrected, and crossed her arms. "We were friends once Devlin, why would you betray me?"

He leaned his back against the brick wall, his gaze never leaving hers. "Because, you've become just as blood thirsty as your mother."

Cerise sneered at the comparison. She was nothing like her mother. She just wanted to rule all of Fairy to protect it. Save it. "I'm doing what is best to keep Fairy alive. To keep it safe. You and the others can't see that because you selfishly want to keep your courts and your powers to yourself. The courts are supposed to belong and work for a crown."

"We're supposed to balance each other out, Cerise, not be under one crown."

She growled and threw her hand out, wrapping her power around his throat. "Where is Alice, Devlin? I know she was with you."

To her disappointment, Devlin didn't even make a noise at her show of power. He stared at her without an answer.

"I can't kill you, not yet, but one of you will tell me where that mortal is."

"So you can kill her," Devlin ground out. "Alice and you are friends."

Cerise released her powers and turned her back to Devlin. "We were, but faes and mortals can't be friends. Alice is predicted to bring down the kingdom and I can't let that happen."

"She's staying in Fairy because of you. She could have ignored the call to Fairy and never returned, but she came because of you."

Cerise didn't look back at him. Seven years she'd called for Alice. Seven years of ignored invites and the broken promise. "Why now?" She tried to keep her voice cold, but she couldn't ignore the tiny bit of hope that crept into it.

"I don't know." Devlin sighed. "But I can't tell you where she is, because she has a plan and I don't know what that is. But if there's a chance of bringing you back from the edge of your insanity, then I won't stop her."

Cerise spun back around and wrapped her magic around Devlin's body. "You were tell me where she is, you will not let her bring down my kingdom."

Devlin held his chin up in defiance and she threw him back to the ground. "Ace!"

Her guard appeared next to her a moment later. "Yes, your majesty?"

"Devlin refuses to tell us where Alice is hiding. Please make sure your men extract the information from him while we locate the others." She spun and raised a brow at Devlin. "Unless you want to tell me where the mortal is?"

"She's long gone, your soldiers missed her in my workshop." Devlin swallowed. "So really, I don't know where she's run off to."

"Funny, Oriana said that same thing when she came to visit. And neither of you seem to be lying. Get the information from him, Ace, don't kill him though. I need him alive to convince the people of his court to answer to only me."

Cerise walked out of the dungeon and ignored the sinking feeling in her stomach. The courts had been fighting against her, ever since her mother was gone. She would not stand for that. This world was hers to rule over. She wrapped her fingers around the rose necklace her mother had given her. The one she swore over to continue her mother's dream to unite Fairy.

Devlin's cry came from behind her as she shut the door. She hesitated for a moment but then tightened her fist.

No, she could not afford to be weak right now. She needed to keep moving forward.

Allie walked through the streets of the village, watching children kick around a ball and laughing while they chased it down the road. Smells of delicious food floated on the air, and voices could be heard through the open windows of the houses.

She's walked through the village most of the day with no one paying any attention to her except for Murl and her husband, but she got to see the people of this village with innocent eyes.

The families were just like hers in the mortal world, adults, children, teens. They had their lives built here. This was home. Even she could feel it with each sound and each laughter of the children, and hear it with each person who spoke.

Devlin wanted to protect this from Cerise.

As she walked through the square one last time, she caught Murl's eye as she was shutting down the stand.

"You should probably head to where ever Devlin told you. Night fall comes quick around here and the creatures may not be able to see you, but they will be able to smell you." She nodded her head toward the sinking sun.

"Of course, thank you. For everything." Allie smiled and walked by the stand.

"If you're still here tomorrow, you should stop by for breakfast, my husband makes a mean breakfast."

Allie nodded. "That sounds wonderful. If I'm around, I'll stop by."

"Good." Murl went back to busying herself with closing the stand while Allie headed in the direction of the palace. To find whatever window it was and to trust the raven. Whatever that meant.

Maybe Devlin really was mad. The few years she knew him before he'd always spouted out nonsense. Nothing ever really came of it, so why should it be different now?

Except now, she wasn't in the giant forest. She was in the Court of Enchantment and she needed Devlin's ramble to make sense, because if it didn't she had nothing to go on.

The cobblestone path she followed led her back to the crooked cottage and she paused. The door was cracked open, although she was sure she'd shut it when she left.

She slowly approached it, trying to listen for anything that might be dangerous. The door shoved opened and a man in armer shot out toward her, followed by a woman.

Allie darted away from them, running down the cobblestone. Her feet pounded against the road and she could hear the two behind her, shouting for her to stop.

She had to make it to the castle. Her heart pounded as the sun dipped down below the towers, casting her in shadows, but she kept moving forward, her cloak flowing behind her as she ran.

The two soldiers continued to chase her as she skidded around a corner and came face to face with a massive creature.

Allie halted and stared at the one-eyed, one-legged creature. Its large eye blinked at her from a face covered in black feathers that ran down its body and from the shadows of those came an arm reaching for her.

She screamed and back peddled, not able to take her eyes of the horrible creature, her back hit something hard and she looked up at the man she'd run into.

"Get behind me, and I'll deal with the Fachan."

She wasn't even going to question him and backed up behind him and next to the woman in armor.

"You should have drawn your sword, lass," the lady muttered. "Stabbed it in the eye and kept on running."

Allie wasn't sure if the words were advice or a threat, but she watched as the soldier in front of her drew his own sword and lunged at the creature. With a flick of his wrist he cut the hand off and the Fachan jumped backwards on its leg, somehow keeping its balance.

Of course this was Fairy, the answer was probably magic. Another quick thrust and the soldier's sword made a squish sound as it went through the head of the creature.

Allie blinked a couple times, trying to get her body to move. She lunged forward, but the woman's hand wrapped around her wrist.

"Unless you know how to use that sword, Alice, I suggest you stay with us," the woman said, sharply.

Allie gave a slight nod. "I need to get to the castle."

"We know," the man said. His green armor blended in with the trees around him, his dark hair was tied back, leaving the sharp angles of his face visible with only a five o'clock shadow to soften his jaw. "I'm Captain Quillon, and this is Isa." He motioned to the other soldier. She held her head high, her braided blond hair swept away from her face into a tight bun. She had the same green armor as Captain Quillon, but her eyes matched the color. "We're here on behalf of Devlin. Sorry we were so late catching up to you."

Allie let out a short laugh. "I've been in the village all day, which is where he told me to be."

Isa nodded. "We had other problems to worry about, and knew you'd be safe there. Come on, let's go before another Fachan finds us."

"What was that thing?"

Quillon snorted. "That was a mortal at one point. That's what happens when a mortal Seer tries or stays too long on the other side using their sight. They get pulled into Fairy and turned into that."

Allie stopped. "Am I going to turn into that?"

"Are you a Seer?" Quillon asked, annoyance in his voice.

"No, but I'm a mortal in Fairy."

"Mortal seers have the ability to tap into the magic of Fairy. You're in no danger being turned into a Fachan, Alice." Isa dropped a heavy hand onto her shoulder. "You're in more danger of getting your head chopped off." She nudged Allie forward.

Yes, because getting her head chopped off sounded so much better. Allie followed them up the cobblestone path to the crooked gate, the hinges barely hanging onto the stone pillars that stood guard of the bridge.

The bridge itself looked even worse. "Budget for repairs is a bit slim, eh?" She joked as she tried not to think about crossing the cracked and broken planks.

Quillon laughed. "You're in the Realm of Enchantment, Alice, open your eyes." He tapped her forehead and a tingle went through her skull. She shook her head and blinked, once again looking at the castle.

The gate now hung straight, the stone pillars were a light green, almost gray, that were beautifully stack and stood tall. The ropes for the bridge were thick and sturdy instead of thin and frayed. The boards now looked sturdy enough to hold an elephant. Though the castle itself still leaned to one side, it was just as beautiful, made from the same stone as the pillars, with stain glass windows up on the towers, heavy oak doors guarded the front entrance.

Alice took a deep breath. "Wow."

"Wow indeed." Isa nudged her. "Come along, if we stand out here much longer another Fachan might come after us, or a Red Hat if they've ventured into the territory."

Allie didn't know what a Red Hat was, but she didn't want to find out especially if it was in the same sentence as a Fachan. She followed Isa over the swaying bridge and dared to look down. Swirling green water flowed around the castle in a moat. She stared at it for a moment, the movement of the waves drawing her mind to it. She wanted to wade into it, bathe in the color and the calm waves. Wash away everything that'd happen in the last twenty-four house.

A sharp tug on her collar brought her out of the trace and she looked back at Quillon. Her hands were around the rope and her body ready to jump in.

"Not all enchantments are good ones, Alice. Remember that." He held onto her collar the rest of the way across the bridge.

The doors opened on their own when they approached and Allie found them standing in a tiled room that opened up to two sets of stairs.

"This is where Devlin lives?" Allie choked out. "This is beautiful." She looked around at the woven tapestries done in green and silver thread, reminding her of the silver in her cloak. Each scene seemed to depict an event in history, most likely the history of Fairy.

Footsteps from the left made them all turn and look. A man stood there, his ears pointed and very obvious against his bald head, but he had a red beard that reminded Allie of Devlin, the eyes were the same swirling green. Isa and Quillon both bowed, but Allie stood there in confusion.

The man stood there and crossed his arms as if he was expecting something, but instead of bowing like she was supposed to she blurted out, "who are you?"

"I'm Mercher, Devlin's father, King of the Court of Enchantment."

Allie stared at the man for a moment before bowing slightly. "Forgive me, I didn't realize who you were."

"You're mortal, I don't expect mortals to know me. But I know you, Alice. Follow me."

Allie glanced behind her where the guards stood and Isa motioned her to go forward. Allie followed Mercher up the left set of stairs.

"Devlin spoke of you as if you went missing and now, here you are," Mercher said.

"I haven't been back to Fairy for seven years. I was in the mortal world without a way to return."

He glanced at her over his shoulder. "Did you think perhaps you weren't welcomed back?"

"I honestly thought I had been going crazy, like the doctors said. I almost stopped believing this world existed, until Oriana and Devlin reached out to bring me back."

He stopped at his son's name. "Devlin wouldn't have brought a mortal back here, he knows the risks."

A sinking feeling started in Allie's stomach as Mercher turned around. "He didn't bring me back, he guided me on how to get back. Him and Oriana."

Mercher met her gaze. "Devlin knows the risk which is why he was taken by the Red Queen. I have one chance to get you to her to save him." He snapped his fingers and Isa grabbed Allie's arms and pulled them behind her back.

Allie growled, throwing her body around. "Let me go."

"The Red Queen will be coming here to claim you as soon as I send her a message. Disarm her. Put her in the tower."

Quillon came up and untied her sword from her waist. "Sorry, Alice."

He sounded like he meant it.

She twisted and turned and tried to shove Isa away from her, but the guard didn't even flinch as she pushed Allie up the stairs behind Mercher.

"Settle down, Alice," Isa whispered in her ear. "Don't anger the king. You need to trust us."

Allie growled, but forced herself to settle down so she didn't take the two of them down the stairs. Once at the top of the first stair case, Mercher stepped to the side. "Left wing. Make sure you stay, we don't want her to escape before Queen Cerise gets here."

"She won't give Devlin back," Allie said and Mercher looked at her.

"The Red Queen keeps her word. She'll give him back as long as I deliver you to her." Mercher shook his head. "You know nothing of how this world works, and if you did, then you would have turned yourself over the moment you got here. The Red Queen will stop at nothing to make sure The Alice is dead."

Allie let out a forced laughed. "I'm an eighteen-year-old mortal. How am I threat?"

"Cerise claims you stole her heart, and she wants it back."

"Cerise also wants to take over all the kingdoms." Allie shot back.

The king turned away from her and motioned to a door to their left. "Take her up there. I won't be discussing this any further with a simple human."

Isa nudged Allie to the door and Quillon opened it. Stairs spiraled upwards like something from a cliche fairytale.

"Is there a dragon up there?" Allie asked as Isa guided her forward and she stepped up the first step.

"A dragon?" Isa laughed. "Why would there be a dragon up there?"

"In human fairytales when the princess is locked in the tower, there's typically a dragon to guard her. So, I thought I'd ask."

This time Quillon laughed. "No dragon, you'll have just us." He shrugged. "That will have to do."

"Hmm, two fae from the Court of Enchantment or a dragon...I almost think the dragon would be safer."

Isa continued to walk Allie up the steps. "I have a pack of cards, we can play cards while we wait."

"Cards? You'd play cards with a prisoner?" Allie continued going up. "I mean, I guess I can't complain because that sounds better than being trapped alone in a tower."

They came to a door and Isa let go of Allie's wrists. "Open it up."

She pushed the door opened and found a round room with a canopy bed in the middle. The drapes were done in black and red, matching the stain glass window in the room. She spun around her mouth opened. "This is beautiful."

She walked over to the window and studied the design. A raven was flying through the reds on the window, making it almost look like it was escaping a fire.

Was this the window that Devlin had mentioned? She touched the raven and the glass warmed under her hand. It was enchanted, she was sure of it. The gauntlets on her wrists seemed to warm as well at the contact. How weird.

She turned to face the two guards. "So how long am I stuck up here?"

"I guess until the Red Queen comes to get you." Isa leaned against the now closed door. "Which unless she flies by gryphon, will be a few days."

"I hope you now a lot of card games then." Allie crossed her arms and leaned against the window.

Isa grinned. "Yeah, we do."

"Just don't let her play poker, she'll steal everything you have."

Allie held her arms out. "Unless she wants my clothes, I don't have a lot."

"You have this great sword." Quillon spun it in an expert move. "Where did you get this? It looks like it's from the Court of Time."

"The Twiddle Tree gifted it to me in exchange for my human clothes." Allie shrugged. "So I'm assuming it's magic."

Quillon sheathed it and handed it back to Allie. "Can you use it?"

"Nope." She tied it back around her waist. "If I did, I would have used it against the creature in the forest."

"You're going to need to learn how to use it." Isa pushed away from the door. "And we have maybe three days to teach you."

"Wait, who's side are you on here?" Allie raised a brow. "I'm a prisoner and you want to teach me to use my sword?"

"We're not going to just let Mercher send an innocent human to her death, it's not what we stand for. He may be thinking of the greater good, but we are loyal to Lord Devlin. He typically makes the choices for his father, he's really the one behind running the Court of Enchantment. And if Devlin thinks there's something special about you, then we're going to do what we can to protect you." Isa grinned. "So let's see what you've got, blondie."

Cerise stepped into the coach where Devlin was sitting with his hands chained and a spell carved into his arm to keep him from accessing his fae abilities. She smiled as she sat across from him. "Your father has found Alice for me. He's trading her for you."

"Fool," Devlin muttered.

She reached over and smoothed her thumb over the bruise on his face. "Ace couldn't get an answer out of you on where she was. You truly had no idea that she was heading to the palace?"

He glanced at her and then out the window of the coach. His lack of attention to her irritated her and she racked her nails down his face, drawing blood. "I could have taken your heart, and then all your secrets, your life, everything would be mine," she snarled.

"You'd have to deal with my father. I'm not the ruler of the court yet." His voice was deadpanned. "If you wanted my heart, you would have taken it long ago, Cerise. You don't scare me. There's only one person's heart you want."

"No. I want Alice's head, not her heart." Cerise looked away this time. "And I'll make sure to make it a public execution."

Devlin leaned back in his seat. "What happened to you Cerise? What happened to the girl that wanted mortals to visit? Who had grand dreams of being allies with the humans and the courts living in true peace?"

Cerise paused for a moment. Catching a glimpse of the friend she had in Devlin before. "That girl was naïve. When my mother died, I was forced to take her spot. You all were learning to take over your parents' positions in the courts. I was alone. My father died years ago. My mother killed him in a blind rage. And I swore that I wasn't going to be like her." Anger curled in her stomach and she clenched her fists. "I swore, I wasn't going to be blood thirsty and vengeful, but when Alice never came back, that was it. I'd lost everyone, and then I found my mother's plans. And everything I saw there made sense."

"What plans?" Devlin asked, his voice hesitating ever so slightly.

"The plans to take over the rest of the courts. To unite the land of Fairy into one kingdom. Even past the dark mountains. She had everything planned out, and now I'm just following it." She gave him a smile. "Your court will be mine soon enough, but first I have to take care of that pesky mortal."

Devlin licked his lips and opened his mouth to say something, but Cerise held a hand up.

"Alice is dangerous, my mother knew that. The seer has given the same prophecy twice. Once when Alice first came, and again before she stepped foot through that mirror. When she is taken care of, Devlin, then I will start taking the courts." She patted his knee. "There's nothing anyone can do about it." Because she controlled the Jabberwock, she controlled the hearts of whom ever she wanted. She was unstoppable and she wouldn't be underestimating people like her mother did.

She wouldn't let one person worm their way through her defenses again. Not even the mortal who held a piece of her heart.

Oriana sat on her throne. The quiet room around her was decorated with blue and white banners and tapestries that had frozen pieces of time weaved in them. The dark blue tile on the floor reflected the light above her.

She'd just finished giving her orders to her captain and now she had a moment of peace where she could relax and not be a princess for a second. Though at this point, with her parents still gone, she was more of a queen. The ice blue walls of her throne room seemed to close in at that thought. She didn't want to sit here and rule a court. She wanted to be out in the lands helping the people, like she did when her parents were home.

She ran her hand over the marble throne, blue lines following her finger tips. If only she could freeze time completely until her parents returned. She took a deep breath and banished the thoughts, demanding her mind to return to a sense of peace.

"Mercher is going to trade Alice for Devlin," Dor's voice shattered her peace and she glared at him.

"What do you mean?" Oriana raised a brow. "Mercher shouldn't even know that Alice is here, never mind be able to trade her for Devlin."

Dor let out a dark laugh and landed on the arm of her throne. "The King of Enchantments managed to get Alice into his castle. She's there now and the Red Queen is on her way."

Oriana let out a string of curses and stood up. "We have to intercept them and stop the trade."

"And risk Devlin?" Dor shook his head and flew into her face to keep her from going forward.

She swatted at him. "We'll rescue Devlin and Alice. We can't let have Cerise have either one of them." She stopped walking when Dor kicked her forehead. "I will squish you."

"No, you won't." He snapped back. "You cannot go up against Cerise alone. We need to find Kit or March to back you up."

"Kit is missing still and March is probably at the tea house." She crossed her arms. "And him and I aren't on talking terms."

Dor waved a little hand around like none of that mattered. "Your magic is no match for Cerise's out-of-control abilities and her anger. Let her get to the castle and see what happens there. If they trade, then Devlin can help us rescue Alice. If that's still what you two want to do."

"How do we know Cerise hasn't taken Devlin's heart yet?" Oriana paced. "I feel like she wouldn't give him back so easily."

"That's how much she wants Alice. I saw Devlin, he's in rough shape, but it doesn't look like she's taken his heart."

Oriana nodded. "Okay, let's get to the castle then." She grabbed her cloak off the throne. "I have guards posted around the court to make sure Cerise doesn't try a hostile takeover. I've sent my parents a letter over carrier to warn them as well."

Dor hesitated for a moment. "Do you think it'll reach them?"

"I don't know. The last response I had was over six months ago, and it was short." It'd only been three words. War is coming. Nothing else, no signature, but it came from her parent's carrier so it had to have been them.

She pushed the thought out of her mind. "My bird comes back empty, so I'm assuming someone is getting them."

"We don't know much about what's on the other side of the Dark Mountains." Dor sat on her shoulder as she walked out of the throne room.

"I'm not thinking about that right now, Dor. Right now I need to stay focus on Devlin and Alice. Once we stop Cerise, then I can worry about my parents."

"We need to worry about it because if they don't come back, then you are queen."

Oriana shivered at the word. She was acting ruler right now, but she didn't want to stay that way. Her parents needed to come back and rule, if only because Oriana barely understood the magic her court was granted.

"Oriana?" Dor asked and it was the worry in his voice that made her stop.

She pulled herself out of her thoughts to see that a gray and black striped cat was standing in her way. Her heart pounded. "Kit?"

A wide grin broke out on the cat's mouth and he purred. His big green eyes fell on her and his tail swished behind him. "Hello, Oriana, it's been a while."

She bent down and scooped him up. "Oh my gods, I've been so worried about you." She squeezed him and smiled at his purring. "Are you still stuck in this form?"

"Yes, and I can't really access my magic this way, but I'm making do." He rubbed his face against her. "It's easier to sneak around as a cat, though. So far I've avoided Cerise's guards and her attempts to find me. Though, I've heard some interesting rumors."

She sat Kit back on the ground and Dor flew down and sat on the cat's back. "Oh?"

"That Alice has returned and Cerise is calling for her death." They started walking down the path together toward the stables.

If she rode hard enough, she could beat Cerise to the castle or intercept her, assuming she didn't have too long of a head start. She glanced down at Dor, he had other ways of traveling than just his wings. All the small fae did, so maybe he didn't waste any time getting to her.

"Alice has returned. We're on our way to free Devlin from Cerise so that Mercher can't trade Alice for him."

"How did you guys screw this up so bad? Alice shouldn't be anywhere near Mercher. You should have taken her straight to the seer." Kit let out a growl.

"Alice doesn't exactly come with directions, Kit, and you were missing. So we did what we could do." She paused in front of her stable and ran her hand over the white horse's nose. She turned to a stable hand. "Please ready my horse."

The stable hand nodded and went to work. No one said anything until the horse was ready to ride and the stable hand went to go busy himself with another task.

Oriana picked Kit up and put him in a saddle bag while Dor wrapped himself into the mane of the horse.

"I learned something interesting about Alice while I was in the mortal world." Kit grinned again at her, but his body started to disappear. "It'll make things much more interesting."

The last thing to disappear was the smile that he wore and Oriana cursed. It was hard to tell whose side Kit was on when he teased information like that and then disappeared.

Dor glanced behind him as Oriana nudged the horse forward. "What do you think he's hiding?"

"I don't know, but maybe Alice will."

CHAPTER 6

"And lunge," Isa demanded.

Allie lunged forward, her sword pointed at Isa's chest. Isa blocked it and swiped at Allie.

She stepped back and swung her sword to meet Isa's. Her muscles protested as she pushed Isa back with the blade. Sweat dripped down her face, sticking to the ends of her hair.

"Good, you're improving."

Allie tried to catch her breath, "We've been at this for hours today. We were at it for hours last night. I better be improving."

Isa sheathed her sword and laughed. "That's true." She looked up as the door opened and Quillon walked in with plates of food.

"According to Mercher, Cerise should be here tonight." He sat the plates down on the table. "Which means she's making very good time for traveling."

Allie sat down. "Do we know if Devlin is okay?"

"We have no idea. We have to trust that Cerise hasn't done anything to him so that he's still worth trading for you. If she's stolen his heart, Mercher won't do the trade."

Allie looked at Quillon. "What does that mean? Does she literally steal hearts?"

"No, well, kind of." Isa shrugged. "She imprints her magic on their hearts, and it ties them to her. With each fae she binds that way, the stronger she gets because she can draw on their power."

"She'd be more aptly named the Queen of Hearts, but she took on her mother's title, 'The Red Queen' we were hoping she wouldn't turn out to be as ruthless." Isa shook her head.

Allie took a drink. "What's keeping her from taking the hearts of all the fae?"

"We don't know." Quillon sat his cup down and sighed. "But, we think that she'll only take the hearts of the powerful."

Allie frowned. "She plans on marking the hearts of the kings and queens of the courts, doesn't she?"

Isa nodded. "Which is why we're worried about Devlin. If she marked his heart, she can control the Court of Enchantment."

"But Mercher is still alive, wouldn't he need to die in order to take Devlin's place?" Allie pressed her lips together.

"Mercher will do anything for Devlin. As you saw. He's willing to trade a mortal for his son. What else do you think he's willing to do for him? Step down from the throne?" Quillon shook his head. "It's a dangerous power for anyone to have."

Allie thought about what Quillon had said as she ate. She was picking at her biscuit when the door opened again.

Mercher walked in. "I see you are doing well."

"I mean, I'm locked in a tower, but at least I have my basic needs met and company." Allie shrugged. "It's a lot like being grounded, with the exception of the company."

"Grounded?" Mercher raised a brow. "A human term?"

"It means when the parents take away fun things as punishment. For example, once I failed a test and I couldn't use my phone for a week, because my parents thought I was too distracted by it to focus on homework."

Mercher glanced at Quillon and then to Isa and then shrugged. "You're going to be grounded for a little bit longer then. Cerise seems to have hit a snag in her journey according to the message I just received."

"When are we expecting her then?" Quillon crossed his arms. "Not a half hour ago you said tonight."

"It looks like it'll be tomorrow morning. You have one more night."

Allie wasn't sure what he meant, one more night staying there? One more night of life? Certainly Cerise wouldn't kill her in the Court of Enchantment.

"You really plan on sending me to my death to save Devlin?" Allie asked as she stood. She walked to the window and looked out over the village below. Lights from lanterns and fires were starting to the light the streets and windows. Shapes of people were walking the cobblestone roads, some toward the square, others towards the houses. "What if she's taken his heart?"

"Then I will trade you to her to remove her mark from him. Devlin is the only person I have left. You will be going in his place. Mortals have no place in Fairy."

Alice raised a brow. "Except your kind spent years stealing our children and giving us yours."

"The rumors of changelings are just myths, Alice. Just like if you eat our food you can't leave Fairy. You left once before, haven't you?"

Allie locked her jaw. "Several times. I spent three years coming back and forth."

"Then you should know that there are a lot of myths about us that are wrong. Isa and Quillon, I need you with me."

Allie stretched. "I'll see you guys tomorrow. I'm going to take a bath and then probably turn in for the night."

Isa nodded. "We'll see you in the morning."

"There will be a guard posted at the bottom of the stairs, so you will be marched back up here if you try to leave," Mercher snapped at her.

Allie nodded. "Yeah, I get it. No going anywhere for me until Cerise gets here." Allie turned around and headed toward the bathroom. "Sleep tight everyone." She peeled off her shirt and a moment later she heard the door shut.

She peaked her head out of the bathroom and then pulled her shirt back over her head. She went back to the window with the raven on it. "Okay, I need to know your secret." Allie muttered.

"Find the window, trust the wind, the raven sends his love by night." She stared at it. "Well, it's night time, there's no wind, and you don't seem to be sending anything," she muttered, and then ran her hand over the back of the raven, the glass once again warm to the touch. "This world is so strange, magic words, magic courts, a way to mark people's hearts. This doesn't feel like the same world I visited before."

The image of the bird flickered and now faced her instead of facing the window side. Allie pulled her hand back with a yell of surprise. "And now the windows change, great."

The beak of the bird opened and cawed at her as it melted out of the glass and formed in a massive raven. He shook his head causing all the black feathers to ruffle. No, the feather's weren't all black, they seemed to have dark shades of blues and purple in them as the moonlight danced over them. The bird stepped up up to her and clicked its massive beak.

The thing was big enough to ride, and he kept clicking his beak at her as if trying to get her to do something.

"I must be crazy," she muttered, and grabbed her cloak from the chair, throwing it on and tied her sword around her waist. "Okay, let's go for a ride?"

The bird bent down so she could climb on to his back. Alice took a deep breath and pulled herself on and then bird shot off through the window, shooting into the wind.

Devlin looked out the window in time to see a massive shadow swoop over the sky and he smiled a little knowing exactly what it was.

"Why are you smiling? Are you happy that Alice will be taking your place?"

Devlin looked at Cerise. "I have a feeling that you're underestimating that mortal."

Cerise sneered. "The magical barrier at the mountain pass was your doing, wasn't it?"

Devlin held his hands up and showed her the iron chains he'd been in since they'd left the castle. "How do you expect me to do magic with these, and after you had Ace beat the crap out of me?"

"A friend of yours then. Oriana? Someone trying to buy time for Alice? Maybe Kit has figured out how to use his magic."

Devlin shook his head. "I don't know what either of them are up to right now. Really, Cerise. You act like we all hang out and love each other."

"Like you said, we were all friends once." Cerise leaned forward and if Devlin could lean farther away, he would have. He could feel her magic marching over her skin as if she was out of control under the surface.

"And like you, we've all changed a little." He looked out the window again. "Do you think you'll really be able to kill Alice once you find her?"

Cerise leaned back in her seat. "I know I can. She's nothing but a human that wormed her way into my heart, making me care for her. It's been seven years. There's nothing of that false friendship left."

"She's changed too, you know. Already, she's starting to understand Fairy more."

"She's mortal, if she doesn't get herself killed before I get my hands on her it will be a miracle," she huffed. "I'm glad your father found her, because now I can have that satisfaction."

Devlin leaned his head back and closed his eyes. "It's a long journey, and I'm tired of rehashing the same conversation."

"You were the one who wanted to change my mind, Devlin. I'm tired of the conversation as well."

He just made a *hmm* noise to show that he'd heard her. He knew

Alice had figured out the raven in the window. He'd felt it the moment his spell broke and the bird was freed from his prison.

Alice wouldn't be at his castle, no. She'd be far gone, deeper into the woods of the Court of Enchantment, safe from Cerise. At least for a little longer. The gauntlets would protect her and hopefully Murl had managed to find Alice and give her a cloak. Those should have been enough to get her through until he could catch up with her.

He opened his eyes to find that Cerise had fallen asleep with her head against the wall of the coach. She looked so much younger and innocent when she was sleeping, like the monster hidden below didn't exist.

"Oh Cerise, what has this world done to you?"

Cerise let out a deep sigh as if she was settling into sleep and he reached over and pulled her cloak over her. "Sleep tight, my queen, because when we get there you're not going to be happy."

He leaned back and leaned his own head against the window, letting the bumps of the carriage lull him to sleep.

"Devlin," Cerise's voice rang out across the clearing in the Giant Forest. "She's coming back!"

She danced across the clearing to the purple mushroom. Her red and white dress swirled around her with each move she made. Devlin followed her calmly. "Yes, she's decided to return again." But there was something eating at him about this visit. Alice's visits had been spreading further and further out. What used to be every other day turned into once a week, then twice a month, and now it'd been two months.

Everyone was disappointed when Alice left, but Cerise the most. Even at eleven, Cerise swore she loved Alice. That they were destined to be together.

But Alice was a mortal and with each visit the danger increased.

Alice stepped through the portal, her eye seemed sunken, her blonde hair had been chopped short. Her human cloths hung off her already slim frame. Overalls, if Devlin recalled right, with a baggy shirt, black gloves peaked out from her pockets where her hands were shoved.

"Alice?" Cerise paused, like she also sensed the change.

A wide smile broke across Alice's face at Cerise's voice and the two of them embraced, but there was no dancing and laughing like the other visits.

No. Alice's eyes didn't shine with the light of her smile. Devlin stepped closer. "What's wrong?"

"They tell me at home that I've imagined this place and everyone here. My parents are sending me to a place with no mirrors and only supervised outside visits."

Devlin's heart fell, but he swore he heard Cerise's shatter.

"How long will you be there?"

Alice shrugged a shoulder. "I don't know. I was told until I understand that I'm delusional, and can admit that I imagined all of this." Alice frowned. "Am I? Imagining?"

Cerise pulled her into a hug. "No, Alice, Fairy is as real as the mortal world." She pulled back. "Let's make a deal."

"We'll all meet back here in a month?" Devlin offered. "Play the mortals' game, pretend you made everything up, that should get you free in a month's time. We can come back here and have a tea party."

Alice smiled. "Deal."

And yet...when the day came Cerise stood at the mushroom, waiting. Devlin and Oriana stood with her, but when the portal opened, it wasn't Alice that walked through, but Kit.

"She's not coming, Cerise," he said, so matter of fact, that it was almost smug.

"Where is she?"

"Things happen in the mortal world." Kit shrugged. "But I wouldn't be expecting her any time soon."

Cerise let out a scream that Devlin swore shook the earth.

Devlin jumped away from his dream and tried to relearn how to breathe. He swore he heard that scream again, but when he looked

Cerise was still sound asleep, though her face was creased as if she was stuck in a dream as well.

"Wonder what the Red Queen dreams of." He muttered and leaned his head back against the window.

Allie clung tight to the bird as he flew and glided through the sky. Eventually he lowered to the ground in a clearing. Alice slide off him and wrapped her cloak tight around her as the chill in the air started to bite at her.

"Where are we?" She didn't really expect the bird to answer, but it let out a caw, and then hooked the back of her cloak with his beak dragging her back to him.

Allie let out a cry when he tucked her under his wing and settled next to her. She was about to protest, but the warmth of him surrounded her and she understood. He was just trying to protect her from the elements.

The woods loomed around them, she would have used the term forest, but here most of the trees were bare, their branches reaching up to the sky and some entangled with each other. In the light of the moon, it looked terrifying.

The raven nudged her with his beak and she snuggled further down into his wing as she ran her hand over his side.

"Thank you."

He clacked his beak at her and she leaned against his warm body. "I guess I can close my eyes for a little while."

Alice drifted off as she allowed herself to relax.

"His name is Fehin," A voice made Alice jump from her sleep.

The bird pulled her closer and nipped at the...cat that was on the ground in front of them.

She stared at the cat for a moment. The gray and black stripes were familiar to her, especially paired with the big green eyes. "Kit?"

He grinned at her, showing little cat fangs. "The one and only. You're a hard girl to find, Alice."

Streams of sunlight came through the tree branches and Kit stretched out and then curled up in one. "Cerise has been looking for you. I'm sure the King of Enchantments is furious that you're gone. Oriana, Dor, hell even March is on the lookout for you."

Allie ran her hands over Fehin's feathers. "Once upon a time, I'd be running towards you all, but now I'm worried about avoiding Cerise so that she doesn't kill me."

"It's a strange world, isn't it, Alice?" Kit rolled onto his back and looked up at her. "But I think part of you thinks you belong here."

She was about to argue when he spoke again.

"Don't deny it. You never would have come back if you didn't feel the call of Fairy. You would have turned around and marched right back home after you found out Cerise wanted you dead. After all, that's what you do in the human world, isn't it? Run?"

Allie bristled at his words. "I got tired of all the words and fists that were thrown at me. So yes, I turned away from the conflicts."

"You can't do that here. There won't be any running away, but never fear, Alice, we're all mad here, and you belong here."

She shook her head. "I'm here to stop Cerise once I figure out how and then I have to go back home. My parents already had one child disappear. They don't need me doing the same."

"Home...and where is home, Alice?" He started to fade away, leaving just his grin. "You must ask yourself that." He disappeared completely and Allie crossed her arms.

"What the hell, Kit?

Fehin chattered behind her and then stood up, shaking his feathers. Her stomach growled and Fehin tilted his head.

"Yeah, buddy, it's breakfast time. I didn't exactly think to bring a bag of food with me." She looked around at the barren trees. "I think fruit is out of the question." She rubbed his beak. "Why don't you go look for some food for you. I'll stay right here."

Fehin seemed to nod before he took off to the sky. Alice looked up as he disappeared into the clouds.

She'd probably be a lot harder to find without a giant bird guarding her, but she had no place to go now. It'd been too dark to even see what direction they flew from the castle and had no idea which way she needed to go.

If only she'd bought a map in the village. Alice paced the clearing trying to ignore her stomach growling as she formulated a plan.

If she could find some rocks, she could leave herself markers to at least get back to the clearing if she needed. That was at least a place to start. She knew the village was within walking distance of the castle and the Field of Sleep, so maybe this forest was within walking distance to something as well.

Though hopefully not Cerise's kingdom. Allie wasn't ready to face her yet. If Fehin didn't return by midday, she'd start her trek through the forest.

***

"Announcing Red Queen and Lord Devlin." The court announcer's voice echoed off the chamber and Devlin cringed at how loud it was. There was no reason to yell since there was only a handful of people in the stone room. The throne room rarely saw visitors anymore because Devlin always saw them in the study. He found it more welcoming than the stone walls and dark jade throne.

"Welcome Queen Cerise, I see you've kept your end of the bargain, release my son from his cuffs." Mercher sat in the throne. The dark streaks of green and black through the seat pulsed with power as he spoke.

Cerise looked back at Devlin and then to Mercher. "Once I have Alice, then I'll let Devlin out of his chains. I don't see the girl here. Where is she?"

Mercher nodded. "She's in the tower. I wanted to make sure she wasn't able to sneak out. I hear she's good at that. Isa is guarding the bottom of the stairs."

Good, Isa would have made sure to turn ignore any noises she could have heard from the bottom of the stairs. Devlin looked at his father. "Did you hurt her?"

"No, she's fine. She's been fed and Isa and Quillon kept her company up until I pulled them out this morning."

Devlin nodded. "Thank you. I'd like to speak to her before she goes with Cerise."

"No. You will not, because you will find a way to fairy her away from here." Cerise snapped her fingers and her guard came up behind Devlin and grabbed the chains.

"Take me to Alice, Mercher, and then I'll release your son."

Mercher nodded and motioned for everyone to follow him. They stopped at the entry to the right wing tower, where Isa was leaning against the wall inspecting her nails. Devlin stilled. This wasn't right. His father always put people in the left wing, which was why Devlin had set the raven up there. His heart pounded as he met Isa's eyes and she nodded just slightly. He hoped that was a good thing, because he wasn't sure what he was going to do if Alice was still in that tower and Fehin hadn't gotten her away.

Isa bowed. "Your majesties, everything has been quiet since this morning."

That was a good sign. Cerise motioned to the door. "Out of our way then. I'd like to start the journey back home."

Isa bowed her head and stepped to the side. "Would you like your guard to stay with me and Devlin? It's a little cramped up there."

What the hell was his guard thinking? Devlin kept his face blank. He wanted to see Alice, he wanted to see if she'd managed to escape from the right wing. He'd felt his spell go off, she had to be free.

Cerise nodded. "Yes."

Devlin glanced at Isa again for an idea of what was going on, but her face was blank.

The others walked up the stairs except for the guard holding Devlin and Isa.

"How's Alice?" Devlin asked.

Isa shrugged a shoulder. "Not sure, I haven't seen her since this morning. Last I talked to her she mentioned something about riding a raven. If you ask me she's nuts."

Devlin nodded. "Yeah, she was pretty rambley with me too." That gave him hope that maybe she had found the raven somehow. But then...what was going to happen when Cerise realized Alice wasn't up there.

The three of them waited in thick tension. Devlin didn't dare speak and Isa leaned against the wall again, cleaning under her nails with a knife.

It wasn't long before footsteps and voices echoed down the stairwell. Calm voices. No one sounded like they were shouting or angry. His dad came through the doorway first, behind him was... Alice.

Devlin tried his best to look just as calm and collected as his father, but he couldn't believe that he was sending Alice with Cerise.

Alice looked at Devlin and then smile a little before the guard shoved her forward. Cerise waved a hand and the chains disappeared from Devlin and reappeared on Alice's wrists. "I thank you all for your corporation." Cerise grinned at Devlin. "You'll all be invited to the execution."

Alice looked back at Devlin again, her smile still plastered in place, and it looked fake. Almost like a doll. The smile faded into a frown like she just realized how she was supposed to be reacting to the situation.

Cerise was blind, how could she not notice that this wasn't Alice?

This was an enchanted doll that walked down the hall and then eventually out the door.

"I think we have a lot to talk about," Mercher said once Cerise was gone. "Including why you brought Alice here and where the girl has disappeared to."

Devlin swallowed. "Yeah, probably a good idea." He ran a hand through his hair and followed his father to the study. He preferred this room with its warm fireplace and comfortable chairs. Books lined one wall with a window against the other.

Devlin sat in one of the high-back chairs facing the fireplace.

Isa stood behind him while Quillon took his place behind Mercher.

"So?" Mercher waved his hand. "Tell me."

"Alice was predicted to bring down the Red Queen and her kingdom. Oriana and I guided her back from the mortal world, because Cerise needs to be stop." Devlin leaned back in the chair. "She's where ever Fehin took her. I sealed him in the window in the left wing because I knew that's where you would put her if she managed to make her away here. Honestly, I was hoping that Murl would take her in, because she has a habit of taking in lost things."

"Alice wasn't lost enough for her, I don't think." Isa chuckled. "She does have one of Murl's cloaks, but I don't think she wasted time getting here."

Mercher looked back at them. "You two were in on this scheme?"

Isa shook her head. "No, I had no idea that Alice escaped nor that Fehin was sealed in the window. Quillon?"

Quillon shook his head. "No idea. We were just told to keep an eye out for her."

Devlin nodded. "I didn't know what would happen, so I didn't want to risk Isa or Quil to your temper."

Mercher chuckled. "It's not them I would have been angry at, it would have been you. Which I'm not pleased with you and you were lucky that I had a doll that looked similar enough to Alice, or we would have both been in trouble. As it is, Cerise is going to know as soon as that enchantment wears off that it is not Alice."

"How long does the enchantment last?" Devlin pressed his lips together. "I need to get to the real Alice before that happens."

"Twenty-four hours was the longest I was able to manage, but I'll be surprised if Cerise doesn't catch on by then."

Devlin nodded. "Then I guess I better go find her."

"You are playing a dangerous game, Devlin."

"And if we lose, then all of Fairy loses. Do you want that? Do you want the courts to bow to Cerise and all of us be under her rule? Because I don't."

"You are too much like your mother." Mercher shook his head. "She always had the need to support helpless causes, and that's what got her killed. I could command you to stay here, but you'll do what you always do which is run off anyway."

Devlin tried not to snap about his mother. Visions of her death still plagued his dreams. "Yes, I will, because I don't think this is helpless."

"The Court of Hearts has always been more powerful, it was just a matter of time before they decided to try and take over the other courts. Some of us are just more logical than the others. I don't want to sacrifice our people in a war that we'd lose."

Devlin shook his head. "Our people, our court are worth fighting for. I thought out of all people you'd see that. Oriana's parents I'd get because they don't spend time with their subjects, but you?" Devlin turned toward the painting of his mother that hung on the wall; her red hair and bright eyes stood out of the canvas. "You met mom in that court, you spent time with your people and now you're willing to hand them over to Cerise?"

"It's better than having our villages burned." Mercher shook his head. "You're still too young to know what protecting our people means."

Devlin growled. "I'll see you when all this is over then." He stormed out of the study and headed into the forest.

CHAPTER 7

Allie looked up as Fehin's shadow flew over her and a moment later he landed next to her. A tin roofed cart was clutched in the bird's claws and he sat it down on the ground in front of her. The driver of the cart clung to the frame of his seat staring at Alice with wide eyes.

"What on earth?" Allie walked around the wooden cart. A large loaf of bread was painted on the side.

Fehin preened and danced around as if he wanted praise for bringing her something.

The cart driver stumbled down from his seat and stammered. "I... I, I have no idea."

Fehin tapped his beak on the tin top of the cart and cawed. Allie rolled her eyes. "You saw something shiny and brought it back?"

Fehin held his head up high and cawed again and then lowered his head and nudged her with his beak.

She rubbed her hand over it. "Okay, okay, good boy," she said, and she swore the bird smiled.

"Good boy?" The man cried. "I have never been plucked from the market square by a bird before. I can't sell my breads here, I need to get back."

Allie looked at Fehin. "You brought me a food cart?" Fehin nuzzled her again and she laughed. "How much for a loaf? Do you have anything other than bread?"

"I have some meat and cheese, but my specialty is bread." The man pulled his shirt straight and took a deep breath.

Allie pulled the purple purse from her belt and handed the man a silver coin. "How much will that buy me?"

He looked at it skeptically at first and then back to Allie. "Two loafs and a log of meat."

"Perfect, I'll take it. And then Fehin can take you back." She glanced at the bird and he preened again.

The man gave a shaky nod and went into his cart. He returned with fabric wrapped around the food. "Here you go my good lady, now please have your bird return me."

"Okay Fehin, take him back where he came from."

The man climbed onto his cart and the bird let out a squawk before jumping into the air and grabbing the cart with his claws once more and then taking off.

Allie watched them disappear and then settled back down in the clearing. Now that she knew Fehin would most likely come back to her, staying put was probably the best thing to do and then maybe she could climb back on him and either find her way back to the castle or to the village.

"Fehin is a pretty smart bird, isn't he?" Devlin's voice came from behind Allie and she spun around and couldn't help the grin she had on her face.

She threw her arms around him. "You escaped Cerise?"

"Well, actually, my dad traded an enchanted doll for me. Since you had actually escaped." Devlin hugged her close for a second and then let go. "Cerise will find out soon. So we need to get you out of Court of Enchantment and somewhere else. I'm thinking either Oriana's court, or with March."

"What court does March belong to?"

"No one, he kind of just goes between all of use. He's probably at the tea house which might not be the best place to meet him." Devlin paced in front of her. "Cerise will probably check there for you since it's neutral territory, she'll expect us to take you there."

"What can I do to fight her?" Allie put a hand on his shoulder. "You guys keep saying that I'm supposed to stop her, but I don't know how. I don't know if I can fight her? You guys, the fae, you move so much faster than humans, I saw it with Isa and Quillon while they were teaching me to sword fight. I've seen your powers and Oriana's. I have no magic. I'm a mortal, carrying around a sword."

Devlin looked at her, his eyes meeting her gaze. "I don't know, and that's why we're shuffling you around until we can figure it out."

"That's a horrible plan. Why bring me here without an actual plan?"

He paused and looked up at the sky. Maybe he was hoping for Fehin to come down and interrupt the conversation.

"Devlin?"

"Sorry. The spell you had hidden in your book was the last spell. Kit was tasked with destroying all spells and, well we needed to bring you in before he destroyed that one."

"So you have no plan at all?"

Devlin nodded. "Yeah, pretty much winging it at this point."

"Okay, can she use her power on me?"

He frowned. "Which power?"

"The heart one."

"No, you're mortal, it'd kill you. Which of course, that is her intention." He cringed.

Allie tried not to think about it. "What other magic of hers do I need to worry about?"

"Oh, Alice. We have to worry about all of it." He shook his head. "This was a stupid idea, maybe my father was right." He started pacing the clearing, the underbrush crunching under each of his steps.

Allie crossed her arms and leaned against a tree. She shivered as the bark brushed against her skin. She turned to look at the tree and snorted. She'd leaned up against an actual fur tree. "And what did he say?"

"Essentially that we should just bow down to Cerise to make sure none of our people come to harm."

She scoffed. "Let's prove him wrong. We'll figure it out. Let's get Oriana and we'll form a plan. Maybe talk to the Seer if we can and they will give us a clue?"

"Cerise keeps the Seer in her castle."

Allie rubbed her eyes. "There has to be more than one Seer in this world."

Devlin again hesitated. "There is, but the other one is a bit… loony."

She motioned to the tree behind her as the fur blew in the breeze. "This whole world is a bit loony. How bad can he be?" She tried not to bring up the worst case scenario. In Fairy who knew what "a bit loony" meant.

"Oh she's insane, but she might be our only option."

Allie crossed her arms. "Kit told me that everyone here is mad, so I guess I shouldn't expect anything other than a crazy."

"You saw Kit?"

She nodded. "Yeah, in his cat form. He spouted a few strange things and then disappeared."

Devlin glanced around. "As soon as Fehin gets back, we leave."

"Something wrong?" Allie asked.

Devlin lifted one shoulder. "I'm not sure, something just feels off. I rather not stay in this court longer than we have to."

"It's your court."

"I know and Cerise will come back the moment the enchantment on that doll fails. Maybe that's what making me nervous.

Allie nodded slightly. "Well, it took Fehin a couple hours to return when he when he went to get the cart. So it'll probably a while before he returns."

"Yeah, meanwhile, you and I are going for a walk." He grabbed her hand and started toward the same direction that Fehin flew off to.

———

Cerise stared at Alice's blank face. She should have seen it sooner, but something was off about the girl sitting in front of her. Her hair was almost too blond, her eyes blue not hazel, and her smile was fake.

Especially since she shouldn't have been smiling knowing that Cerise was going to kill her.

"How have you been Alice?" She asked.

Alice stared blankly at her, almost looking like a posed picture against the red velvet of the carriage seat.

"I asked you a question." Cerise demanded, but the girl just smiled at her.

Unblinking. Not human. Cerise reached out and ran her hand over Alice's cheek, she had expected the warmth of flesh against her hand, not rubber.

A doll.

"Turn the coach around!" Cerise demanded, banging on the roof to alert the driver. "We are going back to the palace now."

The coach jerked and the fake Alice fell to the side, still smiling.

Cerise let out a growl. How did she not see this before they left? Devlin was either a good actor or he had no idea that his dad hadn't traded the real Alice for him. Mercher was going to pay for this. How dare he enchant and give her a doll like she was a child?

She leaned back in her seat and watched as the enchantment faded from Alice, probably brought on by the fact that Cerise saw through it. Cerise crossed her arms and tried to decide what to do with Mercher for this.

Either off with his head or she'd take his heart...or she'd go after Devlin again.

Mercher deserved to have his son taken from him for this stunt.

She pressed her lips together and imagined the look on Mercher's face if Devlin was forced to stay by her side because she marked his heart.

All his abilities at her beck and call until she either killed him or released him. Maybe she could get Mercher to trade his court for his son. He seemed to care enough for that.

The coach jerked to a stop and Cerise waited for it to start again, but when it didn't move, she got out. "What is the meaning of this?" The fur trees rustled around them as she looked around.

She paused when she saw someone in the road. His black hair was pulled up on his head, tucked into a neat bun that seemed to absorb the light. His clothes were stitched with white threat that stood out against the dark brown of the fabric, a symbol was wove over his heart. Cerise tried to remember where she'd seen it before.

"Are you insane? Get out of the way so we can go back," she demanded.

"Going back is not going to help, your majesty." The man met her gaze. "Mercher is already moving guards around to every entry. It seems that his son has run off with The Alice."

She took a few steps forward, but Ace stepped between them. "Get back in the carriage. Let me handle this."

"If you want to catch Alice, you'll have to search another court. I saw Devlin's raven flying to the north."

She should have never given Devlin that stupid bird. Cerise stepped to the side so she could see the man around Ace. "What's your name?"

"Zio, your majesty. I reside between the courts." He bowed at the waist.

Resided between courts...she glanced at the symbol again. Thorn branches woven through each other, a symbol of the Bèarn. Her mother had warned her of them. She could remember her notes clearly now. They weren't to be messed with. They'd tried to take over the courts on this side of the mountain during the great war.

She forced a smile. "Thank you for the information Zio, and saving us time." She turned and got back into the coach.

Ace climbed in the coach with her instead of staying outside. "Your majesty, Zio could have been simply trying to keep us from returning to the Court of Enchantment. Why believe him?"

She peaked out of the read curtained window before they started moving again. "Because, he's one who lives beyond. He's a person of the Bèarn." The coach jerked as they started to move.

Ace looked at her, his gaze roaming her face. "Cerise, I know your mother believed in those wild tales, but I expected you to have a better grasp on reality. Those people don't exist anymore. They were wiped out in the war that divided Fairy. If any of them are left, they are on the other side of the Dark Mountains."

Cerise nodded. "Which is why I'm worried about one being in my kingdom." The things those people had done during the war had been horrific and made every evil person in Fairy look tame.

"We're not even sure if there is life on the other side of the Dark Mountains anymore. The king and queen of the Time Court went to explore and never returned."

Cerise snorted. "They didn't go to explore, they went to redo the spell that trapped the creatures over there. That froze them in time... if Zio really is a Bèarn than they have failed at their task." She sat straighter. "Just another good reason for me to take over all the courts, the other rulers are incompetent."

Ace said nothing as the coach continued to move forward, but she didn't miss him studying her as they went.

He didn't have to believe her about the Bèarn or the others on the Dark Side of the mountains. If she could unify the courts under her, they could withstand a battle, and she would be the ruler of all Fairy. Both sides of the mountains.

She smiled at the thought of that. Yes, she was destined for big things. "I think it's time we see the Seer again."

"As you wish." Ace nodded. "We'll see him first, and then?"

"Then we set out to find Delvin and Alice."

Allie followed Devlin through the forest. She stepped over the fallen branches and trunks in her attempt to keep up with him. Each tree she touched seemed to have a different feel to them. Fur trees were covered with small strands of different colored furs. The ever green tree shifted through hues of greens and the bark was jagged to the touch. The leaves under their feet crunched, but instead of crumbling they unwrinkled themselves. Allie found it all very strange as she followed him.

"It's almost nightfall, how come we haven't seen Fehin yet?"

It took Devlin a moment to answer. "I don't know. I can only assume that he doesn't think it's safe." Worry coated his words.

"Devlin," Allie put a hand on his arm and turned him to face her. "What is going on?"

He met her gaze and then glanced around them. "Not here, Alice. We're close to an inn. There we can get some food and talk." He pulled the hood of her cloak over her head. "Don't talk to anyone."

She frowned at him. "Devlin?"

He put a finger to her lips. "I'm trying to keep you safe. I can't do that if you don't listen to me."

She nodded and he took her hand, pulling her through the darkening woods. Flickering lights shone somewhere close in front of them, and once they broke the barrier of the trees Allie could see a two story building surrounded by floating flickering lights. Voices could be heard coming from the propped open doors.

Devlin smiled back at her and put a finger to his lips to remind her to be quiet. He pulled her toward the doors and into the inn.

A warm fire danced on the far left side of the room. Tables were filled with people drinking and eating, chatter filled the room and felt like a pressure against Allie's skin. She stepped closer to Devlin as she looked at the people around them. Some were dirty, some were pristine, some wore tight-fitting clothes, and some none at all. Allie swore one guy in the back was wearing a white dress splattered in blood.

Not speaking suddenly sound like a great idea. She continued to glance at the patrons from under her hood as Devlin guided her further through the crowd and to the bar.

"Hey Dev!" The bar tender's voice seemed to boom over the room and the crowd quieted just a little.

Devlin pulled Allie closer. "Hey, Rex, we're looking for a place to stay tonight, discretely of course."

Allie had the urge to pull her hood further down as she felt Rex study her. She cast her eyes down at the wood wondering which species of tree it was made from. Her eyes traced the dark lines in the slate. She could almost see her reflection in the wood it was so clean.

"Hmm, who's this? You don't normally bring someone with you, Dev."

"I know." Devlin said quickly. "But who she is can't be said. We'll be out of your hair in the morning. Please?"

There was a moment of silence from the bar tender and Allie held her breath hoping that he'd say yes.

"Only cause it's you. You and your father fighting again?"

"Kind of. Look, this is just really important and the less you know, the better."

Rex slide a key across the wood and into Allie's view. "Your room, I'll make sure no one disturbs you."

"Thanks Rex." Devlin grabbed the key and then tugged Allie to the right, through the crowd. They passed pairs of feet, stools, and tables as they walked over the wooden floor. A hallway came into view and Devlin squeezed her hand as they started to ascend the stairs hand in hand.

Allie let go of his hand when they approached a door at the end of a hall. "You have your own private room?" She pulled her hood down.

"Shush." He reminded her and unlocked the door, motioning for her to enter.

She walked in and looked around at the massive bed in the middle of the room with a table on each side. Off to the left was a dresser with a couple cloaks thrown on it and various cloth hanging out of the drawers. Devin walked over and added his cloak on the top.

Allie took her cloak off and sat on the bed.

He looked at her. "Sorry. I didn't want to draw any more attention to us."

"You just paraded me around a bar with a cloak draped over me, and asked the bartender for your private room." She motioned around. "Which you seem to use quite often."

Devlin glanced around and then quickly shoved some of the clothes in their drawer so they shut all the way. "I'm here often because when my dad and I don't get along and I'm not in the workshop, this is where I come."

"Ah, a home away from home." She stood and went to the window. A field spread out over the land instead of mountains. Purple lights dotted the green, shining under the moonlight. They swayed in the wind and Alice swore she could hear voices.

Devlin came up behind her. "Ah, the Fields of Regret. Don't go there."

She glanced at him. "Aren't we have to go through it if Fehin doesn't come for us?"

He paused for a moment. "No, we'll go around. It's rare that people make it through that field alive. Those lights you see, those are souls still wandering around."

Souls? Allie looked back at the field. How did souls get trapped in a field? "Why is everything if Fairy so dangerous? How do you guys live through this stuff?"

He laughed and sat on the bed. "We're fae; we're used to things like this. The weaker of us die and the stronger survive. I believe the mortal phrase is 'survival of the fittest.'"

Allie nodded. "So all those souls were weak fae?"

"There are some mortals in there. You guys used to wander into our land a lot more. Of course over the years we've strengthened our spells to keep you guys out, because well...you don't typically survive here."

Allie snorted. "Then how am I to defeat Cerise or whatever I'm supposed to do?" She couldn't imagine running up to Cerise and stabbing her with her sword.

"I told you I don't know. We'll figure it out." He shrugged.

"And that's why we're going to go see the looney seer."

He laughed. "Yeah, that's why we're going to see her."

A tapping came on the window and Allie jumped, Devlin cursed and opened the door to let Dor in.

"Where have you been? I've been searching all over for you." Dor zipped in, flying past her face.

Allie shrugged. "I was flown away by a giant bird."

Dor stared at her, his tiny eyes wide. The tips of his brown clothes fluttered with the beat of his wings as he tried to figure out if she was joking.

Devlin laughed. "She met Fehin."

"You let her ride on that monster?" Dor shook his head. "That thing tried to eat me!"

Allie leaned forward so she was face to face with him. "Good thing I'm a little bigger than you."

"Fehin thought you were a bug. I told you that he was sorry," Devlin shrugged. "And it hasn't happened again."

Dor put his hands on his hips and silently mocked Devlin. "Look, we need to go to the tea house and meet with Oriana."

"We'll rest tonight and then tomorrow we'll head out. Alice and I have been walking through the woods all day and we're both exhausted."

"I'd like a shower and some clean clothes, actually." Allie looked down at her dirt stained clothes. "Is that a possibility?"

"The bathroom is the door on the left, enjoy." Devlin smiled at her. "I'll find you some clean clothes.

Allie grinned. "Thank you." She walked into the room to find a large tub already filled with steaming water. It must have been nice to live in a world where everything was magic.

Allie pulled her clothes off and sank into the hot water, letting it soak into her muscles, and relaxed.

Cerise watched the flames of their campfire dance. Ace went to scout the area to make sure there weren't any other Bèarn around. The warmth of the fire kept the chill off her, but the shadows made her paranoid of whatever might have been waiting for them. The other soldiers that came were stationed around her, some of them talking to each other as they made camp, and others working silently.

Ace came and set next to her. "The woods are clear for now. We should be to the back at the palace midnight tomorrow if we leave at sun up."

"And then hopefully we'll have some answers about this chaos." Cerise glanced at him. "Alice returning, Bèarn coming back, what else is waiting for us?"

"I know you're worried, your majesty, but keep moving forward with your plan. Once Alice is gone, that's one less thing to worry about." Ace shrugged. "One less human here."

Cerise couldn't pull her eyes from the flames. "Do you think Alice and the Bèarn are connected?"

Ace was quiet for a moment. "I'm not sure. You said the seer said Alice would bring down the Red Queen, but there was no mention of how."

Cerise nodded. "There are many ways to bring down a queen. One of them would be to lead enemies to her door or to her kingdom. But I don't think a mortal would be smart enough to do that. Alice has no knowledge of our history. She wouldn't know to look for the Bèarn."

"We know that she's working with the other courts, maybe it's one of them that brought the Bèarn into play. We know Oriana's parents are on the other side of the Dark Mountains."

Cerise frowned. "That's a possibility, maybe Alice has been in contact with them this whole time. Seven years..." She thought back to the last time she saw Alice and her heart ached. "Seven years ago, she wouldn't have thought to betray me."

"Seven years ago, you two were mere children. You have risen to queen and Alice is merely a mortal. If she's been plotting against you, then it's been with the guidance of the others."

Cerise agreed, but stayed silent. "Have we had any luck with finding Kit?"

"No, your majesty." Ace shrugged. "He doesn't seem to want to be found."

"Typically he starts to pop up before things go to hell, he can't help but come for the drama." He'd been that way before her mother cursed him too.

Ace chuckled. "That's one way. He's also known for stirring the pot, which is why he was cursed into his cat form."

"My mother was smart to do that. Though we don't know how much that affects his powers."

"We'll find him, milady," Ace promised. "Once he knows that the courts are in trouble, he'll come running."

She shivered as a breeze crossed over her. "I think I'll turn in for the night."

Ace glanced at her. "I think that's best. It's chilly tonight, I made sure your furs were laid out and a warming pan was sat between them."

"Thank you, Ace." She stood and he grabbed her hand.

"Rest well." He squeezed her hand.

She slipped her hand out of his and walked to her tent. Her furs were laid out on a pad in the middle of the tent, she didn't bother changing from her clothes before she climbed into the warmth.

Devlin sat on the bed and kicked his boots off while Alice was in the bath. Dor was perched on window seal.

"What do you think?" Dor asked.

Devlin raised a brow. "About what? This whole situation?"

Dor jerked his head towards the bathroom door. "About Alice. Do you think she really will be able to defeat the Jabberwock and convince Cerise to not take over the rest of the courts?"

Devlin put a finger to his lips. "I haven't told her about the Jabberwock yet, not really. She has no idea that she's going to have to fight it."

"You haven't told her? She's going to go in unprepared for this fight and die. You know what happens if she gets bit by it."

Devlin shrugged. "We don't really, because she has no magic for it to steal."

"Right, because that's going to be worse than the agonizing death that she'll experience." Dor rolled his eyes. "You're going to have to tell her."

"And I will. Right after we go see Cibil." He kept his voice low and his eyes on the bathroom door.

Dor choked. "Cibil? Are you kidding me? That woman hasn't been right since the war. She's insane, Devlin."

"She's also the only seer we have access to right now. Unless we want to sneak into Cerise's castle and see Lavin."

Dor wrinkled his tiny nose and his wings buzzed behind him. "No. I don't think that would end well for any of us."

"Exactly. So we're going to Cibil after we meet with Oriana at the tea garden." Devlin bit his lip. "Which if Fehin comes back will be a quick trip."

"And if he doesn't, you're either going to have to brave the Field of Regrets, or go around it which adds two days to your journey and takes you through old war lands."

Devlin looked out the window at the purple spirits frittering around. "I really don't want to go through that field."

"Scared you'll get stuck there?"

Devlin shrugged. "With Cerise becoming queen and Alice never returning until now? The Courts are feuding more and more. I just wish I could have done more before."

"Cerise made her choices. We couldn't prevent them. She tamed the Jabberwock after her mother passed away, she chose to follow her mother's footsteps in the plans to try and take over the courts. This is not our fault."

Yet, there was still a strange ache in his chest as he thought about it. He went to the dresser and opened the bottom drawer and pulled out blankets. "Alice needs some clean clothes, will you run down stairs and see if Missy has any that would fit her?"

Dor raised a brow. "That's going to let Missy know that you have a girl up here. She's going to want to meet Alice."

Devlin nodded. "Yeah, I know, but clean clothes are needed. Please, Dor?"

He zipped through the room and squeezed himself through the crack.

Devlin made himself a bed on the floor while he waited for Dor to return. It wasn't long before there was a knock at the door.

Devlin answered in and a woman in long skirts and corset walked in. The brown and grays of the fabrics swirled as the dark hair woman swiveled around searching the room. "Devlin, how dare you bring a lady here and not tell me." Her voice was high pitched, but soft. She'd braided her hair tonight so that it fell down her back, leaving her face clear and her pointed ears exposed. "Where is the lovely girl?"

Devlin jerked his head to the bathroom door. "She's still in the bath."

"Dor was telling me that you've dragged that poor girl all over Fairy." Missy huffed. "You know mortals aren't supposed to stay here Devlin, they start wanting to stay forever."

"Did Dor tell you who this girl was?" He sat on the bed.

Missy shook her head and put her hands on her hips. "She better be important."

"She's The Alice," Devlin whispered. "The one that the seer

spoke of at the queen's death. The one that has come to slay the Jabberwock."

Missy's eyes grew wide. "You're saying that *The Alice* is a young mortal?"

"I don't know any other Alices that wander into our land, do you?" Devlin crossed his arms.

Missy was silent for a moment and she glanced to the bathroom door. "Does she know?"

"She knows that she's supposed to bring down the Red Queen." Devlin sighed. "The Tweedle Tree gave her a sword, and I know Isa worked a little bit with her on how to use it, but I doubt it's enough to bring down that beast."

"Then you need to teach her more. And Oriana needs to get involved as well. Oh my goodness you children have such a way of getting in trouble. Does your father know where you are?"

Devlin snorted. "Him and I are not on talking terms right this moment."

"I'm going to take that as a no. Okay." She laid the clothes on the bed. "These are for Alice. I'll get you some food together for your journey."

"Thank you, Missy."

The woman patted his cheek. "Your mother would haunt my inn if I let her boy go out without previsions."

Devlin smiled. "My mother may haunt you for letting me do this."

"No, she won't. She understands what you're trying to stop." Missy looked over as the bathroom door opened and Alice walked out wrapped in a towel. "Oh, hello there."

Alice glanced between the two of them. "Um, hi." She gripped the towel a little tighter.

"Alice, this is my mom's friend Missy. She brought you up some clothes, and she's going to get us a bag of food so we have something to eat while we travel across Fairy."

She pulled the towel tighter around her. "Thank you so much."

"You'll find some warm night clothes there for you as well. I'll try to round up some more clothes and wash your other ones tonight so you'll have more while you travel."

"Thank you so much, I didn't think to bring extra clothes with me." She sat down on the bed and started ruffling her short hair with her hand. "Honestly, I didn't think I'd be staying this long."

Missy laughed. "That's what every mortal says who visits Fairy. You two have a good night and stay out of trouble." She left.

Alice picked up the clothes that Missy had left for her. "Thank you for asking her for clothes."

"Of course." Devlin stood. "I'll step out so that you can get dressed."

Alice shook her head. "I'll step in the bathroom. You're fine." She disappeared back into the bathroom.

Devlin laid on his makeshift bed and stared up at the ceiling. This was really where everything was going to start. He'd left his court behind to help a mortal and to hopefully save the court he loved.

CHAPTER 8

Allie woke early in the morning when the sun was just peeking in the window. The only sound in the room was Devlin's soft snoring making Allie wonder what had woke her. She stood, wrapping the green blanket around her and walked to the window. She expected to see Fehin outside waiting for them, but there was nothing but the purple lights still dancing in the field.

There was something mesmerizing about watching them. Allie imagined herself dancing around with the lights, letting the field drain her regrets away from her mind.

She closed her eyes and swore she could hear music in her ears and her body started to sway to it.

"Alice?" Devlin's voice brought her out of the trance. When she opened her eyes, she wasn't standing at the window anymore. She was at the edge of the field, her hand stretched outward. Her blanket had been discarded somewhere, the blades of grass tickled her bare feet.

She swallowed as her sense of peace disappeared and was replaced by panic. "Devlin?" Her heart pounded as she tried to get herself to turn around and see him, but her body refused to move. The music still sounded in her head, but instead of light and flowy, it had turned into something more demanding. A rhythm pounded in her head, urging her to take a step forward.

"Come on, take a step backwards." His voice was soothing, calm, like she wasn't on the edge of a death field.

"You regret coming to Fairy." A voice whispered to her and she felt like something was pulling her toward the field. Her foot took a step forward.

Panic cause her breathing to speed up as she looked down at her foot seeing the tip of it in the field.

"You regret giving up the truth." Another voice whispered and it sounded like it came from right in front of her. "Your choices in high schools, the things you tell your therapist, abandoning your friends..."

Allie took another step. "I should have never tried to forget Fairy, and I should have gone to the same school as my friends. I was selfish for wanting a school with a better art program. I shouldn't have gone along with dad's plan of moving away."

A hand wrapped around her arm and pulled her back, jerking her off her feet and on to the person that yanked her away from the field.

She tumbled on top of them, and got up, ready to yell, but Devlin stood there in front of her.

"Sometimes selfish choices are okay," he said as he stood and brushed himself off. "What's not okay is dwelling on 'what could have beens' and 'I should haves.'" He held his hand out. "Come back to the inn with me, Alice. You don't want to walk out into that field."

She glanced over her shoulder to see the purple lights moving quicker around.

"Alice look at me," Devlin demanded and put his hand on her cheek, turning her face towards him. "You are where you need to be. Walk with me, please?"

She searched his pleading eyes. She put her hand in his and he gently pulled her back toward the inn. With each step away from the field, the pressure lifted from her chest and her limbs. Her breathing evened out as Devlin led her back inside. The bar was empty this time of the morning, not even Missy was standing around.

Devlin led her up the stairs and into the room.

"What were you thinking?" He asked, his voice low.

She sat on the bed and shook her head. "I don't even know how I got out there. I was watching the field through the window and then closed my eyes. I didn't know I was outside until you called my name." She tried to remember anything that she might have felt or heard to tell her how she got outside. "It's like I just traveled out there."

Devlin sat next to her. "Fairy has a way of calling mortals. It's why our myths are so scary to them. The whole idea of eating our food or drinking here was something mortals feared in the past. Something as simple as giving us your name was tied with horrible things. But, even though we hold powers, it's really the world that's enchanted and magical. It's possible that the field just called you there."

"But why?" Allie met his gaze.

He was silent for a moment. "I don't know. I wish I had an answer for you." He patted the pillow. "We have a couple more hours before we need to get up. Let's get some more rest."

He grabbed the blanket from the floor and motioned for Allie to lie down. "Come on?"

She raised a brow. "Together?"

"Just lying next to each other. You humans and your weird ways. It'll be easier for me to tell if you get out of bed and try to disappear again if I'm lying next to you."

It made sense, and it wasn't like she hadn't shared a bed before, but it was strange how casual Devlin made it sound. She took a deep breath and tried to push her nerves away before she lay down and covered herself with a blanket. Devlin lay next to her and pulled his own blanket over and let out a long sigh as they both tried to fall asleep.

Cerise watched the sunrise while she cupped her hands around the warm mug. Ace's men had made coffee over the fire, one of the best things that came from the mortal world.

"What are you thinking?" Ace asked as he sat down with his own mug.

"I had a dream that Alice was standing on the edge of the Field of Regret." She sipped her coffee. "It felt so real, like I was there with her."

Ace made a *hmm* noise. "And did you hear what the flowers were saying to her?"

She paused. She'd heard everything the voices had told Alice, but she was focused on only one. "That Alice regretted coming to Fairy."

"Do you think she really does?"

Cerise sipped her mug and thought about how to answer. "I don't know, I haven't seen her since she's been back. And before? She always seemed so happy to be here, to escape from the mortal world. Maybe whatever happened in the mortal world is why she regrets it."

Ace patted her shoulder. "It's just a dream, your majesty. There's nothing to dwell on. Come, the soldiers are done packing the tents, let's get back to the palace so you can see Lavin and get more answers." Ace stood and held his hand out to her.

Cerise took his hand and let him pull her to his feet. "And if it wasn't just a dream?"

"Then maybe something will convince her to go home." Ace shrugged. "Which would solve our problem, wouldn't it?"

Cerise nodded and stepped into the coach. Would Alice going home solve their problem? She had the spell she could come back at any time that she pleased. Though, there was something about seeing Alice in the dream. The look on her face of peace tugged at Cerise's chest and she wanted to go to her old friend. Keep her from the fate of walking into the field of regret.

No. She had to keep her mind straight. Alice needed to go if Cerise was going to succeed in taking over the courts and unifying Fairy.

She settled in her seat waiting for the horses to start moving, but nothing happened. She frowned and stuck her head out of the door. "Ace?"

No answer came from the silence. The world around her seemed to have just stopped. Everyone was frozen where they were, except for her and Oriana who stood in the middle of the soldiers.

"What are you doing here, you little traitor?" Cerise got out of the coach. "Unfreeze my men now."

"Maybe your men should be better at keeping you safe." Oriana ground out. "I want you to leave Alice alone." Oriana's blue tail coat blue around her from the power she was using. Her eyes glowed ice blue, the same color as the veins of power running through her skin.

Cerise growled. "She's going to bring down the kingdom. I can't allow that." She stomped toward Oriana, but hit a barrier. "You coward. Face me now."

"I'm telling you that she's not going to bring it down, she's going to save it. Ask your seer."

Cerise saw a bead of sweat trickle down Oriana's face. "Straining yourself a bit?" Cerise grinned. "How about this? I'll give you a chance to leave and I won't mark your heart, yet. Or, I'll force my power through your little bubble."

"You can't mark my heart, Cerise, you can't control the courts. It will unbalance Fairy." Oriana growled. "Go home and stay there."

"So Alice can kill me?" Cerise shot back. "So one of you can take over my court? No." She shoved her magic out and the bubble around Oriana shattered, making the woman cry out. Cerise stalked toward her until her body stopped, frozen in place. "Let me go, Oriana."

"No." Her voice shook. "Not until you listen to me. Alice is not supposed to kill you."

"Lavin said she would bring down the Red Queen. I am the Red Queen! She will destroy my plans for Fairy and kill me. Ending my court." Cerise growled out. "Let me go Oriana, you're wasting your power and your time."

Oriana met her gaze with tears. "You are so blind, Cerise. So incredibly blind." There was a flash of white and when Cerise's vision cleared, the guards were looking around confused and Oriana was gone.

The princess of the Court of Time was getting stronger. Last time Cerise had seen her abilities Oriana could barely make the grass stop moving and could simply slow time down, not stop it all together. Cerise spun to go back into the carriage, anger filling her. She needed to speak to her seer, now.

Allie woke with her head lying on Devlin's shoulder and his arm wrapped around her body. She let out a soft sigh at the warmth of him pressed against her.

Devlin's arm twitched and then he opened his eyes. He turned to look at her and gave her a smile. "Glad to see you're still here."

Allie sat up and rubbed her eyes. "Yeah, no magically being transported somewhere else. Thanks for keeping me safe."

He stretched and sat up. "Of course. Let's get some breakfast and then get out of here."

"Is Fehin back?" She grabbed the clothes that Missy had left for her off the dresser. "Or are we going to have to attempt to navigate that field?"

He hesitated for a moment. "I don't think Fehin is back, but we're not going through that field either. Not after what happened. So we'll work on going the long way until Fehin catches up."

"You're so sure he'll find us?" Allie asked as she walked into the bathroom.

"Yes, he's trained to find me." Devlin's muffled voice came through the door. Alice quickly got dressed, glad to see that Missy had provided a pair of black pants and another black pirate shirt. She walked out of the bathroom and held her arms out to Devlin. "Do you guys have an obsession with pirate clothes?"

"You could be in a corset," Devlin offered. "You'd look great in it, but it's hard to travel and fight in one."

Allie raised a brow. "Yeah, no, corsets aren't an option."

He laughed. "I didn't think you'd want one. Come on." He grabbed a bag off the bed and they both went down stairs to find the inn mostly empty. A few early travelers were sitting at tables eating and talking quietly.

Devlin led her to a table in the back. "Wait right here."

"I'm not going to just up and disappear on you."

He raised an eyebrow at her and she let out an irritated sigh. "On purpose."

Devlin chuckled and then walked away toward the bar. Allie sat back, putting her back against the wall and observed the few people around her. Most of them had their heads down. The couple closest to her had a paper on the table that looked like a map.

Allie wondered what kind of adventure they were planning and if it was as dangerous as the journey her and Devlin seemed to be.

Devlin came back and put two bowls on the table. "Eat up."

She looked at the dish in front of her. Globs of something stuck together, half floating in white liquid. "What is this?"

"Porridge." He laughed. "What? You don't have anything like it the mortal world?"

"No we do, it's just not something I've eaten before." She poked a floating glob with her spoon. "Is it good?" The white lump bobbed up and down in the liquid.

"It's sweet, you'll love it." He took a big spoonful of his and let out a *mmm* sound. "Missy doesn't make anything that's not good."

Allie scooped up some and tasted it. The sweet taste of sugar and cinnamon hit her tongue and she almost moaned. "Okay, that's delicious."

"I told you. And you doubted me. I wouldn't feed you anything gross." He chuckled and continued to eat. Allie glanced again at the couple that was leaned over the paper.

The woman's pointed ears twitched and Allie swore she glanced over at them. Something clenched in her gut and she turned away from the fae.

Devlin glanced over and then back to Allie. "Bounty hunters. They are plotting where their next mark is going to be."

"We probably should have been a bit more quiet about who I was then. If Cerise wants me, would she send bounty hunters?"

Devlin nodded. "But they wouldn't dare attack you when you're with a member of a court. So we just need to make sure that you stay with me or Oriana."

"How many courts are there?"

"Four, The Court of Enchantment, The Court of Time, The Court of Hearts, and The Court of Creation. All faes live within one of these courts, but most of them are loyal to all. Cerise wants to unify all of them under her rule. If you believe the rumors, there's four other courts on the other side of the Dark Mountains, but as far as we know, all those courts were destroyed after the war."

Allie frowned. "But you don't know for certain?"

"Oriana's parents are over there now, they haven't reported anything about courts or fae or creatures of any sort for that matter on the other side of the mountains. So I would say they are just rumors."

She nodded. "So you're prince of the Court of Enchantment. Oriana?"

"Princess of the Court of Time."

"Okay and Cerise is the Court of Hearts. So who is the in charge of the Court of Creation?"

Devlin shrugged. "No one know. Their castle is shrouded in shadows. They don't allow visitors. They send a representative any time that the courts meet, but the person who comes isn't powerful enough to be holding the court seat."

"Is it Dor? Maybe he just doesn't want to be bothered with meetings." Allie finished her porridge and sat her spoon down. "Kit?"

"It's not Dor, the small fae like him tend to belong to the Court of Time or the Court of Hearts. They don't have their own court."

Allie nodded. "Okay, so what about Kit?"

"Kit is loyal to the Court of Enchantment, we're not exactly sure where he came from. Honestly, Allie, every court has people dedicated to figuring out who rules The Court of Creation, but none of us have any leads." He shrugged. "My father has an entire chart on ideas and theories."

She snorted. "I'd like to see that chart someday."

"Well, if we survive this then I'll take you back to the castle and let you look it over."

"Mm, I'm sure your dad would love that."

Devlin finished up his breakfast and stood. "Yeah, well, once we save all of Fairy, I don't think he'll be so heartbroken that you're around." He grabbed their bowls. "I'll be back in a moment. I'm going to drop this off in the kitchen and grab our stuff from Missy." He walked across the room and Allie once again turned her eyes to the couple, but they were gone. She hadn't remembered them getting up and leaving. She searched the room to see if they'd settled anywhere else, but no, they'd left the inn.

Devlin came back with satchels. "Here we go." He handed her one. "Ready?"

"Yeah, I guess so."

Oriana fell to her knees in the clock room, panting while sweat dripped down her face. She'd never sent her spirit out like that before. Not that far and not for that long. Her heart pounded as she tried to focus on what was in front of her. The blue glow of the giant clock below her felt warm as it engulfed her. The ticking of every second echoed in the room, and a minute passed by a heaving thump sounded from under her.

She forced herself to stand up and take a deep breath. She tried to warn Cerise, she tried to tell her the truth.

She stumbled out of the clock room to find her personal guard standing there. "I'm fine, Ewan"

"What you did was stupid, Oriana. You're exhausted. That ability isn't easily controlled, and you could have ripped a hole in Fairy. We don't know what that would have done."

"Because it's never happened." Oriana leaned against the wall. "I had to try. I needed to try to get Cerise to see reason."

"Cerise is way beyond reason, Oriana. She's walking into paranoid insanity."

"I was still hoping that my friend was there." Oriana closed her eyes and took a couple deep breaths. "I was hoping that she could see reason."

"You keep saying that, but we all know that the Red Queen is beyond saving." He took her arm and guided her away from the Clock Room. "You need to rest. Especially if you're still planning on meeting Alice and Devlin at the tea house."

She sighed and nodded. "Yes, rest is probably a good idea." He continued to escort her to her room.

He opened the door for her. "Seriously, Oriana, sleep. I know you like to push things with your parents gone, but you are exhausted."

Oriana walked into her room and turned to face him. "I will try." She shut the door and leaned her head against it. This was a disaster. She walked to her four-poster bed. The blue sheets draped over the mattress reminded her of water, the way the light caught the silk like waves, and it called to her. She groaned and fell into her bed. Closing her eyes and letting the sleep take her down.

The mist coiled around her as she stood in the middle of the frozen lake. The white lines pushed out away from her. Frost covered the ice under her feet where she stood.

"You have to let her follow this path." A male voice spoke. "It'll breed new life in to Fairy, life we need to protect it."

Oriana spun around in a circle, trying to figure out who the voice belonged to. Nothing but frozen water surrounded her, the bank of the lake a distant line on the horizon. "She will destroy Fairy."

"No, Oriana, not the Red Queen. Alice. She must go down this path to become the right Alice."

"Who are you?" Oriana demanded, spinning around again. This time the ice cracked under her feet and she froze.

The voice chuckled. "Who I am isn't important, what's important is that we let Alice walk her path and change the heart of the Queen of Hearts. Do not try to change it."

Another crack sounded below Oriana's feet. "And if Alice fails?"

"You have to let her find her fate. The more you try to change it, the more cracks that appear and the less of a chance she has to save Fairy."

Oriana nodded. "But how do I know I can trust you?"

"Because I haven't let you drown yet."

At those words Oriana realized that the water was soaking into her pants. She shivered at the ice cold feeling crawling up her body. "Who are you?"

"I told you, that's not important. I'll see you around, Oriana. Remember, let Alice walk the path so that she can save Fairy."

Oriana jumped when she woke. She ran her hands over her pant legs to see if her pants were wet because she swore she still felt the icy water at her ankles.

She took a deep breath when she realized it was dry and pulled herself out of bed. The quick nap did nothing to help her exhaustion. She rubbed her eyes and decided what she needed was a sleeping tea. She had two choices, go to the kitchen and have someone make her, or go to the tea house early and have one made for her there.

She opened her door to see Ewan "I'm going to head to the tea house."

He raised a brow. "It's a little early, milady. Are you sure?"

"I'm having problems resting. I'll get a sleep tea there and use one of their rooms." She nodded. "So let's get the horses ready."

"Both of us?"

"Yes, after I went and saw Cerise, I don't want to risk being caught without my guard with me."

Ewan chuckled. "I'm really only around to scare people, your sword skills are enough to take care of yourself."

She beamed at his praise. "Mom taught me well, but extra safety is never a bad thing. Alice isn't trained, so she'll need some protection too."

"And we're sure this is the right Alice?"

Oriana nodded. "Judging by how all of Fairy is starting to respond. I'm sure of it."

Allie pulled the strap of the bag tighter across her shoulder. "No sign of Fehin yet."

Devlin shook his head. "No, so we're going around the field, because I don't want you to be called by it again."

"Yeah," Allie glanced at the field. "I don't think I really want to be near it either." She pulled her hood up. "Let's go."

Devlin walked next to her as they started up a graveled path that was well worn down by travel. He said nothing as they continued to follow it up a hill. Here the breeze bristled through leaves instead of pine needles. Each leaf switched colors as they shifted. Some were the colors she'd find in trees in the mortal world, but others shifted purples and blues.

"So the tea house, who's court is that in?"

"The tea house is a neutral place, it allows all the courts to meet and chat. It's a lot more like a tea inn instead of a tea house. There's room for people to stay, and a huge table outside for people to have tea together if they wish. It's a neat place." He paused. "I thought we took you there."

"You did, but I only remember the table, and how giddy you and Dor were." She laughed, recalling Devlin trapping Dor in a tea pot and pouring him out into Alice's tea. Dor of course proceeded to use her tea as a hot tub. The way Cerise and her laughed at their antics brought a smile to Allie's face.

"Yeah, to be young and carefree like that."

She didn't miss the bitterness in his voice. "Fairy has changed a lot, hasn't it, since I was last here? It's not just Cerise that's changed."

Devlin stopped at the top of the hill and looked out over the Field of Regret. "Yes. Fairy has become darker somehow. I can't put my finger on it, but we can all feel it. Every court has a different theory about what is going on. The Court of Enchantment, my father, thinks that it's Cerise's bitterness and power hungriness seeping through the lands. Oriana's parents, the Court of Time, believe that it's coming over the Dark Mountains, and they went to search over there. Cerise, well no one really knows what she thinks or if she even realizes what is going on. And no one hears from the Court of Creation." He shrugged.

"What do you think?" Allie watched the purple lights dance below them.

Devlin was quiet for a moment. "I think that Fairy is changing. The land is magical, it's bound to change when it feels the whim or when something shifts. But I feel like something is coming. Something big."

"Other than me having to take on Cerise?"

"I think that, Alice, is just the start of what's going to happen." He nudged her forward. "Come on, let's keep going."

Allie followed him, letting his words sink in. Could this really be just the beginning?

After each hill there seemed a bigger hill and the field below continued to get smaller as Allie and Devlin continued to hike. Allie looked up at the noon sun. "We're climbing a mountain."

Devlin looked behind him. "Yes, we are."

"I didn't even see a mountain from the inn."

He laughed. "Yeah, you don't really see it, it's subtle until you start climbing it."

"You know, horses would be nice. A car. A plane?" She offered up.

"We have horses, just they attract more attention when we're traveling, we're trying to avoid that." He stopped at the peak of the hill and looked up. "Fehin will find us soon, and then we'll be in the air with the wind in our hair."

Allie snorted. "You're a poet."

"Haha." He gave a fake laugh. "Come on, mortal."

"How come Dor seems to appear and disappear whenever he wants? Why don't you get that power?"

"Because Dor got it from his heritage. It's a rare ability that's passed down from generation to generation. If rumors are true, it comes from the Court of Creation bloodlines. All small fae like Dor have the ability."

Allie made a *hmm* noise. "Okay come on, let's keep going." She took a step forward and the ground crumbled beneath her feet. Air rushed past her as she skidded down the side of the mountain, rocks and debris cutting into her skin as she struggled to stop herself or find anything to grab on to. Her heart pounded harder with each failed grasp.

A caw sounded above her and a moment later she was snatched off the side of the hill and in the air.

She tried to recover her wits as she saw the Field of Regret below her. She clung to the talon that was wrapped around her now, a new fear taking over. The wind blew through her hair as the bird flew over the Field of Regrets and landed on the other side sometime later.

He stood on one foot and gently sat Allie on the ground. Her heart pounded and her arms ached from holding on to the claw so tight. She stepped back and looked up to see Fehin.

"Good boy," she whispered, trying to catch her breath. He preened for a moment before taking off to the sky.

She almost called for him to come back, but he flew in the direction of the mountain and she assumed that he was off to get Devlin. "Good bird," she muttered again. The other side of the Field of Regrets was a landscape of trees and bushes. Not quite desert like, but not the same lush trees Allie had seen when hiking. Fehin had left her in a clearing, out in the open for anyone to see. She pulled her hood back on and headed towards a grove of trees to take cover.

CHAPTER 9

Cerise stormed through the castle the moment she arrived. She ignored all calls and looks as she made her way to Lavin's room to talk to her Seer. She threw the door opened and stepped into the dark room where Lavin was kept. She could make out the outline of the bed to her left and a bench that sat against the window across from her. Lavin sat on the bench, his silhouette tall against the window.

"You and I need to talk."

He looked up lazily, the red in his eyes glinting in the light from the doorway. He smiled showing a row of pointed teeth. "My queen, you're upset." He floated up to his feet, but sat in a crouched position. "How come?"

Cerise kept her fear down. Lavin would know if she was scared, just as easily as he knew she was upset. "Alice is back."

Levin chuckled and it rolled through Cerise's body, like a soft fur being dragged over her skin. She shivered at the feeling. "I know she's back." He purred and stood.

He towered over her when he straightened to his full height and she swallowed. "Then you know why I'm here."

"You want to know if she'll still be the downfall of The Red

Queen." Lavin reached a hand out, his long fingers reaching for Cerise.

She stepped away even though she knew he was well out of arms reach. "Stop playing games and tell me."

"The mortal woman who steps through the mirror, drinks the tea and eats the cookies, will bring the Red Queen to her knees."

"That's no more information than you gave me last time." Cerise snarled. "There has to be more."

Lavin tilted his head to the right and put one finger against his chin. "Hmm... She shall defeat the beast with Creation's sword, and then she shall be no more." He nodded. "That's the rest I can tell you."

Cerise's heart pounded. The beast had to be the Jabberwock, so Alice wouldn't survive that fight, but would still manage to bring Cerise down.

Cerise smiled. "Thank you, Lavin." She turned to walk away and Lavin's bony hand was around her wrist suddenly.

"My queen, you won't forget my payment will you?" His voice was right by her ear. "Because you forgot last time. And if you forget again..." He dragged his tongue against the line of her jaw.

She closed her eyes and concentrated. She could feel her power connected to his heart, she jerked her fingers, pulling on an imaginary string, but Lavin cried out and moved away from her. "You will get your payment, but you will not threaten me. I own your heart, Lavin. You belong to me."

She didn't miss the snarl in his voice. "Yes, my queen."

"Good." She walked out and shut the door behind her.

A bang sounded as Lavin hit the wall next to the door. He'd been a loyal servant of her mother's and Cerise taking his heart was only securing him to work for her and her only.

She passed Ace on her way to the throne room. "Don't forget to give Lavin his payment this time. I may be able to control him, but he still needs his payments for his services."

"Of course my lady. Did he have anything useful to say?"

"That Alice won't survive her battle with the Jabberwock." Cerise clicked her tongue. "But she will slay him. Something about Creation's sword. I think it's time we force a meeting face to face with the Court of Creation's ruler." She glanced over her shoulder at him. "Don't you?"

"I do, your majesty. Perhaps you should send one of your liaisons to invite them here?" Ace kept pace with her. "Or do you want to go yourself?"

She shook her head. "No, I would be safer here. We don't know much about the Court of Creation. I'll call for one of the liaison." And then if they died, she'd know that it wasn't safe to go.

***

Fehin landed in a clearing and Allie and Devlin climbed off. Fehin clicked his beak and Devlin pulled out a dry fish and tossed it to his bird. "Here you go, good job."

Fehin caught the fish and cawed before he flew off. Allie sighed. "I'm not sure how I feel about flying." More trees surrounded them, but now the leaves were black and silver as if the color had drained out of them. The bark sparkled white in the sunlight and Allie found herself wondering if they were made of jewels.

"Well, I'm sure you're a lot happier about him catching you than landing in a Field of Regret." Devlin started to walk.

Allie nodded. "That's for sure. I'm glad he showed up when he did." She pulled her hood over her head. "Which way now?"

Devlin jerked his head to the north. "It's a little bit of a hike, there's no big clearing for Fehin to land, so this was as close as he can get us."

Allie wrinkled her nose. "I feel like it's always hiking. For magical creatures, you guys have crappy transportation."

"Well, Fehin is my mode of transportation. If I used horses, that's one thing, but honestly Fehin is quicker than horses." He glanced at her. "Do you not hike in the mortal world?"

"Some people do for fun. It's not something I've ever considered fun." She shook her head.

He laughed as he paused at the tree line. "Then you're doing it wrong."

She snorted. "You sound like my dad."

"Well, hiking in Fairy is different." He put a finger to his lips. "Walk with me quietly and listen to the land. See what you can hear."

Allie rolled her eyes and walked with him, but she did stay quiet. Only their feet on the worn path sounded at first, but then when the breeze kicked up she swore she heard bells.

She paused for a moment and looked around, trying to figure out where it was coming from. The stronger the wind blew the more the bells sounded.

She smiled and looked up seeing the leaves dance. Devlin chuckled. "Come on, let's keep going."

Allie followed him, but found she kept falling behind because she'd spot something change in the leaves around them, or heard something on the wind. Allie turned to watch the colors of the leaves shift and started to walk toward them, her hand out stretched.

"Woah, there." Devlin put his hand on her wrist. "You don't want to touch those. Just like in the mortal world, some of our plants are dangerous."

"Your whole world is dangerous." Allie shook her head. "The leaves look so soft."

He nodded. "Yes, but they'll drag you into hallucinations that would make you wish you were dead."

"Have you experienced that?"

"Yes, and I about threw myself off a tower. So let's not try that."

Yeah that didn't sound like an awesome experience. "Okay, so no touching the plants. Is there anything here that I can enjoy?"

He grinned. "My company, our food, music, you enjoyed the little village in my court."

She smiled. "It was charming," she admitted. "The food was delicious." They continued to walk through the trees. "I don't know about the music though, I haven't heard anything since I've gotten here. I do remember Cerise and I singing silly songs all the time though."

"Well, really The Court of Time has the best music, because that's really what music is, time, beats, math, it's beautiful. We'll make sure you hear some when we go through her court."

"I'll get to see her court?"

He nodded. "Yes, Cibil lives on the outskirts of the Court of Time. If I could convince her to come to the tea house, then I would have. But Cibil doesn't leave her house." He hesitated. "She hasn't left her house since the war, if you believe the rumors."

"How old is this fae?" Allie asked.

"Older than the war, so a couple thousand?"

"You guys live that long?" She gaped at him. "What do you do for that long?"

He chuckled. "I'm not sure. I'm just a little older than you, remember? I mean, eventually I'll take my dad's place and find a queen and rule my court. Then my days will be filled with keeping the peace between my court and the others."

Allie sighed. "Assuming I can keep Cerise from taking over everyone's court."

"Yeah, assuming that." His voice lowered to a whisper. "Get down." He grabbed her arm and pulled her behind a purple bush.

Allie pressed against him, trying not to touch the long leaves of the plants.

"These won't hurt you." His voice was barely a whisper.

Three giant men stalked by and Allie's eyes widened as they cast shadows over them. Each one wore a dark brown cap on their heads that slouched over the back, resembling a human beanie.

Their gray skin reminded her of a corpse and they each held a weapon, one ax, and two clubs.

They stopped and sniffed the air and turned toward Allie and

Devlin. Their red eyes froze Allie place. Her breath caught in her throat and everything in her body told her to run.

"We smell you, Devlin." The first one spoke, his voice so deep that Allie swore the ground rumbled with it.

Devlin shoved her to the ground before standing up. "Hello, Harken. A bit far from the ruins aren't you?"

He snorted. "Could say the same for you, bit far from home. Swore I smelt a mortal, but your stench was more."

"I don't know how you smell such when your hat is covered in blood." Devlin shot back.

Blood? Allie put a hand over her mouth, that's why the hat was such a dark brown. It was dried blood.

"What were you doing hiding?"

Devlin held his hand out, but Allie couldn't see what he had.

"I wasn't hiding, I was looking for the red berry, they make a great tea. And since I'm heading to the tea house, I figured I'd grab some." He shrugged. "March makes tea specially for me."

Allie closed her eyes, begging for the men to leave.

"Have you seen the mortal?"

"What if I have?" Devlin asked.

There was shifting against the ground and Allie opened her eyes, hoping not to see the men looking over her.

"My Captain wants her, thinks it'll give him favor with Queen Cerise."

Oh god. Giants wanted her too. Her heart picked up speed again and she tried to make herself smaller so that the others wouldn't see her.

Devlin laughed. "Tell your captain good luck. The mortal has slipped into the Court of Enchantment. My father let her slip through his fingers there."

"We're not allowed there," Harken muttered.

"You should go back to your ruins," Devlin suggested. "Hunting the mortal is just going to force her further into Fairy."

There was grumbling from the group and then footsteps again. Alice waited until Devlin stepped back into the bushes and held his hand out to her. "Come on, let's get going before they decide to come back."

She took his hand and he pulled her up. "Who were they?"

"Redcaps. You do not want to cross them." He pulled her down the path. "Come on." She followed him quickly.

Oriana sat at the table in the back of the tea house, waiting. People milled around the tea house, some sat with tea pots on the table, warmed with magic. Others simply had one cup of tea in front of them. The chatter in the room was low and there were no signs of the others. With each minute that passed by situations played through her mind on what was keeping Devlin. She'd seen the Redcaps head into the forest, hopefully they weren't caught by them.

There were a few travelers that had talked about spotting Fehin in the sky, so they at least made it near the tea house.

"My lady, you're going to crush your mug if you hold it much tighter." Ewan chuckled. "A bit anxious?"

"I'm wondering where Devlin is. He should have been here by now."

He looked around the small crowd that had gathered inside the house. "Do you think they are at the gathering table?"

"No, that's too in the open," she muttered and the door opened, Devlin had Allie in tow behind him. She let go of him once they were inside and pulled her hood lower as she followed him to the back area where Oriana was waiting.

"Where have you two been?" She hissed as they sat down.

"We had to hike a bit when we left the inn, until Fehin found us. Then we had to hide from Redcaps who are looking for Alice," Devlin growled. "News of her being here is spreading and everyone is going to try to get her to stay on Cerise's good side."

Allie glanced around nervously. "Maybe we shouldn't be talking about this with so many people around?"

Oriana nodded. "Come on, let's ask March if we can have the back room."

Devlin stood with her and motioned for Allie to follow. Allie stuck close to him and Oriana figured the Redcaps probably scared the crap out of the poor mortal. Oriana stopped at a door at the back of the room and knocked.

A man answered the door, his long brown hair was pulled back in a low pony tail, his fae ears were high and pointed, and his crimson eyes glanced around outside the door before he grabbed Oriana and pulled her in.

She grabbed Devlin's arm and pulled both him and Alice in behind her before March slammed the door behind them. A small table sat in the middle of the room with four chairs, almost blending in the brown wood walls and floors. The door in the back was cracked open just enough for the room to stay cool.

"What do you think you're doing just sitting out there?" His gravelly voice was low. "You'll attract attention with that around." He motioned at Alice.

Oriana sighed. "We needed a place to meet up, the tea house is the best place for that. We have to form a plan."

"And I'm not a 'that,'" Allie added. "I have a name."

He ignored her. "Yes yes, a plan to defeat the Jabberwock and bring Cerise down to size. But this is not the place to even think about that. Her allies are everywhere." He pegged Alice with a stare. "You shouldn't have the ability to come back here. And with Knave missing, things are already going downhill."

March started to pace the small room and Oriana put a hand on his shoulder. "March, please."

March took a shuddering breath. "Okay, sorry. You guys can stay here and discuss whatever, but you must leave by nightfall."

"What happens at night fall?" Alice asked and Oriana glanced at her.

"Haven't you figured it out? The scary stuff comes out at night." She turned back to March. "We're going to be heading to my court here in a couple hours. We just need to rest, start forming a plan and then we'll head out."

March wrung his hands together. "Okay, thank you. Can I get you some tea?"

"Please," Oriana and Devlin said together.

"And cookies," Oriana tacked on. "We're all hungry."

March nodded and disappeared out the door.

"He's quite the nervous one, isn't he?" Alice asked and sat at the table.

Oriana sat across from her. "He is, because Knave is missing, and he and Knave are lovers."

Alice studied the table for a moment. "He thinks Cerise had something to do with it?"

Orianna nodded. "Knave and I were in charge of destroying any hint of you in Fairy." She hesitated for a moment. "That meant a lot of...questionable things." She tried to push out of her mind the number of people that were in frozen limbo because they dared uttered the name Alice. "This was when we were just trying to help Cerise, she was heartbroken that you wouldn't be coming back. We thought we were doing what was best for our friend."

"And what happened while you and Knave were doing this?" Alice's voice remained soft.

Devlin answered. "Knave just didn't show up to help one day. We contacted March to see if he'd heard from Knave."

"And I hadn't." March said as he walked in with the tea pot and plates on a tray. "And I haven't heard from him since he disappeared." March set the tray down. "And yes, I blame Cerise for it. Him and Kit are still missing."

"Kit isn't exactly missing, he's popping in and out right now." Oriana rolled her eyes. "He's still cursed to stay as a cat, but he's managing."

Alice's hand hesitated over a cookie. "Kit visited me"

Oriana stared at her for a moment. March stopped mid pour of tea. Devlin raised a brow. "And what did Kit have to say?"

"He was questioning me on if I felt like I belong in Fairy or not." Alice picked up the cookie, but didn't meet anyone's gaze. "And then he disappeared."

Oriana looked at Devlin, waiting for him to say something, anything to break the silence.

"Well, what did you tell him?" Devlin asked.

"I told him I didn't know. He also called me out for avoiding conflict."

Oriana sighed. "We're only avoiding it until we know how to handle it."

Alice glanced away as March continued to pour tea. "Part of that plan," Oriana continued, "Is to teach you how to use that sword. We're also going to go see Cibil."

"Cibil will help you. She loves mortals." March chuckled and sat a cup of tea in front of Oriana.

"I thought she was crazy." Alice leaned back in her chair.

Oriana nodded. "That's what the rumors say, but March would know better. He goes to see Cibil often."

March sat a cup down in front of Alice. "Because I'm looking for Knave."

"You love him," Alice stated and picked up her cup. "A lot."

He nodded. "I do, Knave and I have been together for years. He saved me from myself, and I helped him through a trial with Cerise's mother." He paused in handing Devlin his tea. "When you find someone who can save you from yourself, Alice, you hold on to them. Either a lover or a friend, you hold on to them." He handed Devlin his cup. "How did you know that I love him?"

Alice smiled. "The look in your eyes when you talk about him, the worry is written on the creases in your face and your voice softens any time you mention him. It's what I see with my parents."

"Mortal lives are so short, that they should cherish the love they have." March nodded. "I hope one day that you will meet Knave and see why I love him so much."

Alice nodded. "I'd like that. Maybe we'll find him in all this chaos." She waved a hand around.

"We'll stay in the Court of Time for a little bit so that Alice can learn to fight." Oriana said, getting the discussion on track. If she had to hear yet another version of Knave and March's love story. she was going to puke.

"Isa taught me the basics." Alice sipped her tea. "So we can build off of that."

"Good, that gives us something to work with." Devlin stated. "It'd be easier if you had magic, but mortals don't carry magic."

Alice shrugged one shoulder. "Sorry for being so plain."

"Don't sell yourself short, Alice. You are anything but 'plain.'" Devlin chuckled. "The fact that you are here in Fairy means you are not just any mortal."

She rolled her eyes at Devlin's attempt at a compliment.

"We can't linger too long in the Court of Time, because Cerise will check there for Alice eventually, if she's not already on her way. We should have enough time to rest, teach Alice some and visit Cibil."

Alice tapped her fingers on the table, like she was annoyed. "Is there any court Cerise won't check?"

"The Court of Creation," March stuttered out. "But no one goes there because the court family isn't known. It'd be dangerous to go there."

There was shouting outside and March jumped out of his chair. "Stay here, drink your tea, eat your cookies." He shot out of the room.

Oriana looked at Devlin and Alice. "You heard the fae, eat and drink up."

Devlin shook his head. "We need to leave, now. Let's go." They stood and darted out the back door.

Cerise ran her hand over the scaly head of the Jabberwock. One bite from the beast and her fae magic would be drained from her body as she died slowly. But she'd tamed it.

The strange narrow mouth hung open, a tongue hanging out of its mouth almost like a dog.

"Your majesty," Ace called from the door and the Jabberwock swung its head in his direction snarling.

"It's okay, he's not here to harm you," she purred and continued to run her hand down his neck. "He's not the one you have to worry about." She turned to Ace. "What is it?"

"Alice and the others are at the tea house, we just received a message from there via bird."

She pressed her lips together. She had expected the group to make it there, but not so soon. March had sworn to her to let know the moment they got to the tea house...on the promise she'd let him know where Knave was.

Not that she currently had information, but her men were working on finding him. Knave had always been a mystery to her. He'd been brought to trial on the accusations that he was a traitor to the Court of Hearts, but March came to bear witness for him. Cerise had convinced Knave and Oriana to destroy any record of Alice in Fairy, but Knave never returned and after that Oriana suddenly grew a conscious and refused to continue the work.

A breaking point for their friendship.

"My queen?" Ace asked. "What would you like to do?"

"Let them be at the tea house, they'll travel to the Court of Time next, we owe Oriana a visit after her little stunt."

"I'll ready the coach."

"No," Cerise stopped him. "We'll take just the horses, it's quicker that way."

"It's a two-day ride, your majesty. Are you sure?"

"We take minimal men, enough to make camp for one night, and then we rely on Oriana's want to not have a war. Send a bird that we'll be coming."

The Jabberwock nudged Cerise's shoulder and she ran her hand over its neck again. "I don't want it to seem quite like a threat."

"Of course, my queen. I'll ready my men." Ace turned to leave and Cerise looked at her beast.

"There will come a time Jabber, that you must prove that you are loyal to me and only me."

The beast seemed to nod like it understood.

"Good, because when it's time, I want you to kill Alice," she whispered. "So I can officially wipe her name off the seer's lips and out of my world."

Jabber huffed and nodded again before pulling away from her. Cerise stepped back. "I'll be back."

And hopefully she'd have Alice in hand.

***

Allie adjusted herself on the saddle of the horse, trying to hold on with her legs so she didn't slide to one side. "Why didn't we take Fehin again?"

"He's easy to spot," Oriana called back from her lead. "We're almost there, just hold on."

Allie tried not to roll her eyes. She'd been on a horse a couple times in her life, but never for a few hours and her hips and thighs were burning. At least the horse took orders well and followed Oriana's horse with ease. Allie wasn't sure what she'd do if her horse decided to take off on its own.

"You're doing great, Alice," Devlin called from behind her. "Just keep trying to feel the rhythm of the horse."

She grumbled as they crested another hill and the horses came to a stop. They overlooked a city reminding Allie of ancient Greece, with tall white pillars and temples, a river ran through the middle of the city and she could see fae on the edges of it.

"It's beautiful."

Oriana nodded. "It's home." She nudged her horse in the ribs and it took off down the hill. Allie's horse followed and Devlin came up behind her.

They galloped into the city, over cobblestone roads, passing children and adults who were milling about their lives. Colors of blues and greens in clothing and hair flashed by as they road. Allie found herself wishing they'd gone through slower so she could take in everything.

The Court of Time seemed to have much more color in it than the Court of Enchantment, and much more to look at in terms of the main city, but it all moved too fast for her to really focus on any of it.

They approached a large gate with iron bars bent into the shape of a clock. The gate split down the middle as the horses slowed down. Oriana guided them into a garden beyond the gate with the same cobblestone paths as the city.

Here roses were in bloom, except they weren't red or yellow, or even white. They were a brilliant blue, the shade was dark at the base and lightened toward the tips in an ombre that Allie was sure didn't exist in the human world.

Devlin's horse pulled up next to hers. "This is the Oriana's garden. She tends to it when she has the time."

"There roses are beautiful." Allie glanced at him. "Let me guess, if I touch one, it'll kill me."

"No, but I might," Oriana said with a laugh. "Don't pick them."

Allie smiled and just admired the way they looked, but the further from the gate they trotted, the fewer flowers there were, until they gave way to stacks of hay and a stable.

A stable hand came out and smiled at the trio. "Welcome back, my lady."

"Thanks, please make sure the horses are watered and fed. I need to get our guests settled."

The stable hand nodded and took the reins of the three horses. Allie pulled her leg around and slid down to the ground, and took a minute to shake her legs out. Devlin stepped up next to her.

"Your captain is coming and he looks like he's on a mission."

Devlin stepped in front of Allie.

She glanced around him to see a man coming down the pathway, the light glinted against his armor and a white bird perched on his shoulder, almost blending into his hair.

"We need to get you in and cleaned up and ready to receive company."

Oriana sighed and crossed her arms. "Who is coming?"

"Cerise."

Allie felt her stomach drop at the name. "Already? I thought we'd figured we had a few days before she came this direction."

"I thought we did," Oriana snapped back and then started walking with her guard. Devlin nudged Allie to keep moving.

Allie followed them towards the looming castle. The blue tinted stone seem to have scenes moving on each one. Allie paused and titled her head trying to decide if it was the light causing the effect or if she was really seeing different things play across the stone.

"With this being the Court of Time, they are also in charge of the history of Fairy. What you're seeing is a replay of our history," Devlin said. "If you stay and watch long enough, you would see the very beginning of Fairy. When the first light struck here and our kind first began."

Allie marveled at it, squinting to see if she could see the scenes clearly.

"Or you can stand there long enough to get left behind," Ewan called behind him. "Keep up, mortal."

Devlin chuckled and they continued to follow him. "We'll hide when Cerise gets here."

"She's going to know we were here. The people saw us riding through." Allie shook her head.

"They did, but they won't betray me to Cerise," Oriana promised. "You two will hide in the hall of time while Cerise and I meet. She'll be free to look around the castle, but no one can find that hall without me," Oriana stated. "Cerise doesn't even know it exists."

"How can you be so sure of that?" Allie asked.

"Because I didn't know it existed until my parents went on their scouting mission." Her shoulders tensed and she didn't look back.

Allie glanced at Devlin who gave a slight shake of his head telling her not to push that part of the conversation.

"Okay. So we hide and when she leaves?"

"If I can throw her off our track, then she'll leave me alone for a little while." There was something in Oriana's voice that set Allie's nerves off.

"What are you telling us, Oriana?"

She took a deep breath. "I paid Cerise a little visit and I'm not sure if she's here to start a war or not. I won't know until she leaves."

Allie bristled. "What does that mean?"

"It means, she's expecting Cerise to cause problems," Devlin stated.

Allie rubbed her eyes. "Maybe I should just end all this tension and face her now."

"No," the other three answered at the same time.

"I'm just saying, maybe I can talk her out of whatever war path she's on."

"She'll take your head." Devlin put a hand on her shoulder. "We don't want you dead."

She sighed and followed Oriana up a group of steps that led to an oak door. The carvings on the door mirrored the design on the iron gate.

Ewan pushed the doors opened and stepped to the side to let the three of them in.

"Welcome to the Court of Time, Ms. Alice."

Allie stepped in and gasped. Where the outside of the building was blue tinted, inside was copper and browns. A winding stair way was off to the left, while there was a hall that led further into the castle. The floors shone, reflecting the fire on the right.

"It's beautiful."

Oriana smiled. "It's home." She nodded. "Now come on, let's get you and Devlin hidden away before Cerise gets here."

CHAPTER 10

Oriana sat up straight in her throne before adjusting the copper crown on her head. The crown sat on her wrapped braids and had blue jewels wrapped within the wires. Her mother's was similar, but her fathers was made from black iron with white jewels.

Her heart ached as she thought about them not being by her side to help navigate this disaster. She tried to imagine what they would say about the situation.

She knew it would come down to one thing: Protect the court's people.

The door opened and Cerise walked in with two guards at her back. Cerise's red dress swirled around her feet, black hearts done in thorned vines were embroidered at the waist of the bodice, mimicking a belt. The top of the dress rounded over her breast and dipped down making another heart shape.

Her guards' red armor shone as they stepped into the fire light of the throne room, their hands rested on the hilt of their swords, their faces were in straight lines, as if they were also expecting trouble.

"Hello, Queen Cerise." Oriana stood and bowed her head. "What brings you here?"

Her two guards flanked her. "I'm here for Alice. I know you have her. You will hand her over."

Oriana smiled. "She's not here. Devlin is taking her to the Court of Creation. You won't be able to catch up with them at this point." She sat back down and crossed her legs. "You don't think I'd be stupid enough to keep Alice somewhere so obvious as here, do you?"

Cerise growled. "I have witnesses at the tea house that place you, Devlin, and Alice there. That heard your plans to come here."

Oriana locked her jaw. The only person who overheard those plans was March. That little traitor. "Plans change, especially once we realized March was giving you information."

"You knew that he was betraying you?"

Oriana inspected her nail, pretending to be bored with this conversation. "We're not stupid Cerise. I'm sorry, you've wasted your time coming here." She waved her hand. "Feel free to search the castle. And if you swear to leave the civilians out of it, you can search the city. Alice isn't here."

Cerise snapped her fingers. "Go look. Leave no room unturned, use what magic you can, find Alice." Her gaze never left Oriana's.

Oriana nodded. "Would you like some tea or ale while we wait?" She stood. "I had my staff set some out when we heard you had arrived."

Cerise sighed. "If we must pretend to be civil to each other while we wait."

"I certainly think it beats staring at each other for a few hours while your guards search the castle." Oriana stood and walked toward the hall, her guard followed her and Cerise him.

A maid opened the doors that led into the sitting room where a tray of tea and pastries waited for them. Oriana kept her composure as she went to sit down in a tall blue wingback seat. She could have tea with an old friend while waiting for the guards to search the palace.

It was like playing pretend when they were little. The only difference was Cerise's hate felt tangible any time she spoke now.

Cerise sat across from her and reached for the tea, hesitating only slightly before taking a sip. "You're being calm about this situation. You've admitted to helping Alice."

"Your goal is to find Alice, you won't find her here, and because attacking my kingdom would cause a war, you won't attack." Oriana gave her a small smile. "Your mother had a powerful army, but rumor has it, that many of them don't listen to you."

Cerise stiffened in her chair. "Your kingdom's army is still no match for ours. So, if you hand Alice over, then I won't attack. Bring her back from the Court of Creation."

Oriana shook her head. "You know as well as I do, that Devlin won't listen to either of us if we tell him to turn around now."

"Then fetch her for me and I won't raid your court." Cerise ran a painted nail over the fabric of the chair. "It'd be a shame if something were to happen to that school you're so fond of."

Oriana swallowed. The school was her pride and joy, she'd helped build it from the ground up when her parents said there was no need for it. A place for young fae to learn their power.

"You won't touch it." She sat her tea cup down. "And I am not going to sit here and listen to your threats. You want Alice? Then you have to find her. You have to draw her out, because it is you she is hiding from. This has nothing to do with our courts, or our parents. It has everything to do with you and Alice."

Cerise raised a brow. "It has everything to do with our courts, my kingdom. You and the others will bow to me as queen as soon as Alice is out of the picture. She is the only thing standing in my way, the only thing that can bring me down."

"Then search my castle and leave, because she isn't here. Then we will stand against you when you try and conqueror us. You're threatened by a mortal Cerise. She has no magic, no skills, why are you threatened by her?" Oriana held her head high. "We're fae, we're better than the mortals."

Cerise snarled. "Because she stole my heart!" She stood and

paced the room her black heels clicking against the tile. "Because when we were teens she was the only one who didn't care that I was the Red Queen's daughter. That I would inherit a bloody kingdom, she made me fall in love with her, and used that to steal my heart." She clenched her fists and turned to Oriana. "And the only way I can truly claim my throne and all my mother wanted for me is to get rid of Alice."

"We were teens, it's not Alice's fault that you fell in love with her. She has no power over you." Oriana shook her head. She'd no idea that Alice would start a war, maybe that's what the seer meant when he said Alice would bring the Red Queen to her knees. "Let her go back home, let's all forget this prophecy."

Cerise shook her head. "No. She must die."

Oriana sighed and put her tea cup down, keeping her temper controlled and her face a simple pleasant smile. "I'm afraid this conversation won't be able to continue. Please sit and enjoy your tea. Feel free to pick up a book while we sit in silence."

And stew in their emotions. Oriana straightened her back and sipped her tea as Cerise settled back down in the chair. "Have you heard from your parents?" She asked.

Oriana raised a brow. "You've threatened my kingdom, told me we'll be going to war when you kill Alice, and now you want to know about my parents? I won't provide you any answers."

Cerise sipped her tea and stared at Oriana. Oriana kept her pleasant smile on her face and when she finished her tea, she picked up a book and ignored her old friend.

Alice stood in the middle of the floor. The metal around the floor formed a massive clock face and glowed blue through what looked like glass. Gears ticked under feet as she spun around to look at the massive room.

Devlin was leaning against the black wall, eying the floor like it was evil. "This room creeps me out."

"There's something magical about it," Alice muttered as her skin prickled with ever tick. "Like I could hold time itself."

Devlin nodded. "Creepy. I don't like time magic."

"How does it work?" Alice looked at him. "Oriana wields it right?"

He nodded. "It works like all magic works. It's part of who she is, part of her being. Magic keeps us alive, thriving, and our world alive." He pushed off the wall and walked toward her. "The power of time—Oriana and her parents can use it to freeze time for someone, everyone. Together, they could probably freeze it for the world."

Alice looked down at the gears. "Why would you want to freeze time?"

"It's been used to keep information quiet from people. Keep them from dying until a healer could help. Punishment for crimes. Imagine being froze at your age for a decade, only to come back to life in a different time."

Alice shivered at the thought. "Does Oriana use it for such cruel things?"

"She'll have to if she becomes ruler of the kingdom in truth. Her mother and father both have." Devlin nodded. "It's part of ruling. You have to punish those who break the laws. You do the same in the human world."

He was right, but fae punishment seemed so much worse. "Can she freeze whole places in time?"

"Yeah, I've seen it before. It's amazing and terrifying all at the same time." He shivered. "Her mother once froze the whole court when Cerise's mother threatened it. She couldn't get through the gate."

Alice swallowed. "Is that what Oriana will do if we can't stop Cerise?"

"Yes." Devlin pressed his lips together. "She'll freeze her court, my father will bend to Cerise's will to protect our people."

"And the Court of Creation?" Alice asked, staring down at the gears studying their ticking.

"Who knows?" Devlin slowly walked across the clock. "We can't focus on that right now. We're going to go see Cibil. We're going to figure out how to win this, and then you'll get to go home."

Alice snorted. "I could go home the moment I find my way back to the giant mushroom."

"You could, but we're a long way from there, and it's too late to turn back. Don't you think?"

Did she? She'd run from Cerise's guards, almost lost herself to the Field of Regrets, fell asleep in the Flowers of Sleep...and fell off a cliff.

"It might be a little too late. I'd probably die on the way back to the giant forest."

Devlin laughed. "Yeah, probably."

"How long do you think Cerise will stay?" Alice sat on the floor and leaned back on her hands.

"Hopefully she'll leave as soon as she realizes you're not in the palace." Devlin shrugged. "And hopefully she doesn't do something stupid like attack Oriana."

Alice shook her head. "No, I don't think she'd do that. Not now."

"Why do you say that?"

Alice thought back to the games she and Cerise played. Simple human board games, chess, checkers, card games that needed strategies. The stories Cerise would tell of battles in the past and what she would do different.

As a human Alice thought Cerise was simply a child thinking she could win whatever game she played.

But now as she saw how the fae children grew up and were taught...

"Because, Cerise removes the biggest threat first. And right now, that biggest threat is me." Alice stood and pulled her sword out.

Devlin held his hands up and fear flashed in his eyes. "Alice?"

"We're stuck in here, let's work on my moves and spend this time wisely instead of waiting for something to happen." She locked her jaw. "If Cerise tries to kill me, I'm not going to go quietly."

Devlin nodded. "Then let's get to work."

Cerise sat her book down when her guards came in. "Where's Alice?" She'd been sitting quietly while she and Oriana glanced at each other over books. Neither of them had said another word to the other. Not after the threats passed between them.

"She's nowhere here, your majesty," the first one said. "We've checked every room, closet, and nook that we could find."

Cerise turned to Oriana. "So you aren't lying about her not being here."

Oriana didn't look up. She slowly turned the next page of her book. "I told you that you were wasting your time, Cerise."

Alice was eluding her again, still one step ahead. How could the mortal be so smart? Cerise had always beaten her at strategy games and Oriana was right, Alice had no magic of her own. Devlin was with her, so they must have taken his giant crow...

But they hadn't seen any signs in the sky, and Oriana couldn't have been home for very long before Cerise showed up. How then?

Could she have been telling the truth about where Devlin was taking Alice? "I sent a messenger to the Court of Creations, they'll tell me if Alice and Devlin show up."

She watched for any sign of Oriana being alarmed, but the woman just sat there, turning another page of the book. Anger heated in her and Cerise snatched the book out of Oriana's hand. "Do not disrespect me like this."

Oriana stood and dusted her dress off as if there was dirt on it. "Please give me my book back. I told you where Alice and Devlin were heading. I tried to have a civil conversation with you, but you refused, and now you're being rude."

Cerise threw the book to the side. "War, Oriana, is what will be coming to your court."

"You are delusional, Cerise. You can't take on three other courts."

"I reached out to the Court of Creation for an alliance." Cerise smirked, the lie falling off her tongue easily. "I should hear from their court in a couple days."

"You sent a messenger to reach out for an alliance? Interesting."

"You and I both know that the rulers there do not grant audiences." Cerise met Oriana's eyes. "I'm hoping to talk to a liaison." There were still no signs of anger in Oriana, as if she was frozen by her own powers of time. No emotions playing out of her face.

"Good luck." Oriana's voice became sweet. "May our next meeting be more productive."

Cerise glared at her and spun, walking out of the room with her two guards at her back. It'd been a pointless trip. No Alice to be found, but the words of the seer rang in her mind. The sword of creation...there was only one place that sword could be and that was in the Court.

Once they were out of the castle, Cerise turned to her guards. "One of you will stay here to watch for any signs of Alice, I don't care what Oriana says about your presence. If there is any sign of Alice, send a bird. The other two will be going with me."

"And where are we going your majesty?"

"To the Court of Creation, send a bird to our messenger there." She marched for her coach. "If we ride hard, we can make it there in four days, and be out of this wretched court."

"As you wish," the soldier said and turned to speak to the other two.

Cerise gathered her dress around her and climbed onto the horse. She'd make good on her threat and come back to Oriana. The group was trying to play her, and Alice was always good at hide and seek. Maybe it was time for Cerise to change her tactic.

"You're still too slow," Devlin growled as he took another swing at Allie.

She blocked it and stumbled back. "You're a lot faster because you're fae," she snapped back as she shoved him away from her with her blade. Sweat dripped down her face as she lunged at him and he blocked with a downward swing.

"The Jabberwock isn't going to care if you're mortal or fae. He moves just as fast as us." He held his hand up to show her to stop.

Allie took a few deep breaths as she sheathed her sword. "This is hopeless. The best I'm going to manage to do is beat a human when I get back home." She sat down with a huff.

"Your form looks pretty good to me." Oriana pushed away from the wall. Allie hadn't seen her there a moment ago, but of course she hadn't seen a door since they walked into this room. "Isa started teaching you, right?"

Allie nodded. "While I was in the Court of Enchantments, yeah."

"Isa's good with swords, but if we want to defeat the Jabberwock, you're going to want to be proficient in short blades. It has a long neck, and claws, but it has a hard time guarding close to its body."

Allie sighed. "Do you have an image of this thing?"

"At the school, I do." Oriana glanced at Devlin. "I'd like to stop by the school on our way to Cibil if we can."

Devlin nodded. "Of course. Everything okay?"

"Cerise threatened to destroy it. I just want to give the council there a warning." Oriana pressed her lips together. "I worked so hard to create that place, that I couldn't bare if something happened to it."

Devlin nodded. "We'll stop by. How did the meeting with Cerise go?"

"It was basically a declaration of war. Once she takes care of the biggest threat."

Allie raised her hand. "That'd be me."

"That'd be you," Oriana agreed. "Then Cerise made it clear that she plans on taking over all the courts. But she's worried that Alice will ruin her plans."

Allie lay back on the ground and stared up, the blue from below her barely touched the darkness of the vaulted ceiling. "Maybe we can just keep running her on a wild goose chase until she gives up on this idea of taking over all of Fairy."

"She's smarter than that. She'll find a way to trap you. Honestly, we're on borrowed time." Devlin sighed. "Let's split up? I can take Alice to Cibil and you can check on the school? You can meet us at Cibil's when you're done?"

Oriana nodded. "Cerise probably expects me to go to you two, give it a few hours after I leave to see if her guard follows me."

"She left a guard?"

Oriana nodded. "And if I have to, I'll trap him in time, but I'd rather not."

Allie shivered at that thought. "I'd like a shower and some food before we go?" She asked.

"Yeah, I have the staff working on a meal for us now. I'll show you to a room. It's too late to travel now anyway. So we'll rest for the night and split up tomorrow."

Allie stood. "Sounds good." She wanted some time to think anyway. It sounded like Fairy was going to go to war if Cerise ever found her. Maybe going back to the mortal would be the best option. She tried to push that thought away as she followed Oriana and Devlin.

Oriana put her hand against the wall and the door appeared. Alice shivered as they walked back into the hallway.

Could fae go to the mortal world to kill a mortal? Was there some universal law against that?

If there wasn't, there was a chance she'd bring danger home to her parents. As it was, it looked like she'd be dying in Fairy.

"If I die, will one of you take my body back to my parents?" She asked, breaking the silence of following the two down a hallway.

The two fae stopped and turned to her. Oriana gave a sad smile. "If you die, yes."

"We didn't bring you here to die, Alice. We brought you here to stop Cerise and we wouldn't have done so if we didn't think you had a fighting chance to fix this."

She met Devlin's gaze. "You're putting me up against a magical creature with blades. You said we'd figure another plan out. Maybe I could just talk to Cerise? Fix whatever it is that she has against me."

"You broke her heart." Oriana crossed her arms. "When you were young teenagers."

Allie stared at her for a moment. "Wait, what? Teenage heart break is a reason for war in this world? What is wrong with you people?"

"Like the mortals are so much better?" Devlin laughed. "You wage war over the smallest things too."

Okay, he had a point, but Allie let out a growl of frustration. "Would apologizing do anything to help?"

"Probably not. She's becoming her mother." Oriana shrugged. "Blood thirsty and vengeful."

Great. Allie had managed to turn her first crush into a psychopath. "Okay then. Jabberwock fighting it is. Then what? She's impressed by my strength and stands down?"

"Um...we'll have to find you an adviser or something. Because according to the Court of Hearts, whoever defeats or controls the Jabberwock, controls that court."

Allie shook her head. "Nope, I do not want to be a mortal queen of any fae court. You can't make me. Can I just drag Cerise back to the mortal world with me? Maybe she can adjust to being a mortal young adult more than I can being a fae."

"I'll see if I can find a better answer at the library. Or if Cibil can give you an answer, that would be nice." Oriana continued to walk. "For now, let's just focus on how to kill the Jabberwock."

Allie pondered for a moment on if it was like a horse, could she feed it a carrot or a bit of fae flesh and tame it? The thought made her smile and Devlin raised a brow at her.

"What are you thinking?"

"I'm just wondering if a good steak would help my chances with the Jabberwock."

Oriana snorted. "It might be worth a try."

CHAPTER 11

Allie came out of her room, dressed freshly in a pair of soft pajamas. Her hair was fresh and cleans, sticking out every which way from her trying to drying it.

Devlin came out of the room next to her. "You look much better."

"I feel better. There was so much dust on me from flying and then the sword fighting." She ran her hands over her arms. "It was just nice to get a hot shower."

He grinned. "Yeah, I feel better too. Come on, let's get some dinner."

They walked down the hallway and Allie looked up at the tapestries. She'd glanced at them before when Oriana led her to the room, but she hadn't really taken notice of them.

"Those are the things I ran into in the woods." She looked at the terrifying one-eyed creature, strangling someone with their chest hand.

Devlin nodded. "When Isa found you. The Fachan. This is when they tried to raid the Court of Time. Before the war. They came from the other side of the mountains, as warriors of the courts there."

"Why did they attack?"

"It's said because the king of the courts wanted our land as well.

They lost the war and well, everyone over there was destroyed. Or so they say. Oriana's parents are over there now, exploring."

Allie raised a brow. "Why?"

"Because it's been a thousand of years and we haven't seen any activity over there. We're growing on this side of the mountain; if we can spread our courts to there, then we won't have crowded cities."

Allie walked down the hall, glancing at each tapestry which showed another part of the war. "And if there are people over there?"

"I don't know," he said honestly. "Maybe we can reach out in peace and offer trades. Not everything has to end in war."

She nodded. "Peace would be good, but if the mortals are any example, there's never truly peace." She walked down a flight of stairs with Devlin in front of her.

"I guess that's something both of our people have in common." Devlin shrugged.

Allie was about to say something when music floated through the air. String instruments echoed through the hallway they just entered. A strong steady beat guided the notes and as they approached the dining hall, Allie found that she wanted to dance.

Devlin smiled at her. "I told you that the Court of Time had the best music."

"I'm in pjs, I shouldn't be attending a fancy dinner with music."

He motioned down to his cotton pants and shirt. "I'm also dressed for a night in. It's just the three of us and the band. Come have some fun while we can." He grabbed her hand and dragged her into the room.

Allie stopped and looked at the huge room. The floors shone with the fairy lights that floated in the air. "This is where you eat?" She glanced at Oriana that was sitting at a small table.

"Well, typically it's more of a feast in here, or I'll eat in my room. But I didn't think you guys wanted to eat there, so..." she gestured around her. "It's a feast of three."

Allie walked over to the table with Devlin at her back. The music continued to play, but seemed to quiet when they sat. Allie looked around trying to spot the band and Devlin pointed up to a corner. "Up on the balcony there."

Allie glanced up and saw a handful of fae playing. She smiled. "A concert and dinner."

"And dancing," Devlin reminded her. "Oriana can teach you to dance."

Oriana snorted. "We both can, it's drilled into our heads from the moment we can walk." She started to count and sway her body.

"Don't step on toes." Devlin added to the count and they both started laughing.

Allie smiled and started picking at the salad in front of her. "So fighting, ruling, and dancing. What else do they teach you as fae children? Do you go to school? Have homework?"

"Royal families are home schooled, but we do have schools in the towns. They are different from yours, I'm sure," Oriana mused. "We do teach reading, writing, history, math, but we teach survival skills as well."

"You mentioned a school that you were going to check on?"

She nodded. "It's in a rural area, it was one of the biggest schools before the war and had a massive library. The library survived because it was magically protected and in the basement, but most of the building was destroyed. I headed the project to have it restored so that those who couldn't travel to a town could still learn." She hesitated slightly. "We're fae, we're people, and like the mortals, we have those who are wealthier than others. Those who have skills and magic that lend more to gaining wealth than others. Our rural areas grow the crops and livestock, they feed our people. We trade with the Kingdom of Creation for their fish and gems. But the people who run the farms, they tend to be less wealthy. But they still deserve to be educated, so I wanted to make sure that was funded and they had that opportunity."

"That's amazing." Allie smiled. "I'd love to see it."

"Once we get done with this mess, I'll happily take you. Hell, I'll take you for a proper tour of my court," she said. "But sadly, we don't have the time for it right now."

Devlin nodded. "After all of this, we'll make sure you have a vacation in our world, so you can experience all the fun. Because I promise we have more to offer than monsters and war."

Allie finished up her salad and pulled the meat toward her. The three of them finished their meals in silence while Allie's mind wandered about what kind of vacation she could have here. "What kind of fun do you have?"

"Balls, parties, celebrations, festivals," Oriana mused. "The markets are fun."

"Hiking, swimming, night time is amazing," Devlin added. "There's so much more than running away from Cerise."

Allie snorted and pushed her plate away.

Oriana stood and grabbed Alice's hand. "Come on, I'll teach you how to dance."

Allie shook her head and pulled back a little. "Oh no, I don't dance."

"Today you learn how to dance like one of the court members." Oriana pulled her wrist up and spread her hand out. "Like this." She showed Allie with her own hand how to hold it properly. She pressed her palm with Allie's. "Okay, now follow my steps." Oriana put her other hand on Allie's hips and started moving them across the floor.

Oriana showed her how to switch partners with certain beats, using Devlin to help her. They all laughed any time Allie stepped on a foot or missed a beat.

Devlin stepped on her toes a couple times, claiming that he was out of practice and really Oriana was the best teacher.

Allie didn't know how much time had gone by before they all ended up on the floor in fits of giggles.

"You're timing is awful Devlin," Oriana joked. "No wonder why you skip the parties."

He snorted. "I swear the beats kept changing, are you sure you know what you're doing?"

Allie laughed. "Oriana never stepped on my feet, Devlin, maybe you should have let me lead."

"Do I need to tell you how many times you stepped on my toes?" Devlin nudged her.

She shook with laughter and she wondered if there would be another time that she'd feel happy and content like this with them. There was a chance that after they went different ways tomorrow, she'd never see Oriana again.

Cerise might rip everything away from her, from them. As a mortal her life ended if Cerise killed her, but the two fae lying on the floor with her would lose their Courts, their people, everything they were raised to protect.

Allie's smile faded as the thoughts invaded the moment, but she lay there, and tried to enjoy it the best she could, because it could very well be the last.

***

Cerise sat in front of the fire watching the flames move. They'd gotten out of the main city of the Court of Time and into the forest just after the sunset.

It wasn't safe to ride through the forest at night. Not with the creatures that still lurked, and the way the land of Fairy could shift, almost at will, changing the terrain, especially in the Court of Time. Her thoughts drifted to Alice.

Had she experienced the land changing? Or the call of the deadly fields that were around. They'd always stuck to the giant forest where it'd be safe. There was once they went to the Tea House, but even then, it was playing it safe. Because she never wanted Alice to get hurt in Fairy, or become one of those mortals so enchanted by it that she couldn't go home.

And in the end, that's what Alice did one last time. She went home and she stayed there without a word for seven years.

Only to return to bring down the walls that Cerise had put into place, to bring down the court that she was now in charge of and ruin all the plans of uniting this side of Fairy under one ruler.

"Don't think too hard on it, my queen," Ace said as he sat next to her. "We'll find the mortal, or she'll be killed by the land."

Cerise snorted. "I don't want her to be killed by the land. I want her death to be mine."

"Then we move on to the Court of Enchantment?"

Cerise nodded. "Devlin's dad is weak minded. He may have tricked us into taking a doll instead of Alice, but he won't stand if we hurt his people. So, plan with your generals on how you want to start the attack on that court. I doubt we take over one city before he bows to us."

Ace nodded. "And do you really intend to ask the Court of Creations to join your side?"

"If I can talk to the monarch, yes. I will not go through a liaison." Cerise shook her head. "They are a court, their rulers should be acting as the rest of us. Meetings, trade deals, aid. This is something I'll fix when I unite everyone." She held her hands out to the fire to warm them. "Court of Enchantment first, Time next, and Creation on my side, I will make my mother's dying wish come true." She wrapped her hand around the roses necklace at her throat and it pulsed with magic.

She'd rule over it all. No matter how much bloodshed it took, how many people she had to kill. Even if that meant her old friends. She was born to rule over all of Fairy, and Alice's return home had made her see that. Cerise had spent years thinking she could live just as a fae, with a mortal friend, and they would live in their own world forever.

Except Alice never came back. Until now.

"She's enchanted your heart, Cerise, turn your mind away from her until the moment is right." Ace said, almost as if he could read her mind. "Until then, she's not worth your worry."

Cerise pressed her lips together and then looked up when someone brought her a loaf of bread with meat and cheese. Traveling food. She couldn't wait to get back home where she could have a full meal at a table instead of on her lap.

"Once our business is done at the Court of Creation, then we can head home."

Cerise nodded. "It's been a lot of travel."

"Next time, I can see if I can gather some birds for us to fly on?"

She shook her head. "No." The heights terrified her. She'd flown once with Devlin one Fehin, and she'd been so terrified she threw up when they landed. "No, I rather have my feet on the ground."

"Very well," He patted her shoulder. "Your mother would be proud of what you're doing."

Would she? Cerise pulled a chunk off the loaf. Would her mother guide her in a different way? Or tell her not to worry about the prophecy that Lavin stated? No, her mother was the reason that Lavin was in their service. She put a lot of thought into the prophecies that were handed to her, which is why she instructed Cerise so early on ruling.

Because her mother knew that she'd die. Cerise ate in silence while Ace stayed by her side. A howl in the woods sent a shiver down her back, the wolf fae were on the hunt tonight. Chasing creatures that didn't belong on this side of the mountains.

Like the Bèarn.

Cerise wrapped the rest of her meal up in the cloth and forced her mind away from what was in the forest. The wolves were nothing to fear, unless they wanted revenge.

She thought through the list of people she had beheaded lately, and none of them were wolves as far as she knew.

So, they'd be safe for the night. And if they dare attacked, her soldiers would take them on.

Ace stood dragging her mind back to the present. "Your tent is ready, my queen."

Cerise stood. "Thank you, I would like to rest." And maybe she could quiet her mind enough to sleep. Another howl ripped through the night and she cringed. Perhaps there would be no sleep tonight.

Oriana stood with Alice in front of Fehin, the giant bird nudged Alice with his beak and she ran her hand over it. "I thought flying was a bad idea."

"It'll get you to Cibil quicker." Oriana crossed her arms. "You'll fly, Devlin will take a horse, and I'll go to the school."

They stood in the middle of the castle courtyard, the trees and plants around them were forever green and in bloom, as her mother cast a spell on them to keep them that way. To never grow past this point.

Immortality for plants, but plants didn't have minds, or need to wander. They could be frozen without consequences to the mind. Unlike the guard outside that Oriana had frozen in the evening. She'd moved the frozen man to prison. If she left him frozen for too long, there was a risk of him going insane when she unfroze him. Which was one of the reasons she never unfroze the people Cerise had asked her to freeze.

Because she didn't want to face the insanity that she caused. Oriana swallowed and then let out a long sigh. "Trust me on this?"

"What do I do when I beat Devlin there?"

"Tell Cibil that I sent you. She's harmless, just a bit...unhinged."

Alice raised a brow. "Unhinged?"

"You'll see what I mean."

Devlin walked out into the court yard. "What she means is that Cibil tends to spout nonsense and her mind is stuck in another time a lot. But she's not going to attack you." Devlin shook his head. "Honestly, you're probably pretty safe there because people avoid her."

"And if any of Cerise soldiers do show up, you can handle them with the sword." Oriana offered a small smile.

Alice patted the hilt of the sword. "Or maybe I'll just ask them to dance and step on their toes."

Oriana and Devlin both laughed. Oriana didn't miss the worry in Alice's eyes though. "I took care of the one person that Cerise left behind, so no one should be following us. The faster we get you there and get you hidden, the better."

"Do I want to know what you did to that person?" Alice raised a brow.

"No, you don't." Oriana motioned to the giant bird. "Up you go. Devlin can tell the bird where to go. Once you're there, send him away so that it's not obvious one of us are there."

"What's stopping anyone from following Fehin?" Alice asked, climbing up on the bird with a boost from Devlin.

"He flies faster than a horse could run, so they'd only get your general direction. He also flies high. You'll be safe." Devlin promised.

Alice nodded and pet the side of the bird. "Okay." Though her voice shook.

Devlin put his head against Fehin's beak. "Head north to the old house." Fehin nipped at Devlin's shoulder and then took to the air.

"She'll be fine," Oriana said as Fehin disappeared into the clouds.

Devlin nodded. "Yeah, I know. Now we both need to get going, it'll take me a day and a half to get to Cibil's. Join us as quick as you can after you're done checking on the school."

"I will. Hey, have you heard from Dor lately?"

He shook his head. "No, but I have a feeling he's keeping his head down. He can hide better than us."

Oriana nodded. "Yeah, hopefully he's off gathering information or something. And staying safe." But it wasn't like their friend to not check in every few days, especially when something was going on.

"Send a messenger if you're worried about him." Devlin started toward the arch that led out toward the stables.

Oriana followed him. "I'm not sure if I'm worried, or concerned that he's avoiding us."

"By avoiding you mean?" Devlin glanced at her over his shoulder.

She took a moment to choose her words. "March betrayed our movements to Cerise, but what if Dor has been doing the same?"

"He does have the ability to move places without the use of horses or birds."

She nodded. "Do you think he'd do that?"

Devlin was quiet as they walked through the hedges to the stable. "No, I don't. Which brings me to wonder if something has happened to him."

Her heart clenched at the thought. "You don't think Cerise would be stupid enough to start taking people, do you?"

"I think Cerise would do whatever it takes to find Alice at this point." He shuddered. "So it's best that we keep moving and figure out how to stop her."

The stable hand came out leading two horses. Oriana climbed up on hers and Devlin did the same on the other one. The stable hand gave her the reigns. "Be safe, my lady."

"Of course. Thank you."

Devlin took his reigns and then looked at Oriana. "The path we take doesn't matter when we don't know where we're going." He took off suddenly without another word.

She sat there for a moment with her horse and wondered what on earth that nonsense was about. Some weird riddle for her to figure out? Or just classic Devlin spouting words that made no sense.

Like when he talked about the raven. She shook her head and squeezed her horse, urging him forward.

***

Allic and Fehin landed in a clearing as the sun started to set. She knew he needed to hunt and sleep, and she needed to rest her legs and body for a bit. Clinging to a giant bird was a lot harder than she had anticipated.

She pulled her cloak around her and surveyed the clearing. Nothing there except a few rocks and weeds. Typical looking trees surrounded them, so normal Allie could almost pretend she was in the mortal world. Fehin squawked and took back off to the air. She had to trust that he'd come back after he'd hunted.

For a moment, she wondered what giant ravens ate. She shook

her head and sat down on a rock, pulling her bit of cheese and meat from her pouch.

A fast-food hamburger sounded great right about now, but she doubted Fairy had any drive-throughs—and if they did, she doubted they could accommodate Fehin.

She ate her food entertaining that thought. The first thing she was going to do when she got home was go out to eat. Well, after she hugged her parents and tried to explain all of this.

Of course, that might land her back in the mental hospital, again. She wrinkled her nose thinking about that. She didn't want to lose another year of her life to that experience.

A noise from the trees drew her attention and she shoved the food back into her pouch before drawing her sword.

The weeds rustled near her and then a smile split out in the air and she relaxed a little as the rest of Kit's cat form showed up.

He flicked his tail before pouncing up on the rock. "Hello, Alice."

"Kit, nice of you to show up while the rest of us are trying to figure out a plan."

"I have four paws and a tail, what do you expect me to do? Shed on her?" He jumped up on to her shoulder. "Besides, you three seem to have it handled."

She snorted and reached up to scratch his ear. He purred against her.

"I could get used to the scratches if I'm stuck as a cat forever," he muttered. "Now, where are you heading? Devlin and Oriana dumped you here?"

She shook her head. "No, Fehin and I stopped for the night. Are you like Dor? You can just pop in and out of where you want?"

"I am, but if you think I can take you to your destination, you're wrong." He laughed. "Where are you going Alice?"

"I honestly don't know. Fehin knows the way." She shrugged one shoulder. After March betrayed them, Alice wasn't willing to share their plans.

He dug his claws into her cloak, but she didn't feel them. "And where are Oriana and Devlin?"

"Executing their part of the plan," she said easily, "which they didn't trust a mere mortal to know."

His weight was suddenly gone from her shoulder and he appeared floating in front of her. "You have your own path to forge, Alice. All the guidance and prophecies in the world aren't written in stone. If you want to change things, you can."

He disappeared and reappeared back on the rock. "So Alice, what path will you take?"

"I don't know where I'm going or what I'm doing."

"Then I guess the path doesn't matter then." He seemed to shrug his shoulders before disappearing, his grin staying behind for just a moment before also fading.

She sheathed her sword and sat back down on the rock. What on earth was he going on about? Did he know what Cibil was going to say?

She watched the sun dipped down behind the mountains and pulled her cloak around her tighter. Hopefully Fehin would be back before the truly dangerous creatures came out to play. The last thing she wanted to run into was a Fachan or a Redcap. Or heaven forbid if Cerise's soldiers were wandering the woods just in case.

She shivered and looked up as a shadow blocked the fading sun. Fehin came down with a whoosh, blowing the weeds into a wave.

He cawed at her and started to nudge her under his wing. She snuggled into him and his feathers, stroking his side to thank him for sharing the warm. She had a feeling no one was going to approach a giant raven, and if they did, they'd probably turn into Fehin's meal.

She leaned against him and watched the forest until she fell asleep, praying that when the sun came up, they'd still be safe.

Kit lay in the tree knowing full well that Alice had lied to him. He couldn't blame her, he hadn't shown her much to trust since she returned to Fairy. He had to make sure that the true fate of the mortal stay on track.

And if he messed around too much, or revealed too many details, Alice would fast track off her fate so hard that it would really mean the end of Fairy.

Imagine that, a mortal the downfall of the Fae. He let out a little snort at that thought. He watched Alice snuggled under Fehin's wing, tucked safe like a baby bird. Oriana and Devlin were playing a dangerous game leaving Alice out here alone, but he knew the two of them. There had to be a reason that they split up.

Cerise, he was sure of it. She'd rattled their cages enough to make them split up. Was that her plan then? Pick them all off one at a time? Or just take Alice while the rest of them were distracted.

Alice wouldn't survive the Queen of Hearts. No, he knew that. Her death was coming and it broke his heart, but if she didn't die, then she couldn't save Fairy.

He bristled at the thought. Cibil had made that clear when he went to see her four years ago, the mortal must sacrifice her life to reset the balance. Alice will bring the Queen of Hearts to her knees and defeat the Jabberwock with creation's sword.

The sword she carried now wasn't from the Court of Creations, no, that had been a gift from the Tweedle Tree and her cloak that he couldn't pierce his claws through must have been a gift from someone in the Court of Enchantment.

Maybe Cibil was wrong and Alice wasn't the mortal that had to die to save Fairy.

He jumped down, landing on the ground with his four paws. He was used to this form now to the point where he stopped wondering if he'd ever get his fae form back. Would he eventually walk Fairy again with two legs instead of four?

In theory, the curse should break once Cerise had Alice.

That gave him pause. He could go pop to Cerise and tell him

where Alice was now and end his curse...but Alice needed to go through this journey in order for her to fulfill her destiny.

He let out a huff and then climbed under Fehin's wing with Alice, curling up next to her. No one was going to hurt her on his watch.

CHAPTER 12

Oriana's horse trotted up to the school just after noon the next day. The children and adults who were outside enjoying the sun waved and smiled at her as she passed them on her way to the stables. The wide field gave them plenty of room to spread out in the warm sunlight.

Everyone looked happy, unharmed, peaceful. Hopefully that meant Cerise hadn't gone through with her threat yet.

She pulled her horse over to the stable and then jumped down. The teen helping at the stable came over and smiled, taking the reins from Oriana.

"Your highness, we didn't know that you were visiting today." She ran her hand over the horse's nose.

Oriana smiled. "It was unplanned. I need to talk to the head master about something. Is she in her office?"

"I would assume so, she might be doing an orientation class though. We got a load of new students this season." She patted the horse's neck. "I'll get this one fed and rested for you. How long will you be staying?"

Oriana considered that question. "A night or two. I have somewhere I need to be, but I want to make sure everything here is taken care of before I leave."

"I'll make sure that she's in top shape then before you leave." The teen led the horse away and Oriana walked toward the building.

Green vines covered the brown building, someone's plant magic must have been seeking an escape at some point, because there were a lot more vines and flowers on the building than there had been before.

She walked through the wooden doors and looked around, students chattered as they walked through the main hall, heading to class.

The bottom level of this building held the classrooms, while the upper level held the offices. She ran up the stairs, brushing past the couple of students that were going the opposite direction.

She walked down the hall to the end where she knew the headmaster's office was. She stopped in front of the door and knocked. "Eikka?"

A moment later the door flung open. "Oriana!" The dark-skinned fae greeted her. Her twisted hair hung down her back with charms weaved throughout. "How are you?" She dragged Oriana into the office.

Oriana hugged her. "I'm doing okay. How are you? How are things at the school?"

"You'd know if something was wrong here." Eikka crossed her arms. "I'm well, still enjoying my job." She clicked her tongue. "But you're not here for a dinner visit, are you?"

"I'm here for the night at least, so if you'd like to have dinner together, I'd be honored, but you're right. There is a reason I'm here."

The laughter faded from Eikka's eyes. "Danger?"

"A threat from Cerise."

Eikka glanced behind Oriana. "Here is not the place to discuss this. After classes are done for the day, we'll have dinner at my place. I don't want to risk the students overhearing."

Oriana bowed her head. "Of course, thank you."

She nodded. "Come, though, I want you to see what improvements I've made to the school." She took Oriana's hand and pulled her out of the office.

"I can't wait. I know you've been working on a lot of things."

She grinned. "The new dorms are up, and the library has grown. The students are not only learning their basics, but I've secured teachers in most magical types from each Court. We're rivaling the in town school now."

"You are a brilliant woman, I knew I made a good choice by appointing you as headmaster."

Eikka nudged her. "Had nothing to do with the fact that you and I explored this place as children?"

"That might have something to do with it. I may have had the idea, but you had the brains to put it all together. And my mother said it'd never work."

Eikka sighed. "If only she was here to see it."

"They'll be back," Oriana said despite the sinking feeling in her chest. "They'll realize there's nothing over there and come home."

Eikka stayed silent and Oriana realized she was probably holding on to a false hope. "I don't want to be queen forever," she whispered.

Eikka looked at her. "It's your bloodline, your crown. If Cerise takes over this court, she'll destroy anything that she doesn't agree with. You are the only thing standing in her way right now."

Oriana nodded. "I know, but sometimes I wish I could be here, teaching with you. Giving our children the knowledge of Fairy and magic, not in the castle trying to prevent wars."

Eikka wrapped an arm around her and squeezed. "You'll be a wonderful leader. You already are."

Oriana gave her a gentle smile. "Show me the library? I want to see what you did and I need to see if I can find some information."

"Well, thanks to you, we have the biggest library of any of the Courts, and I think you'll love what I've done with it."

Fehin landed with a whoosh outside of a house. If one could call the dilapidated building that. The wood seemed to be more rot than wood at this point, but thorned vines held it together so it still stood.

The door hung crooked on the hinges, there was no glass in the windows, and torn fabric hung as curtains. Allie slide off Fehin. "Are you sure this is the right place?" She whispered.

Fehin let out a loud caw and then shot back to the sky.

"Gee, thanks bird." Now she had no choice but to hope this was the right place and it wasn't a killer that lived inside.

"Appearances can be deceiving." A soft voice came from the house. "Come in, Alice of the Mortal World, and let us speak."

A shiver went down Allie's spin and she stepped up to the house. She wrapped her hand around the dirty doorknob and the moment her skin met it, magic burst over her. A strange warm shock cascaded through her limbs.

Her breath caught in her throat and she tried to pull her hand away from the knob, but the magic held her tight to it.

The cabin changed into a beautiful house of marbled stone, the black lines mimicking the vines that had been there before. Tinted glass filled the windows and a feeling of welcome washed over Allie.

It was like the wind came and blew the old away and replaced it with new.

Allie opened the door and stepped in. A foyer with a warm fire greeted her and she looked around to see who the voice belonged to. "Hello?"

"In the study." A sing song voice called and then started humming. Allie took a deep breath and followed the voice down a hall and into a room. Warm brown walls surrounded the room, with white carpet contrasting with them. The room was empty with the exception of an empty chair and a taken chair.

A woman with long white hair plated in braids and twisted into a crown on her head, rocked in a chair. The dangling ends of her braids moved with the motion and she hummed as her feet pushed gently on the floor. "I was wondering when you would come, Alice. I thought maybe you might have decided to seek my brother instead."

She turned to look at Allie, her gray eyes distant, as if she was blind. Then the woman blinked and they cleared. She smiled. "Welcome. Please, have a seat and we'll wait for the others."

"Oriana…"

"Will be here later than Devlin, I know." She tucked one braid behind her pointed ear. "And Devlin will be arriving in the morning."

So they were just going to sit there and stare at each other for half a day? Allie sat in the empty chair.

"I'm Cibil," the woman said.

Allie nodded. "Nice to meet you, you already know who I am."

"Alice of the Mortal world. Yes, I'm aware." Her appearance appeared to flicker, like there was a filter over her. For a moment her white hair flashed black, and her eyes red.

Allie swallowed, trying to keep her panic down.

"Forsaken is the mortal, no longer of her world. Forgiven is the Red of Hearts, her sins cleansed in blood. Cursed is the Court of Creation, for the ruler has been lost. And dead is the wanderers, for they found what lurks beyond. The one you sought is no longer your blood."

With each sentence that changes between appearances changed between the two.

Was this what Devlin meant by Cibil being unhinged? They were both pretty certain that Allie was safe here. She took a deep breath. "Am I the mortal?"

Cibil put a finger to her chin. "Are you the right Alice, or the wrong Alice?"

Allie raised a brow. "I think that's what I'm asking."

She chuckled. "Right now, you're the wrong Alice. Tell me, why did you decide to go by Allie?"

Allie hesitated. She hadn't corrected anyone in Fairy about her name. She'd let them all call her Alice, because that's who she was here. "I needed a change," she said honestly. "Alice was the girl who told stories about fae, and fantastical worlds, the one who was put into inpatient mental care because she refused to say it was all pretend."

"But which Alice does Fairy need right now? The scared woman who was afraid of what people thought? Or the brave child who ran wild through our lands?"

Allie bit her lip, but didn't answer.

"Believe in the impossible, and you won't be forgotten." Cibil smiled at her, but it looked crazed. "The Red Queen will fall to her knees."

Cibil leaned her head back against the rocking chair, her appearance settling on the one with black hair. "You must be exhausted. Please rest in the guest room. I'll wake you for dinner."

Allie waited for a moment to see if Cibil had anything more to say, but when the seer closed her eyes and rocked in silence, Allie stood and wandered to the hallway to find the guest room.

The only door that was opened sat at the end of the hall. Allie walked in and found a bath waiting for her. The wisps of steam danced up from the water, beckoning her to step in.

She stripped out of her dirty clothes and sank into the water, leaning her head back on the ledge. The warmth soaked into her bones, loosening her muscles. Just what she needed after the last few days.

The Court of Creation was one of the great mysteries of Fairy. The black mist wrapped around the entry of the main city, hiding the walls and the streets from any passer-by. Swirling up wards, it hid the castle from view as well, and there had been rumors if the Court of Creation even had a castle.

All the courts did, though Cerise didn't know when the last time anyone had seen the Court of Creation's castle. It could be in ruins for all she knew.

A shiver rolled down her back as they approached the black mist. The horses stomped their feet and tried to back away from the gate. Cerise pulled on her reins. "Easy girl," she muttered and tried to ease the horse forward.

The horse continued to rear.

"I think this is as far as we can go with the horses, my queen," Ace stated and slid off his horse. He walked the creature over to a tree and tied the reigns. "Let's continue on foot."

On foot, like she was a commoner. She was going to rule this court one day, but Ace was right. There was going to be no other way if the horses wouldn't continue.

She jumped down and Ace took the reins and tied them to a tree. "Stay here," she told the others. "We don't want to come across as a threat, and someone needs to watch the horses."

Ace stepped to her side and nodded. "Let's go pay the leader a visit, shall we?" He held his arm out for her. She wrapped her hand into the crook of his elbow.

"Yes."

Together they stepped through the swirling black mist and...

Nothing was there. Nothing more than more mist wafting around them.

"What trick is this?" Cerise growled. "Where is the city? The roads? The people?"

A figure appeared in front of them, cast in a robe of shadows and mist. "Who seeks to enter the city?"

"The Queen," Cerise snapped.

The figure laughed and the voice shifted from male to female. "The self-proclaimed queen, the Red Queen. You are not allowed to enter the city. We know your intentions."

"I demand to speak with the leader of your court."

"We told your messenger that we will send a liaison within a fortnight. And that we will grant no one access to the Court of Creation." The figure was swept away by the black mist.

Cerise let out a frustrated growl as a wind whipped around her, pulling at her clothes and her hair, but it took the mist away with it. Ace and her found themselves standing back in front of the horses, outside the barrier to the Court of Creation.

"Such power." Ace nearly purred. "To be able to hide your entire main city like that."

Cerise smirked. "Yes, power." Power that would be hers one way or another.

"We should return home, meet with the messenger."

"The prophecy said that Alice would wield the sword of creation, how is she going to get it if they allow no one in?" Cerise growled. "Why does that court have all that power and never attends court meetings, never shows any sign of weakness? It's like it lives in its own little realm."

Ace hummed for a moment as he glanced back at the swirling mist, but said nothing more. Cerise urged her horse to head towards home. There had been no word from soldiers about whether anyone had left Oriana's court or if they had found Alice.

Dread sat in the pit of her stomach at the idea that Alice could be wandering around Fairy alone. She tried to convince herself that she wanted to be responsible for Alice's death, her revenge for Alice leaving her alone in Fairy and not keeping her promise to return. But there was one small part of her that still worried for her friend. She could still hear the laughter of the two of them as they played like an echo in her mind.

Cerise shook her head. No. Alice betrayed her and was standing in the way of her uniting and ruling over all the courts.

The mortal had to die.

Devlin walked into the seer's house. Cibil was sitting in her rocking chair, humming to herself with her eyes closed. The sun had peeked over the horizon about an hour ago and he'd expected Cibil and Alice to be awake, but Cibil didn't open her eyes to greet him or stop humming.

"Cibil?" Devlin asked and the seer still rocked. Her white hair was down around her shoulders today; one back stripe of it was all that showed from her other self right now.

He walked down the hall to find rooms lining either side of it, they all seemed dim in color compared to the one at the end of the hall.

The white door held a crispness that the others didn't. Almost a glow around it making it more real than the others. Devlin knocked. "Alice?"

She opened the door and smiled. "You made it."

Her pixie cut hair was tamed so it didn't stick out everywhere. Her dirty clothes had been exchanged for a clean sleeveless black dress that swirled around her ankles. If she had pointed ears, she would have looked like a fae. "You look..." he hesitated for a moment. "Well rested."

She rolled her eyes. "I didn't rest well at all. I took a nice hot bath, and then piddled around until dinner and then excused myself to bed. But I didn't sleep much. Cibil was muttering all night walking up and down the halls."

"Did she say anything of use?"

Alice crossed her arms. "While she was wandering the halls like a restless spirit? No. When I first got here...she had a prophecy for me, or something for me. I've been thinking about it all night."

"Tell me exactly what she said." Devlin met Alice's gaze. "The wording is very important."

Alice took a moment to think about it. "'Forsaken is the mortal, no longer of her world. Forgiven is the Red of Hearts, her sins cleansed in blood. Cursed is the Court of Creation, for the ruler has been lost. And dead is the wanderers, for they found what lurks beyond. The one you sought is no longer your blood.' I'm pretty sure that's how it went."

"That's exactly how it went." Cibil said from the doorway. "Her memory is better than most mortals." Cibil's now black hair fell in waves and her red gaze never left Alice. "Alice must discover if she is the wrong or the right Alice."

Devlin pressed his lips together as the words ran through his head. There was a lot to unpack there. "That's different from the prophecy that Cerise was given."

"My brother favors the Queen of Hearts." Cibil leaned against the wall, reaching up wards. Stretching her body as if she was trying to grab something off a tall shelf. "He will tell her what fate has stored for her. I on the other hand…" Her form shifted again, flickering between her light and dark persona. "Listen to what the fates tell me and deliver it. We used to be a whole, you know…" She looked at Alice. "My brother and I. Twins in fate, delivering the news as one piece. And then we were shattered…"

She glided out of the room, running her nails alone the wall and Alice looked at Devlin. "Um…"

"It's a long story that's about as old as Fairy itself. We'll talk about it another time." The story had been passed down in each court, some details changing and now one could ever agree on whose fault it was that the twins of fate were shattered.

Alice nodded slightly. "So, any ideas on what her little prophecy meant?"

A few things had sprung to mine, Alice was clearly the mortal, but he couldn't see Cerise's sins being forgiven. He wasn't sure whose blood was strong enough to cleanse her. Who knew what was going on in the court of creation…dead is the wanderers…that was probably Oriana's parents and the mere thought of it made his heart ache. But that last line, he had no inkling on. "Honestly, it sounds more like a list than an actual prophecy. I'll think on it."

He didn't want to give her half answers, she was already nervous enough as it was about having to face the Jabberwock and Cerise. There was no need to add more onto that until he had to. "Hopefully Oriana isn't far behind me. I'm willing to bet she spent the night at the school."

"Maybe she'll bring me that picture of the Jabberwock." Alice mused "So I can at least know what I'm going to end up facing down."

Devlin nodded. "That'll be a start. Then we can head to the Court of Creation to see about this sword you're supposed to be carrying."

Alice patted the pummel of her sword. "I'm not sure if I want to carry a different one."

"I mean ultimately the choice is up to you, but I wouldn't look a gift horse in the mouth. Especially from the Court of Creation." Devlin shrugged. "Rumor has it that they are stronger than any of the courts."

"So why haven't they tried to start a war? Or prevented one by taking Cerise out?"

"You heard Cibil, their leader is gone. That's probably why." Which meant there was a chance that Cerise could overtake it if the magic faded. "No one knows who really rules the court."

Alice let out a frustrated sigh. "Let me guess, there are more rumors?"

"There are always rumors in Fairy." Devlin laughed. "Even the plants have ears here Alice, not just the walls, and the birds. The rumors start from the information people gleam on the passing wind."

She stared at him like she didn't believe him, and he couldn't really blame her. The human world had nothing that was as insane as talking wind...as far as he knew.

"Well, regardless of what sword I choose, let's get some more practice in," she muttered. "Maybe I'll get to be fast enough that the Jabberwock won't get me with the first bite."

Devlin tried to conjure up comforting words, but there wasn't anything to say. A mortal against the Jabberwock was a predictable battle. He could only hope that Fate had more in store for Alice.

CHAPTER 13

"My queen," a soldier's voice caught Cerise's attention the moment she walked into the castle. "We caught a spy."

She raised a brow. That was the best news she could have heard when she arrived. The only thing better would be if it was Alice. "Oh? Take me to them."

The solider bowed and led Cerise to a room instead of the dungeon where she had expected him to. "What kind of joke is this? Why would you give a spy a room?"

"Please be patient, my queen. He is not flittering about the room free, I assure you." He opened the door and Cerise looked around the empty room. The bed sat against the window, made and ready for a guest. The muted red a stark contrast against the dark stone of the room. To her left was a simple wooden desk and a chair. Her eyes landed on a small cage sitting on the desk and spotted Dor trying to pick the lock.

Her lips split into a cruel smile. "Dor, my dear, how are you?"

Dor froze, floating down to his tiny feet and staring up at her with wide eyes. "Cerise," he stuttered. "Please tell your men that I mean no harm and have them free me."

She pulled the chair up to the desk and looked at him. "Now why would I do that?" She sat down. "My solider has informed me that you were spying on me."

Dor gave a nervous laugh. "Me? Spying on you? You know that no one holds my leash. I'm not loyal to any one court. Why would I spy on you?"

She tapped her long nails against the wood. "You've been seen helping my enemies," she purred and looked at the little fae. "Helping *Alice.*"

Dor shook his head. "I did no such thing. Maybe Devlin and Oriana, but not Alice. We all know that you don't want her in your land."

"Nice way to suck up, but as you said, you have no loyalties to any of the courts. So you'll rot in mine." She turned to walk away.

"Wait!" Dor cried. "Wait, don't leave me in this cage, please Cerise."

"I need information, Dor and then maybe I won't keep you trapped." She waited within in a foot of the doorway, but Dor remained silent. "See, you aren't willing to betray your friends."

She walked out and the door clicked shut behind her. She could hear Dor begging still, though his voice was muted by the heavy wood. "Make sure he is kept well. He might change his mind and I'd hate him to die in his captivity."

The solider nodded. "Yes, my queen."

She walked down the hall with Ace behind her. "We saw no signs of Alice or Devlin at the Court of Creation," she growled.

"We saw no signs of anything," Ace corrected. "Not even the court itself."

There was that. There was a chance that Alice had been hiding within the mist, but they very well could have been turned away just like Cerise and Ace. "So where does that leave us? I still have no Alice; Devlin and Oriana are sneaking around making sure she's safe. I can't attack the Courts until Alice is dealt with."

Ace sighed. "We can always send him out? With his connection to her he might be able to find her easier than us."

She paused at that thought. "We could. It's a risk, we don't know if he's actually loyal to me or if he's been playing a long."

"Seven years is a long time to play along." Ace shrugged. "He's fae and he has a connection to her. I say, we release him."

Cerise spun to look at him. "And if it doesn't work?"

"Then we kill him." He shrugged. "He's a hunter, we're giving him prey."

She considered the possibilities. He had been training as a hunter and now was as good of time as any to trust his loyalty. "Fine, send him after her. Let's see what this hunter can do."

Ace bowed. "I'll go fetch him."

"And make it clear that if he screws this up, I will be feeding him to my pet."

Ace smirked. "Of course."

This was the only next step she could see. Waiting around for Alice was not an option. If she came to the Court of Hearts, she could ruin everything. And that was just not acceptable.

That is the Jabberwock?" Allie tried to keep her voice calm as she looked down at the picture that Oriana had laid out on the marble table. Allie swore almost every surface in Cibil's house was marble, and though it was pretty it made the home feel almost cold.

"Yes," Oriana and Devlin said at the same time.

Allie looked at the rounded snout that opened to beaver like teeth, and the long serpent like neck that was dotted with spikes. It led down to a slim body with scales like she imaged a dragon would have, but it stood up right on two theropod clawed feet with long front arms, with three clawed fingers. A tail wrapped around it, on the ground, but it was nothing compared to the great bat wings that sprouted from the Jabberwock's back. "That looks like a science experiment gone wrong."

Devlin snorted. "Something like that. The spikes are something to watch out for, because they will hurt like hell if you get hit by them." He tapped the tail of the creature. "So that's going to be a concern. You'll have to move faster than the tail."

Allie nodded. "Okay, claws?"

"Poisonous," Oriana said. "But they shouldn't be able to get through your cloak."

"Or your gauntlets," Devlin pointed out.

That's good, that gave her two options to block with. "And his buck teeth?"

"We don't know what would happen to a human if it bit you." Oriana pressed her lips together. "But a fae? A bit from the Jabberwock would drain their magic, killing them slowly."

That didn't sound pleasant at all. "And it can fly. Great."

"It's slow at flying, if that helps at all." Devlin offered. "I mean look at it, it's not really built for speed."

Allie wasn't sure what it was built for, honestly. "I'm going to die."

Neither of them said anything to counter her thought.

She stared down at the picture and muttered. "There has to be a weakness here somewhere."

Oriana nodded. "Cut its head off."

She glanced up. "What?"

"Either cut its head off, or tame it somehow. If you tame it though, then you take Cerise's place as queen."

Allie wrinkled her nose. "I don't think a mortal on the throne for that court would do so well."

"A mortal on any of our thrones wouldn't do well." Devlin agreed. "What we need is—"

"Sword of creation." Cibil walked in, her hair white for the moment. Her blue gown swirled around her as she walked towards them. "She wields the sword of creation, and she'll bring the queen of hearts to her knees."

She didn't sound like she was in a trance of any sort, the words didn't have power to them like when she was speaking the prophecy. It sounded like she was stating it as a fact.

Allie put her hand on the hilt of her sword. "Is this the sword of creation?"

Cibil shook her head. "No. You have the wrong sword and you're the wrong Alice." She put a finger to her chin. "Whatever are we to do?"

Going back to the image, Allie crossed her arms. "Can you tell us where to find the sword of creation?"

Cibil's appearance shifted, flickering so her hair was black for a moment and then back to white. She stumbled. "I...I don't know. I can't see it."

Allie looked at Devlin who shrugged. "Sometimes things are blocked from the seers."

That wasn't comforting at all. "So now what? We go to the Court of Creation?"

Oriana nodded. "That's what it sounds like. I'm sure Cerise has noticed that you're not there now."

Allie pressed her lips together. "Do you think she left men there like she did at your kingdom?"

Oriana shook her head. "I think that whoever is running that Court wouldn't stand for it."

Devlin nodded. "I would agree with that."

Allie turned away from the drawing of the Jabberwock and let out a frustrated sigh. None of this was straight forward, go here, go there, find the mysterious sword, slay the beast, and...and then what? Slay the queen?

Could she strike Cerise down? Could a human even hope to take down the Jabberwock?

The idea of being killed by something that had poisoned buck teeth was ridiculous.

Maybe she was dreaming and she'd wake up in the mental health hospital again.

Or a tornado struck the house and she was concussion in the storm.

Or...

"This isn't a dream Alice," Cibil interrupted her wishful thinking. "This is your destiny."

Allie wrinkled her nose. "I don't believe in destiny."

"Well you better start, because you can't become Alice without believing in destiny." Cibil patted her cheek and then laughed. "You guys must go. There's a shadow coming and I don't want you to get caught."

Allie looked at Oriana, who picked up the picture and tucked it into her bag. "Okay, let's go then. Devlin, call Fehin and we'll ride to the Court of Creation."

Devlin hesitated. "Are we sure that'll be safe?"

Oriana sighed. "It's a risk we'll have to take. It's a long ride from here and the sooner we get there, the better."

Allie frowned. "Are we on a deadline? If riding is safer, what does it matter that it'll take longer?"

"The longer we take in getting the sword, the less time you have to learn how to use it." Oriana looked to Devlin.

"And the more time Cerise has to come up with a plan to stop us. Okay, flying it is."

Allie nodded. "Okay. Let's get back on the giant bird."

Devlin chuckled. "I bet you're going to miss traveling by bird when you get back to the human world."

If she ever got back to the human world.

Cerise walked around the leather clad male. Dual swords crossed over his back, his long black hair blended into the leather and was tied back away from his face.

The cruel scar across his face was a painful reminder of the price he paid to protect a mortal. Seven years he'd been in Cerise court, loyal to her, slaying what enemies she needed.

This would be his test.

She smiled and ran her finger down the tip of his pointed ear and he jerked his head away from her.

"Griffin, don't shy away from my touch. I'm the one who saved you from death. Remember?" Cerise purred and stepped away from him.

Griffin crossed his arms. "Why did you call me here, my queen?"

"There's a mortal in our world that I need you to bring to me. She's evading my men, always staying a step ahead of me with the help of other courts."

Shadows flashed in his eyes. "A mortal? Has she returned then?" Griffin asked, his hand tightening just slightly on his wrist.

"Yes, she has. She's the face the Jabberwock, just like the seer says."

"If the seer is good at what he does, then Alice will not need my help to find her way here." His lip lifted in a sneer. "She'll fall into the steps of destiny."

Cerise nodded. "This is true, but I'd like to speed it up a bit. And the way to do that is to get her here faster."

"Is there a deadline I'm not aware of?" Griffin asked. "Something else the seer said?"

"No, but there are rumors of creatures from the other side of the mountain. I wish to deal with the mortal issue before more creatures cross."

Griffin shifted on his feet. "I'll bring her to you, my queen."

"Do not harm her, not yet Griffin. Hunter her, stalk her, and bring her here, but do not take your anger or your rage out on her. Am I clear?"

Griffin nodded. "As you wish, my queen." He turned and left. She didn't need to give him a starting point or a direction. He'd learned and adapted quickly to his fae form and how to hunt within this world.

If he couldn't track Alice down or lure her to the Court of Hearts, then fate really was in control here.

"He'll bring her in," Ace said from behind her. "Then we can move forward with all the plans. Put Alice against the Jabberwock, let it kill her. Take over the courts and prepare to take out those who rise against you."

She spun around to look at him. "Has our prisoner talked yet?"

"No, Dor only asks to be released from the cage, but he won't give the guard any useful information. Of course if he was spying, he's been away from Alice to have any relative information at this point." Ace shook his head. "And to believe these people once claimed to be your friends, and now they are all working against you."

She nodded. "They don't want me to have power. They know that I'll be the best ruler this land could have, but that they have to surrender their courts for it. They wouldn't dare give up their magic, their lands, their people. Even if it's to better the world of Fairy. They rather be selfish and keep it, even though it'll be the downfall of our ways." She shuddered and wrapped her hand around the necklace as it pulsed. "If the creatures on the other side of the mountains have survived the war and they are planning on attacking. The only way to stop them is to unite, or all of Fairy will become the dark world. And all of us can kiss our powers goodbye."

And she was just blood thirsty and driven enough to do what needed to be done. Slaughter those who survived the war so she could rule over all of Fairy. That was her destiny.

"The first war took a toll on our people, I'm not sure if Fairy can survive another one." Ace said.

"Not as different courts," Cerise agreed. "As one, fighting as one army. If we act quickly we can."

Ace was silent and Cerise raised a brow. "You disagree?"

"I don't know what we're dealing with on the other side of the mountains, so it's hard to say what battle strategy will work best." He shrugged. "We may be worried about nothing more than a few stragglers."

"Or an army of Bèarn." She shook her head. "Alice is said to bring Fairy down, we need to take care of that first."

Ace nodded. "That I agree with, we'll see what Griffin returns with."

Cerise smiled and turned, leaving the throne room she headed toward her chambers, barely aware of Ace's footfalls behind her. Griffin wouldn't fail in bringing Alice to Cerise, one way or another he'd make sure the woman made it here. Alice would face the Jabberwock and that would be the end of any sort of ruin Alice could bring to Fairy. One bite from the creature, one slice from its thorns, and she'd be gone. Dead. Just as she should have been from the start.

Allie slid off Fehin's back when they landed for the night. She stretched and ran her hand over the beak of the bird. "Thank you."

He clicked at her and then at Devlin before flying off. Allie looked around the forest clearing that they'd stopped at and frowned. "This isn't the court of Creation." The tall trees reached out to the sky, their leaves a deep red color in the shadows. The moonlight filtered through, making the trees look almost blood stained.

"No, we're in the forest outside the Court of Creation." Oriana stepped up to her side. "We can't just fly into the court. It's protected."

Allie stood there waiting for an explanation, was it protected by other giant birds? Eagles perhaps? Or creatures? Magic? Neither Oriana nor Devlin offered up more of an explanation.

"But we can walk right into it?" Allie asked and the two fae shook their heads.

"No, only those who are welcomed are allowed to walk into the court." Oriana stated and crossed her arms. "So we're hoping that you're welcomed into the court since you're part of the prophecies."

Allie stared at Oriana. "Alone?"

"Alone, the Court of Creation hasn't allowed any other court ruler inside for…hundreds of years? Since the war at least." Oriana pressed her lips together.

"And if I'm not welcomed?" Allie held her arms out. "Also, why do you guys keep hiding things like this? It's like you're only giving me half the information."

Devlin glanced at Oriana who shrugged. "Because we're worried if we say too much we can change the fate and outcome to a less desirable one."

I had a feeling I knew what they meant by less desirable. "Okay, so at dawn, what am I supposed to do? Just waltz up to the gates?"

Oriana shrugged. "We go to the boarder and see what we can see. Hopefully, you'll be let in, and from there you'll discover what you can do. The goal is to get the sword of creation which can bring down the Jabberwock."

Allie nodded. "Yeah, yeah, bring down the beast, talk Cerise into not waging war, and then go home."

Neither of the fae said anything. She spun around and faced the forest. "Let's eat and turn in I guess. Dawn comes early and apparently there is no such thing as sleep in when it comes to Fairy."

At that the other two laughed. "You're right, we live by the sun. Imagine a world where alarms and whistles ruled the time that you get up." Devlin shivered. "The sun says, it's time to wake, and the moon says it's time to sleep."

"For most creatures anyway." Oriana added. "Time has its place, and some creatures rise with the moon and sleep with the sun."

Devlin nodded. "But what fun is a world where your time is divided up? School? Work? Sleep?" He grabbed Allie's arm and spun her around, pulling her into a dance as they laughed. "Time is great for dancing, and fighting. Everything has its timing, but it's not a schedule."

He spun her around under his arm. "Not like the humans have."

She stopped abruptly in her spin and thought about that. Other than needing to be somewhere before dusk or dawn, they didn't have a schedule. They ate when they were hungry. She was sure there was a schedule when it came to court meetings and politics, but what they'd been living felt...freeing from the human world.

"Something wrong?" Oriana asked, meeting her gaze.

Allie shook her head. "No, I was just thinking about the differences in our world, is all. Some things I miss, and others I don't." She shrugged a shoulder. "I miss my family, the few friends I had, but I do like the freedom here."

"Devlin makes it sound grand, but we still have responsibilities. People to protect, courts to run, and wars to stop."

At such young ages. But then again, humans sent their new adults to the military too. Allie nodded. "Prophecies to fulfill or change, beasts to destroy. I guess every world has their problems."

Devlin nodded. "Thanks for taking my fun moment and turning it serious." He grumbled. "All I wanted was a dance."

Oriana cracked a smile. "Dance then. I'll gather some fire wood." She clapped her hands and music floated through the breeze and Allie looked at Devlin.

"Magic never ceases to amaze me," she muttered as he grabbed her hand and started to lead her in the dance.

He smiled. "You grow used to it. We don't see how humans live without it. Honestly."

"Technology is like magic," she said as he twirled her again. "It does a lot of what your powers can."

He smiled. "Maybe when this is all done I'll spend some time in your world."

"Is that possible?"

"We'll have to find out." He winked at her and spun her around again.

They danced until Oriana came back with a stack of wood, then Devlin went to help her set up the fire. Allie sat with them and watched the flames dance in the darkness. Her mind wandered back to home.

The panic her parents must have been feeling with her disappearing again. Or would they have written it off as her running away and just give up? Was there a way to let them know she was safe?

A rustle caught her attention and she glanced away from the fire. A shiver marched up her spine as she tried to place the source of the noise. A glance at Oriana and Devlin told her they also heard it and were on alert.

Her heart pounded against her chest as she stood slowly, putting her hand on the hilt of her sword.

Another rustle, this time closer. It sounded too big to just be a woodland creature. Or at least one small enough not to be a threat.

Something glinted in the moonlight and Allie acted on instinct. She pulled her sword up and threw it up to block an attack.

Dark eyes met her gaze in the flickering of the fire light. She swore she knew the face under the scars and hair. He shoved her back and turned to attack again.

This time Devlin blocked. "Alice, run!"

She swallowed and took off, hoping that the direction she picked was correct, or she'd be lost and swallowed forever in Fairy.

CHAPTER 14

Allie's feet pounded against the ground as she trusted her instincts to guide her. The sound of clashing swords echoed behind her as she forced herself to keep going forward.

She heard the caw of Fehin above her and slowed a little. She focused on her breathing as she moved forward. They weren't supposed to be far from the Court of Creation, but the way Devlin and Oriana had talked the court was hidden.

She rounded over a hill, her breath hitching in her chest as she spotted dark gates wrapped in shadows.

This had to be it.

"Run!" Devlin's voice echoed behind her. "Don't look back!"

Allie forced herself forward again, heading toward the gates. Her pulse echoed her footsteps as she approached the gate. She reached her hand up to push it open, but it swung in wards and wisps of shadows wrapped around her, pulling her in.

She swore that the world behind her disappeared with a pop of sound, leaving her isolated on the other side of the gate.

Turning, she feared the worse, but there was nothing.

Well, nothing she expected. The red leafed trees were gone and in front of her stretched out a field of what looked like strawberries as far as the eyes could see. Her stomach churned as she searched for the gate that she just walked through.

She turned back to see that the fields ended at another gate. This one a silver color that seemed to move as if it was alive.

Somehow, Allie knew this was the true gate to the Court of Creation. She glanced back over her shoulder at the fields. Unless she wanted to wander aimlessly through the plants, she had no other choice but to enter the other gate.

Slowly she walked up to it, and just like the black one, it swung inwards, but no shadows grabbed her. She walked through and every-thing on the other side became clearer, like a veil was lifted.

Fae bustled on the street, talking to one another or waving. No one paid her any attention like she didn't just materialize out of nowhere. Their steps sounded on white and gray cobblestones that made up the roads between the carts and houses of the village she was now in.

She pulled her hood up and kept her head down as she started navigating her way through the crowd, trying to find some place quiet and less crowded to get a handle on where she was and what to do next.

Oriana and Devlin hadn't given her much instruction. Find the Blade of Creation and return to them. Neither of which seemed possible right this moment. Someone bumped into her shoulder and then reached out to steady her.

She looked up to apologize to the person and found dark green eyes staring into hers. The woman's dark face broke out into a grin. "You're here."

She grabbed Allie's wrist and started running through the streets. Allie tried to keep her feet under her and follow the fae. The woman's black hair danced behind her in braids that shined with silver jewels that moved much like the silver of the gate.

The houses and villagers sped by Allie in a blur of movement as the woman kept pulling her along at speeds that Allie swore weren't human.

They came to a jolting stop and the woman spun around to face Allie. "Well, it took you long enough."

She pulled Allie's hood down and fussed with her hair. "Ah, if only my husband was here for this."

Allie resisted the urge to push the woman away. "Who are you?"

"Mallow, I'm one of the advisers for the Court of Creation. And you are Alice." She grinned again. "We've been waiting for you Alice."

Allie took a deep breath. "So I keep hearing. Look, Oriana and Devlin are still out there. We were attacked and—"

Mallow held a finger up to Alice's lips to silence her. "Your friends will be fine. That fae was after you. Once he realizes that he won't be able to get to you, he'll leave the others alone. Your focus is here now. With me and the other advisers."

"And this is the court of creation?" Allie asked gently. "They weren't sure that I was going to be welcomed in."

Mallow nodded. "Yes, welcome." She smiled. "You are of course welcomed here. The Alice who will bring the Red Queen to her knees."

Allie tried not to roll her eyes. "So you've heard the prophecy too then."

"Everyone has. Let's go, it's time to meet the others." Mallow pushed opened the door they stood at.

Allie followed Mallow into the building and paused. Walls of water waved and swirled on either side of them. Ripples flowed through, guiding them forward with each step that Mallow took.

The fae turned and glanced at Alice. "It's not going to drown you or anything. Please, follow me."

Taking a deep breath, Allie moved forward, keeping her eyes trained on the back of Mallow's head so she didn't have to admit how much the ripples in the walls unsettled her. This was fairy, walls could be made of water here without danger.

So she hoped.

They stopped at a dead-end and Mallow put her hand against the water wall. It rippled around her fingers and then parted open. "Come, Alice, it's time for you to face your destiny."

Allie stepped under the doorway, expecting Mallow to follow, but the water crashed down between them, leaving Alice in the dark.

Devlin snarled as their attacker glanced around and then darted back into the woods, the same direction Alice went. He shot after him, but Oriana grabbed his arm. "Alice isn't in the woods anymore."

Devlin took a deep breath and put his weapon away. "She got into the Court then?"

"Yes. So now we wait for her to come out."

"And our attacker?" Devlin pointed in the direction that he went. "Do you think he'll be waiting too?"

Oriana shrugged. "I'm not sure. There's something...familiar about him."

"There's something off about him," Devlin disagreed. "When he approached felt different. Like...a fae still developing his abilities and powers."

"He's a full-grown male, his powers should be developed. An enchantment perhaps? Something to make him seem weaker?"

Devlin glanced around them. "I don't know. It's possible, but why would Cerise someone who is weakened after us."

"Are we sure Cerise sent him? All the courts are aware of the prophecy, it could be someone else. We all have rebels."

Devlin sighed. "We don't need any more enemies right now. What we need is to get Alice prepared." Something rustled behind them and he drew his sword spinning around to face March.

"What do you want you traitor?" Devlin snarled at him. "You tried to sell us out to Cerise."

"Because she said she knew where Knave is." The man snapped and looked around, rubbing his hands together nervously. "Cerise has

Dor. It's only a matter of time before she tries to take you two captive. Where is Alice?"

Devlin glanced at Oriana who gave a subtle shake of her head. Devlin shrugged. "Your guess is as good as mine. We've been looking for her. It seems she doesn't want to be found."

"Liars. Do you realize the damage you are doing by hiding her?" March snarled. "She needs to be taken into custody."

"So Cerise can kill her?" Oriana shot back. "March, I know you think that Cerise has information on Knave, and I'm sorry that your love was taken, but you can't seriously be siding with Cerise on this."

"You want Alice to bring ruin upon fairy by taking down Cerise?" He growled. "Because that's what's going to happen."

Devlin considered his words carefully. "Before you agreed with us that Alice needed to be protected, that she needed to bring down Cerise. What has changed?"

March stared at him. "The fact that Cerise has the power to actually take over Fairy and kill all of you. Take all the courts. And she knows where Knave is. Give me Alice."

"She won't give you that information, if she does actually have it." Devlin shook his head. "Join us in looking for Alice."

March shook his head slowly. "No. She already has Dor, I won't become her prisoner." He backed up, his foot snapping a stick. He jumped, turned, and ran the opposite direction.

Oriana stepped up next to Devlin. "He's acting jumpier than normal."

"Yes, he's worried about Knave, but I'm not sure if Cerise really knows where Knave is." Devlin crossed his arms. "But she's getting more desperate to get Alice. A warrior, March...who next? The Jabberwock itself?"

Oriana shivered. "I've heard the stories about the damage the Jabberwock can do when left out of check. Let's hope she doesn't get that desperate. And right now, Alice is untouchable in the Court of Creation. We have to trust that she'll be safe while she finds the sword."

Devlin marched back to the now dying fire and sat down. "No one really knows what lies in the Court of Creation anymore. We don't know if she's safe because they won't let us in."

"But they let her in."

"And what's to say they don't turn around and hand her over to Cerise? Make a treaty with her where they can keep their court covered in shadows in exchange for Alice?" Devlin fell back against the ground.

Oriana looked over him, her blue eyes meeting his gaze. "It sounds like you've thought about it."

Devlin snorted. "Did you forget that my father was trying to use Alice as a bargaining tool?"

Oriana nodded. "But we know that the correct path here is not to let Cerise take over the other courts of Fairy. That we should all be working together to keep Cerise's court in check. That is what Fairy needs."

Devlin sighed. "Yes, it is." He closed his eyes. "Take first watch? I'm going to rest."

"Sure thing." Oriana walked away.

Devlin tried to get his breathing to even out as he thought about the attack. The man looked familiar, older somehow than what his memory was trying to pull up. Different, and yet there was something in the attackers eyes that was familiar. Like a friend had been there once. Something that seemed to call out for help.

He rolled over on his side, trying to banish the image from his head.

Cerise counted to ten in her head as she looked down at Griffin. "She went where?" She asked again, knowing the answer wasn't going to change. "And then you *left*?" She snarled.

Griffin nodded. "She was already disappearing into the shadows when I caught up to her. I've put my traps in place, she won't be able to leave without my magic tracking her."

Cerise tapped her fingers on the arm of the throne. "So she will be here?"

"I will know the moment that she leaves the Court of Creations, my queen." Griffin's voice never shook, never wavered; not once did he show that he was scared of her.

Which Cerise wasn't sure was a good or a bad thing. "You know what happens if you fail?"

Griffin's throat bobbed. "I do."

There was that hint of fear in his eyes. She smirked. "Then you will make sure you bring her to me or you will be seeing the Jabberwock."

He bowed. "I won't fail you in this." He turned and left. Cerise looked at Ace. "So why is the court allowing her in?"

"Because they want to see you taken down, my queen." Ace said. "That's why they didn't allow you in, but they did Alice. Griff said that Devlin and Oriana were both near the court as well. Would you like me to send soldiers to bring them in? More assurance that Alice will come?"

Cerise thought for a moment. "No, let them be. Let them think they have won this round. They don't know what Griffin is capable of. A false sense of security will have them dropping their guard." Cerise smiled.

Ace nodded. "As you wish."

Cerise walked away from her throne and to the adjoining room. A black table with red marble streaks swirled in sat at the far end. On the table lay a map of Fairy. Cerise walked over to it and studied it. "The Court of Creation lies closest to the mountains." She tapped her fingers against it. "If there are more creatures like Zio that have come over, they would know."

"If they have they haven't alerted any of the other courts." Ace said.

"Or they just don't want us to know. They share nothing with the other courts. They could be helping with an evasion," Cerise growled. This is why Fairy needed to be united, there were too many secrets between the courts. They couldn't trust each other.

Ace said nothing at her back while she looked over the map. "As far as we know there is only one entrance to the Court of Creation, and that's in the Blood Leaf Forest." She tapped the illustrations on the map. "So we'll just have to trust that Griffin's magic works."

Ace stepped up to her side. "Until then, might I suggest that we start to bargain with the Court of Enchantment again?"

"There's no bargaining. He needs to hand his court and power over, or we'll take it forcefully. I'm trying to wait until Alice is taken care of. Because she could undo my hard work."

Ace shrugged. "There's no telling with that pesky mortal will be out of the Court of Creation."

Cerise stared at the map, her nails making clicking noises against it as she thought. "Send a liaison to the Court of Enchantment, let's see what move the king there makes. Until then, let's focus on Griffin bringing Alice back. Leave Oriana and Devlin alone for now. Either they will grow bored waiting for Alice or they will stay loyal to the mortal. Either way, the wheels are in motion. The only chance we'll have to stop Alice from taking down my court is when she arrives and we kill her."

Ace nodded. "We'll be prepared my queen."

Cerise looked over the map. "Good, now go. Tell my court adviser what I want done, I'll draft a note to the Court of Enchantment. I'm sure there's something useful we can get from them."

Ace left the room, leaving Cerise to ponder on the map of Fairy. When did the Court of Creation seal itself off from the others? When was the last time a court had heard from someone aside from an adviser?

The answers would be in her mother's notes. She spun away from the table and stormed to the study. The Court of Creation was hiding something, but what? And why would they welcome Alice in?

Allie stood in the dark for a moment, her hand on the hilt on her sword as she waited for something, anything, to come after her. Her time in Fairy had taught her nothing nice lurked in the dark and this was probably no different.

Shuffling sounded in front of her and she drew her sword. Was it a Fachan that was waiting for her?

"Put the blade away Alice." The voice seemed to come from all around her. "You have nothing to fear here."

Allie swallowed. "Then show yourself. I'm learning I don't have many friends in Fairy."

The darkness gave way to light around her and Allie found herself staring...at herself. She pressed her lips together. "What is this?"

The Alice that stared back at her had pointed ears and deep blue eyes, but the face, the brown hair, everything else was the same.

"Put the blade away." The other Alice said. "There is no need for that here. Even if you wanted to hurt me, you couldn't."

Allie let her sword slide back into the scabbard. "Why?"

"Because I don't actually exist." The other Alice melted away revealing the man who had attacked her.

Allie stepped backwards, her hand once again reaching for her sword, before he melted away revealing her brother.

Her heart ached as she reached out to touch him. "Brendyn," she muttered and he faded away. Leaving her alone in the empty room.

"The Court of Creation welcomes you, Alice of the Mortal world. Every seer speaks of you bringing the Red Queen to her knees and we want to see that happen." The voice wrapped around her like a breeze, making her turn to see if the owner of the voice was now behind her.

"So I keep hearing." Allie looked around the empty space. There were no walls, nothing distinct around her to say if she was in a room or outside, or anywhere really. Under her feet was a solid surface, so she didn't feel like she was floating in space. Just standing in a void with only the voice around her.

"Depending on the seer, though," A male appeared in front of her. He towered over her, his sharp teeth bared at her. His stringy black hair fell down his back. "Depends on how it ends. Does Alice fall to the Jabberwock?"

The appearance shifted to Cibil. "Or does she bring the ruin of Fairy?"

Allie stepped back. "I just want to stop Cerise and go home."

"You're still the wrong Alice," Cibil's voice whispered, and then the creature in front of her switched to the male again. "And until you are the right Alice, you won't be slaying the Jabberwock."

The creature disappeared again and Allie found herself trying to catch her breath. The back and forth, the different faces, this void of a world made her head spin. Her heart pounded in her chest as she tried to think of something to do. "How do I become the right Alice?"

"You follow your destiny." A man appeared in front of her. His hair fell to his chin and shifted through different colors, from the darkest hue to the lightest and every color in between. Shades and colors Alice didn't know existed moved through the strands in front of her.

He met her gaze and his eyes were doing the same and she couldn't hold the gasp back. He laughed. "Hello, Alice."

"Who are you?"

"You don't remember me?" He crossed his arms. "We played in the forest together, walked under the stars of Fairy, watched as the sun rise…"

She frowned as she tried to remember someone who'd been as beautiful as him. He cupped her cheek and warmth spread through her.

"Maybe you don't know this form, but this one instead." His appearance shifted before her, leaving a young boy with brown hair and eyes standing in front of her, pointed ears peaked through the locks that fell to his shoulder.

Alice's heart lifted. "You were the one who led me home the first time."

He appeared back to his other form. "There we go. When you were lost after you had the tea party with Cerise. Poor mortal girl, alone trying to find her way home...after her brother..." He paused at that. "But here is Alice again, the mortal girl who has fallen into Fairy."

"Can you help me?" Allie asked. "I'm nothing but confused and scared. Terrified of the Jabberwock, and I have no idea how to stop Cerise."

"Oh my dear, not only can I help you, I can make sure that we change the fate that the seers have given you." He chuckled. "Let me see your blade."

Allie pulled the sword out of the scabbard and handed it to him. He twisted the sword to the right and left, the light reflected off the metal. "This is a good sword, where did you get it from?"

"The Tweedle Tree gave it to me when I first arrived."

He smirked. "Well, it has good taste, but this isn't a sword worthy of killing the Jabberwock, oh no. For that you need one from my court."

Allie nodded. "Apparently a seer predicted that I would need a 'Creation's sword'."

He thought for a moment before handing her sword back. "To find Creation's Sword, you must go through the cave and seek the spinner. There you will find Creation's Sword."

"The spinner?" She cringed. "A spider?"

He shook his head and chuckled. "No, Alice, not a spider, though that is a good guess. I'll see you there." He disappeared.

Allie turned around to find that the waterfall was behind her now, the rush of the water parting for her to walk back through. She took a deep breath and walked out to find Mallow waiting for her patiently.

"Well?" Mallow asked.

Allie glanced at her. "I need to seek the spinner. That's all he said." Allie paused. "Who was he? I never caught his name this time or the last time I met him."

Mallow pressed her lips together. "Who you saw depends on what connections you have to the Court of Creation."

"So you have no idea who was in there?"

She shook her head. "But you've met him once before, so that is your connection. Come. We must get you ready for your journey."

Allie followed her back down the strange hall, pausing when she swore she saw the man moving alongside her. But when she stopped, there was nothing but her own reflection shining back.

CHAPTER 15

"She's been in there since sun up. What could possibly be taking that long?" Devlin asked, pacing around the clearing.

"Maybe they can't find the sword?" Oriana suggested. "Or maybe they decided to keep her."

"She can't defeat the Red Queen if we keep her." A woman appeared with Alice by her side. The woman's dark braids tumbled down her back, the fading light glinting off the jewels that were woven into the strands.

Alice looked no worse for wear as she stood next to the fae. She gave them a small wave. "So, apparently we're looking for a cave."

Devlin stared at her. "A cave? We're supposed to be figuring out how to defeat Cerise."

"And the sword of Creation is in a cave with someone or something called the Spinner."

Oriana jerked to attention at that. "The Spinner? Are you sure?"

"You know of it?"

"Her." Oriana nodded. "And I know where to find her." She glanced at Devlin. "But it's going to take time to get there, we'll need Fehin. It's at least three nights as the crow flies."

Alice crossed her arms. "There's no other way to get the blade. So

I guess we have to. At least Cerise won't expect us to be caving to find this woman."

Devlin nodded. "Fehin can fly us. We'll be going the opposite direction than what Cerise is expecting, so we may not attract unwanted attention."

Oriana nodded. "The quicker we get to the cave the better. Something in my gut tells me we're running out of time."

Devlin glanced at her. "You're from the court of time; if your gut says we're running out, then we should probably believe it."

Alice nodded. "Okay, then let's go."

Marrow looked to the sky. "There's a magic out here. Leave now." She waved her hand and disappeared.

Alice looked at Devlin. "What did she mean, 'there's a magic out here?'"

"It means that she sensed something that shouldn't be here." Devlin whistled and Fehin came diving from the sky. "Get on."

Alice climbed up on to Fehin's back, Oriana behind her and finally Devlin. A moment later they took to the sky. The wind blew through Devlin's hair as Fehin flew them north towards the mountain.

Worried filled him as he thought about Marrow's comment about magic and Oriana's comment about time filled his head. Until now they had no true deadline in mind. They had all the time in the world to train Alice and help her figure out how to defeat the Jabberwock, as long as they stayed away from Cerise and her people until Alice was ready.

But if that changed...

Running out of time would be bad.

Fehin let out a loud squawk and dived down into the trees. Devlin clung on with his arms wrapped around Oriana and squeezed with his legs. The bird landed in a clearing, but didn't bow to let them off. Instead he stood, silently, waiting.

Devlin patted the side of his bird. "What's up boy?"

The crow clacked his jaw almost as if to tell Devlin to shut up and then went back to being silent.

"There was something in the sky," Alice whispered. "Something bigger than Fehin."

Oriana stiffened, but remained silent.

"I didn't see anything," Devlin said softly, "but clearly Fehin sensed something since he brought us down here."

They waited in the darkness for a little while. No one daring to speak as the shadows seemed to close in around them. Finally Fehin took off towards the sky with them on their back and headed toward the mountains again.

The chill in the night air started to eat at Devlin as they continued to push forward and exhaustion ate at his mind. At one point he swore he fell asleep and fell off Fehin, only to open his eyes and be securely on the bird.

He caught Oriana nodding off a few times as well. Alice seemed to be the most alert out of all of them and he guessed it was the adrenaline of it all that kept her going. At some point she was going to crash though and hopefully they could afford that luxury when they did.

When the sun peeked over the horizon, Devlin nudged Fehin so he knew to land. The bird needed a rest and the three of them needed some sleep. They could head back to the sky in the afternoon, fly through most of the night again, and hopefully arrive at the mountain in less than three nights.

Fehin's feet made no noise as he landed in a clearing. He bowed his head and the three of them slid off his back. Alice started gathering up sticks for the fire, and Oriana laid out the bundles of blankets. Devlin walked around the circle, murmuring an enchantment spell. He'd been hoping to avoid using one because it drained his energy and it wasn't completely undetectable.

Without knowing who the attacker was, there was no way to tell if he was strong enough to detect and break the enchantment.

Magic flowed out of him and through the clearing, wrapping around it. Lesser fae and creatures would see nothing amiss but they would avoid the clearing. Stronger fae would be able to detect it and some break it.

If Ace or Cerise came upon it, they'd know exactly what it was and they wouldn't be safe. The magic would at least give Devlin a warning.

His heart pounded in his chest as he finished the spell and he sat down next to where Alice had built the fire with Oriana. "We should only stay here until afternoon."

"Do you think Fehin will be ready to fly again for so long after only a handful of hours rest?"

Devlin glanced at Oriana. "If he's not, then we walk for half the day. You said it yourself, you think time is running out. If it is, we can't waste time. That means short rests and long treks."

Oriana looked at Alice who stared into the fire, lost in thought. "She's human Dev, she may not be able to keep up a pace like that. And with us going to see The Spinner, she'll need her energy."

"What kind of fae is The Spinner?" Alice asked, her eyes not moving away from the flames.

"She can see your intentions and depending on what she sees depends on if she'll help you or kill you." Oriana shrugged. "My mom went and saw her once."

Alice sighed. "Everything in this world can kill you. Maybe I should just go back home."

"That won't stop any of this," Devlin said. "The die is cast, everything is in motion now. There's no running away. We brought you back here to defeat Cerise."

Alice growled. "Maybe you should have asked me first instead of luring me back here like I'm a child. Did you ever think that maybe I didn't want to actually be gone from my home this long? Who knows what my parents are thinking now. They already lost Brendyn to this world, and now maybe me."

"You walked through that mirror willing, Alice." Oriana shot back. "You followed Dor when you got here. We didn't force you to come here. We simply invited you."

Devlin nodded. "We needed you and hoped that you would come. Turning around and running away is not an option now."

Alice sighed. "No, it's not."

"My queen."

Cerise looked up when Griffin came into the room. "Yes?"

His dark hair was braided close to his scalp today, away from his face, leaving the wicked scar clear. "Alice has left the court of creation. My magic has tracked her to a forest to the north of the court."

"North? Are you sure?" Cerise frowned. There was nothing but the mountains north of the Court of Creations. What were they going?

"My magic wouldn't be wrong, my queen." His lips pulled into a sneer. "That's where they are going."

"Follow them then. Convince Alice to come to me."

"If I do that, I want you to release me from your service."

Cerise kept herself from snarling at the fae in front of her. "I saved your life, you're in my debt."

"Seven years, my queen. You made me, molded me, I have been loyal to you. Once Alice is at your feet, my job is done. Let me go and live as a male fae should." He stared at her, unblinking in his command.

Cerise pressed her lips together. Alice was the biggest threat, but she had other courts to take over, and needed Griffin. "I'll make you a deal."

He narrowed his dark gaze at her and she smiled. Deals could be dangerous in Fairy. Wordings had to be considered carefully or one could be tricked into servitude. Which was her plan. "What deal?"

"Bring me Alice and I'll release you on your tenth year of service after." She smiled at him. Innocently.

He thought for a moment, considering her. Cerise waited for him to jump on the offer, but the longer he took to consider it, the more her confidence started to edge.

"I will bring you Alice, and you will release me three years after I bring her to you. Not ten." He met her gaze, challenging her.

She smirked. "I see you caught my loophole."

"I'm not stupid Cerise. I suggest you take my deal." He reached up casually and touched the pummel of his sword.

Anger rushed to the surface. Cerise stormed to her feet. "You dare threaten me? I saved your pathetic life and gave you something great."

"You put me in chains and turned me into a killer, with the faith that I wouldn't kill you in return." His cold gaze met hers. "In hopes that you would be able to always control me."

Cerise swallowed. "You can't raise a hand against me, I won't allow it, my guards—"

Before she could finish her thought, Griffin had his swords in an 'x' across her neck, the blades just touching her skin.

"My deal, my queen."

She called on her magic and he tightened the swords against her neck.

"Now, now, Cerise." He purred her name. "You aren't stupid enough to try and manipulate my heart when I have swords at your throat, are you?"

The magic faded from her fingertips. "Fine, I accept your deal."

Magic flashed around them, binding the deal to their words. Griffin stepped back and put his blades away. "I am a fae of my word, I will bring you Alice." He disappeared from in front of her.

Cerise took a few deep breaths to calm herself. "Ace!" She called.

Ace walked in a moment later. "Yes my—" He paused and wiped a finger over her neck where Griffin's blades had been. "Blood? He hurt you?"

"Just a threat, an empty one because he knew I could take his heart in an instant," she lied. "I gave him what he wants, for now. I'll find a way to keep him in my servitude."

Ace's magic tingled against her skin as he healed the small cuts on her neck. "You made a deal to release him?"

"I need him to think that he's won." She nodded. "So that he'll bring me Alice."

"And where is Alice?" Ace asked.

"Heading north to the mountains." Cerise sat in her throne. "I don't know what she's up to, but Griffin is going after her."

"Did you specify that you wanted her alive?"

Cerise cursed. "No."

"Then hopefully he's not going to be a dick about it and kill her first." Ace shook his head. "Cerise, you know you have to be specific with the deals."

She glared at him. "I am not a child. I had two swords against my throat and I was focused on my magic, not my words."

"You could always take his heart when he returns."

She nodded. "And maybe that's what I'll do, but he won't be much of a killer once I take his heart. That's where all his rage lives."

Ace nodded. "Better to have a sniveling pet than an untamed beast."

"True." She sighed. "Let's see if he brings me Alice, alive. Then I will figure out his future here in this court. After we take the other courts over, he may change his mind about leaving my side." She glanced at Ace. "Because I will own all of the courts. There will be no escape from me."

Allie clung to Fehin as the sun set in the sky. The soft feathers under hands gave her something to focus on other than the ground passing by them at a blurring speed. Flying by bird was amazing, but she missed the comfort of walls and seats that an airplane offered.

Something whooshed by her head and Fehin screeched in pain. The bird careened to the side as something else shot by.

"Arrows," Devlin called from behind. "Fehin down." The bird

shot towards the ground, tree branches brushing by them as he found a place to drop. He landed with another cry of pain and they all slid off his back.

Oriana and Allie pulled their weapons, waiting. Devlin whispered words to Fehin who let out another shrill cry. Allie glanced over her shoulder to see Devlin pulling an arrow out of the edge of Fehin's wing.

Footsteps sounded behind her and spun to find Oriana ready for attack. Through the trees broke Griffin, his dual swords heading toward Allie.

He swung them down, but she held up her sword, blocking the blow. The pressure of it nearly taking her to the ground. She shoved him away and found her footing as he came at her again.

She side stepped his next attack as Oriana came up behind him. He sheathed one sword and threw out a hand. A black mist shot away from him and surrounded Oriana. "I'm not here to kill any of you," the man growled. "I'm just here to take Alice to the Queen of Hearts."

Allie snarled. "That's basically sentencing me to death."

He paused at her words. "She desires your death?"

Allie nodded, meeting his gaze. Something familiar stirred within them and she tried to place it. "She plans to pit me against the Jabberwock."

Anger snarled in his eyes and he muttered something under his breath. Devlin stepped forward, his weapon in his hand, but he wasn't poised for attack. Not yet. Allie watched as emotions played out on the man's face.

"Your capture means my freedom." There was something apologetic in his voice. "But I don't agree to walking you to your death."

Devlin growled. "Why not? You seemed hell bent on killing us before."

"You can defend yourselves against my attack, you hold magic, even the mortal holds a sword. She will be helpless against the Jabberwock. I know that's what the Queen wants."

Allie swallowed. "What if..." Devlin put a hand on her shoulder.

"Beware your words, a deal struck with fae is a deal struck with magic. You're bound by your words."

Allie nodded and tried to think through what she was trying to say. "We will go with you, after I retrieve what is in the cave." She glanced at Devlin who nodded.

The man in front of her raised a brow. "And what are you retrieving?"

"A weapon." Allie said easily. "You want to give me a chance to survive the Jabberwock, I need that weapon."

He glanced at Devlin. "You're in on this?"

"Yes." Devlin said with a shrug. "Oriana and I are the reason Alice made it this far."

Allie frowned as the man's eyes flashed from the dark swirling black and gray to hazel, a very human color. "Do...I know you?"

The man looked at her. "No. My name is Griffin, and I accept your deal, Alice of the mortal world. You will come with me, willingly after you retrieve the weapon in the cave and I will not harm you or your companions before."

She kept herself from smiling as magic wrapped around her, seeping in through her body and warming her.

The magic around Oriana disappeared and she stood there, arms crossed, glaring at the group. "I'm not sure if this deal is stupid or brilliant."

Allie thought it was down-right brilliant, they would survive long enough to make it to the cave and at least have a weapon in hand that could harm the Jabberwock.

Griffin looked at Allie. "You're pretty clever for a mortal."

"My brother taught me a lot." Allie shrugged. "He learned more about the fae in our first visit here than I did."

Griffin frowned. "Your brother is here as well?"

Allie swallowed. "He died here." She tried to forget the cries of him below her as she was climbing back to the human world. "He fell when we were going home. Before we knew a safer way to go back and forth."

"That's not..." Griffin shook his head. "That's horrible. And yet you've chosen to return here."

Allie nodded. "To stop the Red Queen from taking over the other courts."

Griffin said nothing.

Oriana stomped over to Fehin and looked at where the arrow had hit him. "Stupid arrows, stupid Cerise," she muttered. Allie walked over to them. "Is he going to be okay?"

Oriana nodded and ran her hand over the spot. A watch symbol appeared over the wound, the hands on it ticking counter clockwise. With each stroke the wound began to heal. The skin knitted back together first, leaving a pink scare, but that faded after a couple more beats of time. Then small feathers grew over the skin, another few seconds those fluffed into full grown feathers.

Oriana stepped back and caught her breath, wiping a bead of sweat from her forehead. "Next person who shoots this bird dies."

Devlin snorted. "So you do care about Fehin!"

"Go to hell, Devlin, I still don't like flying." She leaned against a tree. "I'm exhausted now."

Allie put her pack down and grabbed the rolled-up blankets. "Here, take a nap. We can wait a couple hours to get going again." She'd be okay if they walked the rest of the way because it would prolong their arrival at the Court of Hearts.

It was inevitable they were going to be there. The longer they took, the better. Oriana didn't protest and lay down, instantly falling asleep. Allie glanced at Devlin. "I'll gather some firewood?"

Devlin nodded. "Yeah, I'll get the pit ready and the enchantment up." He glanced at Griffin. "Why are you still standing here?"

"Because I'm going to accompany you to this cave." He crossed his arms.

Allie shook her head. "Don't want to report back to the queen?"

"No. If I return empty-handed, I break my deal with her."

Allie cringed. "She'd take your heart."

"Most likely. And as damaged and scarred as my heart is, I'd like to keep it intact."

She nodded and started to gather kindling. Griffin said nothing as he followed her around the trees. It should have been unnerving that he was at her back, but there was something oddly comforting about it.

"What was your brother like?" Griffin asked, catching her off guard.

Allie shrugged. "He was a brother. He always had my back, even when I was little. He was the golden star of the family, played sports, got good grades." She tried to push the image of her parents grieving out of her head. "Everything changed when he died."

Griffin made a noise that made her wonder if he was emphasizing. "And your parents?"

"I'm not talking about this anymore. Especially with someone that's literally going to deliver me to the queen," she muttered, and then took the pile of kindling to Devlin.

Devlin glanced at Griffin. "If you're going to stay, we're not going to be able to ride of Fehin anymore. Three people is already pushing his limits."

"How much further is this cave?"

Allie ignored him and sat down in front of the pit Devlin had marked out.

"Another day's fly, or two days walk."

Griffin grunted and sat down near Allie. She glanced at him and then at Devlin. Devlin shrugged and used his magic to start the fire with the kindling.

No one spoke while they let Oriana rest. Allie got up a few times to stretch. She wanted to work on sword forms with Devlin, but she didn't want to do it in front of Griffin.

"Alice, sit down. Your pacing is making me nervous," Devlin stated. "Do you need some tea or something to calm you down?"

She shook her head. "No, I'm just antsy to get back on track.

With adding time to the trek, I'm worried about who else Cerise will send after us. Or what news Griffin might manage to send her way."

"So far it'd be a very boring report." Griffin shrugged. "The lady of the Court of Time healed the bird I shot, and then we all sat around a fire with our thoughts."

Devlin snorted.

Allie sat down and leaned back on her hands and she looked at the night sky. The tree branches allowed her glimpses of stars on a sapphire background. She couldn't see the moon, but she bet that it was full.

The night is beautiful, isn't it?

She looked around when she heard the voice whisper to her. She glanced at Devil and Griffin, but they both looked lost in their own thoughts. She looked back to the sky.

Shame you couldn't see it from the Court of Creation, the colors in the sky are so vivid, especially as the sun is setting.

Allie swallowed, fear starting to creep into her.

Don't be afraid, Alice, you know me. We walked under the stars of Fairy together...

She relaxed a little at the familiar words. Magic wrapped around her, calling to her. She stood, glancing at Devlin and Griffin. Neither of them seemed to notice that she was standing.

The magic tugged on her, leading her past the fire, north toward the mountains. Her heart pounded as she realized where they were. This was the mountain where the rabbit hole led them. This was where her brother fell and she became lost.

She shook her head, trying to move backwards as the trees seemed to bend toward her.

Branches reached out for her as the magic continued to call her, draw her towards where her brother's body had laid.

Panic grasped her heart as she saw a form there on the ground. This couldn't be real. They weren't close enough to the mountain for this yet. They still had two days on foot to travel.

But there it was, the first rocky hill they had to climb, at the top would be the rabbit hole from the human world.

Her heart slowed for a moment.

She could climb that rocky side and go home. Leave before anyone realized that she was missing.

You have to fulfill the prophecy, one way or another, Alice. The voice told her and she shook her head.

"No, I can go home."

"And let Cerise's and Griffin's magic follow you?" The man appeared in front of her. "Alice, you know you can't do that. The fae magic must not bleed into the human realm."

"Why did you call me to this place?" Allie asked, her heart aching. "Why remind me of what your land took away from me." She motioned to the form that lay on the ground.

He looked and then snapped his fingers and the form she saw started to scatter as butterflies flew away. "In Fairy, not everything is as it seems, Alice. You should know that."

"That doesn't answer my question," she growled at him. "Everyone in this land speaks in riddles and I'm tired of it."

He let out a long sigh. "I have brought you here, Alice, because here is where you need to be."

"That's not much clearer." She shook her head.

He nodded. "Open your eyes, Alice, and see where I have taken you and your group." He snapped his fingers and dark mist wrapped around her.

Allie opened her eyes, not even aware that she had closed them. She found Griffin and Devlin blinking in front of her, and Oriana rubbing her eyes, clearing the sleep from them.

The problem being, they were in a completely different place now. In the mountains, in front of a cave. The man stood there. "Time is of the essence. The Red Queen is growing impatient."

"Elken, what are you doing here? You're supposed to be...lost?" Oriana gasped. "Where have you been?"

"I'm not real, not right now. I'm trapped." He held his arms out. Allie stared at him. "You look real enough."

Griffin stood and drew a sword from his back. "How did we get here?"

"I used my magic to bring you all here," Elken said. "My magic is starting to dwindle though. Free me when you've finished with the Jabberwock, Alice. And my kingdom will be yours."

Allie pressed her lips together. "And where are you trapped?"

"I made a mistake, Alice. One Cerise doesn't know about or she'd have used it to her advantage already. I'm trapped in the throne room. Now go. Retrieve the sword and slay the Jabberwock."

He faded away and Alice looked at the three fae at her back. "Well, we're here so I guess we go in."

Griffin shook his head. "I don't do caves. I'll wait for you out here."

Allie rolled her eyes but walked into the wide entrance of the cave, Devlin and Oriana at her back. Despite it being night, the entrance of the cave seemed to have a lightness surrounding it, as if the rocks had absorbed the sun and let it leak out into the darkness.

Their footsteps were the only thing she could hear as they continued to make their way deeper into the cave. The light started to fade the farther away they went, but instead of the damp coolness of most caves, a warmth wrapped around them.

Allie put her hand to her mouth and yawned. "I don't feel very rested for falling asleep involuntarily."

"A magically induced sleep is not the same as a restful sleep." Gavin grumbled. "Elken must be desperate if he's wanting us to free him and he's willing to bring us here."

Allie paused as singing filled the air. She frowned at what sounded like the tune of a lullaby. "Who is singing?"

"The Spinner." Oriana swallowed. "It sounds like she's in a good mood." But her voice shook as she spoke.

Allie took a deep breath and continued forward. "We just need the sword. That's it. Get the sword. Get the hell out."

They enter a wide cavern. Scones with flames lined the walls cast the fae in the mile in orange highlights, making the shadows deeper on her skin and gown. The gown danced with the flickering flames, the black seemingly drinking up the light the scones had to offer. Her skin sparkled with magic as her hands worked the spinning wheel in front of her. Her fingers dancing to smooth out the thread she was making from the basket of...hair?

Allie kept her squeak of surprise in and turned her attention towards the wall. Heads hung from pegs on the wall. Clean of blood from their necks, the looks on their face were all twisted in pain or horror. Allie scanned the rest of the wall and her eyes landed on a black blade with a silver handle, a swirling mark on the hilt.

That had to be the sword.

Devlin took a step toward it.

"No one enters my cave without me knowing." The fae's sing-song voice echoed around them and Allie froze in her steps.

"I'm here for—"

"The sword of creation, yes, yes, I know." She turned to look at Allie. Her silver eyes caught the flickering light. "Everyone comes here for the sword." She laughed. "Take a look at my collection."

Allie swallowed. "I need it to defeat the Jabberwock."

The woman's hands paused as did her foot on the peddle of the spinning wheel. "A mortal against the Jabberwock." She let out a long breath and then tilted her head to the side. "You're the mortal girl from the prophecies."

Allie tried to keep her irritation down. "Yes, that mortal."

"And you think the sword will help you with that?"

"According to Cibil's prophecy it will."

The Spinner went back to her thread. "Your hair is much too plain to be added to my collection. Mortal hair lacks the luster and thickness that fae hair has."

Allie took a step forward, towards the sword.

"That doesn't mean that you can have the sword my dear." The fae flicked her wrist and something silver came flying toward Allie.

On instinct she went to cover her face. A needle pierced her hand. She cried out and stumbled back. Devlin put a hand on her shoulder to steady her.

"Please, Spinner," Oriana said. "We are trying to save our courts and bring Cerise down to size. That's it. We have no other intentions."

The Spinner looked at Oriana. "Ah, my niece." Her tongue flicked out between her teeth. "Your intentions are true. I will say that. You have your mother's honor and your father's stupidity."

Allie didn't hear what she said next because a rushing sound filled her ears, like the world around her was falling.

Which judging by the fact that she was now looking at the dark ceiling of the cavern might have been true. She could hear The Spinner again.

"She may have the sword, but you will return it to me when she has slain the Jabberwock, or when she dies from it."

Devlin's face appeared in her vision and she swore he was saying something, but she couldn't hear.

"And of course. If she survives the poison." The Spinner's voice cut through the rushing noise again. "Take the sword Oriana, I will see you when you return it."

The world started twisting and then not only was her hearing stolen, so was her vision.

CHAPTER 16

Devlin scooped Alice up and rushed outside the cave. Oriana could grab the sword and join him, but he had to get Alice out of the cave.

He should have taught her how to use her cloak to her advantage. If she'd pulled it up with her arm, the needle would have deflected. How dumb of him to assume she'd figure that out.

He cursed as he ran into Griffin at the exit of the cave.

Griffin looked down at Alice and frowned. "She's dying."

"Fae poison," Devlin growled, and tried to shove the man out of the way. "I need to get her to a healer."

"Oriana healed the bird, can she not heal Alice?"

Devlin shook his head. "Her talents don't work like that. This is poison not a wound that she can turn back time on."

Alice convulsed in his arms and Devlin whistled to call Fehin.

"She won't survive the flight," Griffin said.

Devlin snarled, "I have to try."

"Why do you care about this mortal so much?" Griffin frowned and stepped up to Alice.

"Because she's my friend," Devlin snarled. "I don't want to see her die in my arms." His heart felt heavy. "Don't you have any friends?"

Griffin slowly shook his head. "No…I think I had…someone once. Lay her down."

Devlin shook his head and searched the sky for Fehin.

"I have an antidote," Griffin growled.

Devlin's heart skipped a beat and he lay Alice down. Oriana came out of the cave a moment later. "What are you doing? We need to get her back to the Court of Creation."

"I have an antidote," Griffin said again.

Devlin stroked Alice's hair out of her face as she struggled to breathe. His gut told him to trust Griffin, but this was a person under Cerise's control. Someone she sent to kill Alice, and she was most vulnerable now.

"Swear to me you won't kill her," Devlin growled. "Swear it."

Griffin nodded. "I swear."

Alice gasped, her back arching as she tried to breathe. Sweat beaded on her forehead.

Griffin pulled a glass vile out of a leather pouch. He pulled the cork out and tipped it to Alice's lips. "Drink, Alice."

Alice's throat worked, trying to get the liquid down. Her convulsing stopped and her breathing evened out.

"The poison will have taken a toll on her, but she'll heal and wake." Griffin pressed his lips together. "She'll be weak, but if we bide our time with returning to the Court of Hearts, she should be strong enough to face the Jabberwock."

Alice's eyes flickered open for a moment. "Brendyn?" Her hand tried to lift off the ground. "How…" Her eyes closed again and her hand dropped.

Griffin stood quickly and backed away from Alice. "Best we get off the mountainside." He turned away. "We don't want any beasts to interrupt her sleep."

Oriana looked at Devlin. He shrugged. "I don't think Fehin could land safely, that's why he didn't come." He picked Alice back up, wrapping her cloak tightly around her. "It's going to be hard to get her down."

Griffin looked over his shoulder. "We'll manage." He started down a narrow path and Devlin followed. "Aren't you a fae that can pop in and out everywhere?" Devlin asked.

Griffin nodded. "Yes, but my skills in that area are limited. I cannot carry another with me yet."

"Yet?" Oriana snorted. "You're a full grown fae, your powers should be fully developed."

Griffin said nothing as he continued to lead them down the steep path. More than once Devlin's feet slid, but he held on to the sleeping Alice.

The sun was sinking by the time they found flat ground and Alice hadn't stirred at all.

Oriana rolled the beds out and Devlin lay Alice on one. The woman shivered as she hit the ground and Oriana put a hand to Alice's head. She glared at Griffin. "I thought you said she'd be okay. She's hot."

"I told you the poison would still take a toll on her." Griffin bent down and tucked her cloak around her. "Her body is still trying to repair the damage that was done. It's going to take a bit."

Devlin shook his head. "We can't travel by feet like this."

Griffin sat down. "We're going to wait until she becomes conscious again. Then go."

Devlin bit his tongue. This wasn't how he'd imagine them getting to the Court of Hearts, with one of Cerise's people as their guide, and walking willingly into the court. But Griffin did save Alice, even if she was going to be weakened.

"Who died and made you leader?" Oriana snapped.

Griffin laughed. "There was a deal struck and now I'm just making sure that I fulfill that deal."

Devlin glanced at the sword strapped to Oriana's back. They had retrieved the sword. Maybe this was the way it was supposed to happen. Alice just needed to wake up and learn to wield it.

Oriana sat next to Alice ignoring Griffin. Devlin sighed. "I'll get the enchantments up then, and hopefully we can stay safe for the night and Alice will be awake in the morning."

Griffin nodded and sat on a rock, his dark gaze on Alice. His brows pinched together as if he'd lost something, or maybe forgotten. The look in his eyes softened as Alice let out a sigh.

And there was that familiar look again.

"Where do you come from Griffin?" Devlin asked. "Which court?"

Griffin looked at him. "I don't know. I remember waking up in the Court of Hearts. Cerise had saved my life and for that I work for her." He locked his jaw.

"She never told you where you came from?" Oriana asked. "And you don't find that suspicious at all?"

Griffin let out a dark laugh. "Of course I find it suspicious. I'm bound to her though, for another four years after I deliver Alice."

"So that's your deal with Cerise," Devlin snorted. "If Alice can take Cerise down, then you'd be free earlier."

Griffin was silent for a moment. "I hadn't considered that."

"Help us teach her how to fight. Clearly you know a thing or two. If Alice can slay the Jabberwock, then she can change the prophecy."

"The prophecy says she brings Cerise to her knees, but that she'll lose to the Jabberwock."

Devlin nodded. "And that's the part that we're trying to change."

Griffin tilted back to look at the sky and said nothing.

Devlin let the other fae stay in his own silence as Devlin moved to watch over Alice.

"Neither of you have provided me with any good information, so I had to send someone out to hunt the mortal." Cerise walked in front of March and Dor.

Dor had his tiny hands wrapped around the bars of his cage. His eyes narrowed at Cerise as his wings beat behind him.

March's arms were held behind his back with magical enhanced chains and cuffs to ensure that he didn't use his magic. "You promised me information on Knave."

"Only if you gave me proper information," Cerise growled. "And now I hear Alice is heading north to the mountains. I've sent my best hunter after her, he won't fail me. Now you two..." She took a step forward, her fingertips tingling with her magic. "Need to be punished for what you've done."

March took a step back, his face paling. "Cerise, think about this for a moment."

"I am your *queen* and you will address me as such," She snarled. "The sooner you people accept that, the better things will be."

March backed into the table that Dor's cage was sitting on. Rocking it.

Cerise reached her hand out for March and he spun away from her, knocking Dor's cage to the floor.

The clatter of the metal hitting the floor echoed around them, but Cerise ignored it, snatching March by the collar. "Your heart is now mine." She gave him a wicked smirk as she placed her other hand on his chest.

He cried out as her magic weaved its way through him. The rush of it making Cerise nearly giddy as it wrapped around his heart, tying him to her.

He wouldn't be able to go against her now. She owned him, and if she wanted she could kill him with a mere thought. This was the power of the Court of Hearts. This was her birth right.

She let go of March and he fell to his knees panting, his head held down. Cerise bent down and used two fingers to make him look at her. "You will never betray me again."

"Yes, my queen." He muttered, pain lacing his voice.

"Now." She turned and clapped her hands. "Your turn Dor." She bent down to pick up the cage, only to find the door had busted open and the cage was now empty.

She snarled as she realized the little fae escaped and turned to March. "You did that on purpose."

He shook his head. "I was trying to avoid your magic. I have no love lost for the bug. I couldn't care less if you had stolen his heart."

Her magic prevented him from lying to her, so she had no choice but to accept the truth. "Then you won't mind hunting him done. Take two of my hunters and find Dor."

March stood up. "Of course, my queen." He walked out of the room and she threw the cage at the wall. She wanted Dor's heart. He could have been useful in so many ways when she took over the courts and now he'd escaped.

"My queen?" Ace walked in.

"Dor escaped. March will hunt him down with two of my hunters. I stole his heart so there will be no more betraying me." She turned to face him. "Has there been any word from the Court of Enchantment?"

He shook his head. "Not yet, but they would have just gotten the message yesterday. I wouldn't expect a reply for at least two days."

"I don't want to wait two days," she snapped. "Griffin should be back soon with Alice. I want everything to be ready to go after the Jabberwock kills her." Rage boiled in her. "I want that mortal dead."

Ace bowed his head. "I understand my queen, but I cannot force their hands and make them reply faster, nor can I affect the speed of the bird that carries the message."

They were all logical responses, but they didn't stomp out her anger. "Fine, then we wait."

"Look at the stars here." Cerise's voice was a giggle. "Do they look like the stars in your world?"

Allie shook her head. "No, they're brighter here. I can't really see the stars where we live. Mama says it's because of the lights in the city."

Cerise glanced at Allie. "I want to visit your world one day, but my mother says I can't. That fae aren't allowed in the human world."

"Well, mortals aren't supposed to be here either." Allie giggled. "And here I am for a visit."

"And I hope you keep visiting."

The grass that they lay on tickled Allie's arms as the wind blew over them. She looked up at the bright dots that lit up the sky above them. "My mother says I need to stop running away. That it's time to face what happened to my brother."

Cerise tensed a little. "His death?"

Allie couldn't bring herself to say the words. "She says that there's a special place that will help me cope with everything that's happened. She claims that you're nothing but a figment of my imagination."

Cerise put a hand on Allie's. "I'm not. You know that, right? I'm just as real as you are."

"I know that. But I wonder if I play along, if she'd give me more freedom and I can come and go as I please."

"But you'll forget about me." The fear in Cerise's voice caught Allie off guard. "You're mortal, your life span is shorter than mine, and your memory weaker than a fae's. You'll forget that my world is real and you'll never come back."

Allie squeezed Cerise's hand. "How could I ever forget about this world or you, Cerise?"

Allie woke gasping as her body seemed to be relearning how to breathe. The dream wasn't scary, but it had filled her with a sense of dread as her mind cleared.

Oriana and Devlin were sleeping by her side while Griffin sat on a rock staring at her. "What happened?"

"You were poisoned," he said so casually, he might as well have told her that the sky was blue.

"I remember that part. The needle that The Spinner threw at me. What I don't remember is anything after that." She pushed herself up, but her arms shook with the effort. "I feel like a truck hit me."

"I was able to get you the antidote in time, but your body is still fighting off the effects. You're going to feel weak for a couple days." Griffin shrugged. "We'll make sure to get some water and good food in you so that you can recover quicker. So you'll be at full strength when you face the Jabberwock."

Allie took a deep breath as she tried to keep herself sitting up right. "Did we get the sword?"

"Oriana ran out with it. She didn't give me details on how you three managed to get it from the Spinner, but we have it." Griffin stood. "And now we continue our trek to the Court of Hearts."

Allie flopped back down on the ground. "I don't think I can walk yet."

Griffin grunted. "No, not yet. You rest. I'm going to hunt." He disappeared and Allie closed her eyes.

Her dream haunted her. How could Cerise go from such a sweet girl to an angry raging queen?

Was it really because Allie hadn't come back after her stint in the mental hospital? Had she really broken Cerise's heart with a childhood promise gone wrong?

She rolled over with a groan and came face to face with Devlin.

He blinked at her. "You're awake."

"Yeah, but exhausted still. Griffin kind of filled me in on things. How did we get the sword?"

Devlin gave her a small smile. "We made a deal that we would return it when you either slay the Jabberwock, or die trying."

Allie laughed. "So who's in charge of returning it when I die?"

"I am," Oriana said from behind her. "But you'll be coming with me, because you aren't going to die."

Allie rolled on to her back. "I feel like I'm trying to die."

"Poison will do that to you," Devlin snorted. "Just rest for a bit. When Griffin gets back, we'll make a better plan than just walking to the Court of Hearts."

Allie nodded. "Yeah, I don't like the idea of walking, but I also don't want to get there any faster."

A little pop noise sounded right by her ear and Dor appeared.

"Dor!" They all three called.

"She took March's heart!" He fluttered around their heads. "She took his heart!"

Oriana sat up and held her hand out for him to land on. "Slow down."

Dor landed on her finger hand. "Cerise stole March's heart. He's under her control now." He put his hands on his knees and leaned forward to catch his breath. "She was going to take mine, but I escaped when March knocked my cage over."

Allie sat up. "What does this mean for us? Can we get March his heart back?"

"This means that Cerise is growing impatient." Devlin frowned. "And she's willing to turn her back on the friends she had. She may be lost to us. The only way to get March's heart back is if Cerise releases it, or if she dies."

Allie's heart ached. The friend she made was long gone at this point. Which meant that she was going to have no choice but to bring Cerise down.

"There's one more thing. Cerise said she sent a hunter after you guys. One of her best. I heard whispers when I was in the cage. This man has been trained to do nothing but kill. No one knows where he came from."

Griffin's laugh caught Allie's attention. "Your warning comes too late, little fae. I've been with them since they left the Court of Creation."

Allie looked over at Griffin and then back to Dor. "We made a deal with him."

"Stupid mortal. He works for Cerise. He's not someone who can be trusted."

"We didn't really have a choice." Allie put her head in her hands as the world started to spin. "And we're lucky he was here because he saved my life."

Dor said something, but Allie wasn't paying attention as she focused on her breathing so she didn't throw up.

"I caught a couple of ducks to roast before we get started back to the Court of Hearts. Alice?" He asked.

Allie gave him a thumbs up without looking up. "Not sure if I can eat right now, but okay."

Devlin stood. "I'll get the fire going."

Dor found his way under Allie's arm and hovered right by her face. "Humans are always getting sick. Are you sick?"

"No, I'm fighting poison," she muttered. "But we got the Sword of Creation, so I guess this is really going to happen."

Dor nodded his tiny head and Allie closed her eyes. "There's no other path than forward right now Alice."

Are you the right Alice or the wrong Alice? Cibil's voice echoed in her head and she focused on that question for a moment. She still felt like she was the wrong Alice. Maybe she'd never be the right Alice.

Dor flew away from her as she lifted her head. Oriana was still sitting next to her. "Hanging in there?"

Allie shrugged a shoulder. "You know, I've been attacked by monsters, traveled almost the whole of this side of Fairy, been poisoned and I get to face a giant monster. I think I'm doing as well as I could expect."

Oriana cracked a smile. "That's my girl."

Allie watched as Devlin built the fire and Griffin prepared the ducks that he found. "There's something about Griffin. I can't put my finger on it."

"He's a killer," Dor said as he landed on her shoulder. "He kills for Cerise. I'm not sure why he hasn't dragged you back to her yet, but I'm sure he has something up his sleeve."

Allie watched the fae as he worked with Devlin. "There's something more to him. Something none of us know. But it's right there on the surface."

"You're mortal," Dor stated. "You want to see the best in people. Here in Fairy, sometimes a killer is a killer."

Allie smirked. "But aren't you guys always telling me, not everything in Fairy is as it seems?"

Dor had no comment for that, but Oriana laughed. "She's learning."

Dor snorted. "I'm off. I'm sure Cerise sent hunters after me. I rather not lead them here to discover that Griffin is taking his sweet time bringing you in." He disappeared and Allie frowned. "Wasn't there something you said about the fae that could appear and disappear?"

"They tend to be the little fae or they belong to the Court of Creation." Oriana nodded. "Which means that's where Griffin is from since he has that ability."

Allie frowned. "So the lord of the Court of Creation is trapped somewhere in Cerise's palace and she has a hunter who is part of the same court. I think there's something more going on there. You said she was following in her mother's footsteps?"

"She wants to rule all of fairy; it's what the Lady of Hearts wanted. To be the queen."

Allie stood slowly as the smell of food hit her nose and her stomach growled. "I guess a lot happens in seven years."

"That it does," Oriana agreed. "That it does."

***

After the meal Allie felt her strength starting to return and she paced around the fire trying to think. "What if we make it to the next town? And stay there for the night and take horses to the Court of Hearts?"

Devlin grabbed her arm and pulled her to sit down. "Conserve your energy."

She let out a huff, but settled beside him.

Griffin nodded. "It's not a bad idea, it'll be faster than walking, but slow enough for Alice to regain her strength completely and for us to help her learn her new weapon."

Oriana sighed. "The nearest city that's not part of the Court of Creation, and therefore not hidden, is the outskirt city of Nyx."

Allie raised a brow. "As in the goddess Nyx?"

"That's cute, I forgot stronger fae in the human world were given the titles of Gods and Goddesses," Devlin muttered.

Oriana nodded. "She went to the human world and convinced them she had something to do with their religion, it used to happen all the time. The City of Nyx existed before the courts and outside the courts. There's only a handful of fae that live there and I doubt they have a carriage."

Allie thought about Marrow at the Court of Creation, how she seemed to want to help with everything. "What if I return to the Court of Creation? Do you think Marrow would lend us help?"

Griffin looked up at that. "That's a possibility. There's no harm in asking. If anything, they'll just refuse you entry."

Devlin nodded. "It's worth a try. Fehin can fly you there, and the rest of us can just meet you in at the Forest of Red Trees."

"The three of you can fly there. I will simply meet you there." Griffin stated. "My magic is tethered to Alice so I'll know if you try to break our deal and I'll be able to find you if you run away."

Allie swallowed. That wasn't a scary thought at all.

"That's not a bad plan," Oriana agreed. "And we're all tied up with deals and so none of us are going to be able to back out of this."

Allie glanced at Devlin. "Thoughts?"

"I think that Griffin is right on this. Not to mention the Court of Creation is more likely to let you in if Griffin isn't there because he's a threat." He rubbed his eyes. "There are so many other things to consider though. Like if Cerise has anyone else after us. Or what she's doing now with the courts while she's waiting for Griffin to bring us back."

Oriana nodded. "Then it's settled, we'll take Alice to the Court of Creation and hope they will lend us horses or a carriage."

Allie lay back and looked up at the sky. Clouds passed over head, blocking the sun from her view. Her eyes started drifting shut and Devlin nudged her. "Don't fall asleep."

"Let her rest, Devlin," Griffin said. "She needs it."

Devlin laid her cloak over her. "Okay, quick nap, and then we fly."

Allie closed her eyes and nodded. "Then we fly."

"Back in the dream realm I see." Elken stood in front of her. "Spending a lot of time here lately."

"What are you doing in the dream realm? Hmm?" Allie looked at him. "Shouldn't you be figuring out a way to be free from Cerise?"

He laughed. "I have. You and your friends are going to free me." He stepped up and touched her cheek. "I sense something is wrong."

"I'm recovering from poison. Nothing to worry about. Maybe I'll gain some immunity from it and not have to worry about the Jabberwock's poison." She cracked a smile.

"That is not something to joke about Alice." He dropped his hand. "Where are you recovering?"

"I'm asleep in the woods somewhere. My friends are watching over me."

"Go back to the Court of Creation, tell Mellow that you're hurt. She'll take care of you." He pleaded. "Promise me?"

"I'm going back there to ask for horses or a carriage to take us to the Court of Hearts. We're dragging our feet so I have time to heal before I take on the Jabberwock." Allie crossed her arms. "So if you have any advice on how to beat him, now might be the best time to tell me."

He shook his head. "I have no idea how Cerise managed to tame it and no one has killed it before, obviously."

"Obviously," she echoed.

"I'll see you when you free me, Alice. Once you bring the Cerise down and you defeat the Jabberwock, look for the red jewel and shatter it." He bowed. "Remember my promise." He faded away, leaving her standing in the white abyss alone.

She swore she could hear the roar of the Jabberwock in the distance, even though she'd never heard it before. Goosebumps rose on her skin as she tried to push the image of the creature out of her mind. Her body shivered as the wind whipped around her and the sound of the Jabberwock sounded closer.

'Beware the Jabberwock...wield the sword of Creation and be changed by the event destined for you.'

The female voice seemed to be coming from her mind. She'd always been told that there was no such thing as destiny, that she was in charge of her own path, but it seemed that no matter the path she chose, she was still going to face the Jabberwock.

CHAPTER 17

Devlin stared at Griffin, willing the hunter to say something. Anything. But the fae just stared at Alice as she tossed and turned in her sleep. Oriana played with a strand of grass, freezing it in time, so it didn't move or bend in the wind and then unfreezing it.

"Can you turn it back into a seed?" Griffin spoke, his eyes still on Alice. "Turn someone back into a child?"

Oriana looked up at him. "My mother can, but it's something that takes a lot of power and energy."

"What about turning back the time of memories? If someone has lost their memories, can you bring them back?"

Devlin raised a brow at the thought. He'd seen the Court of Time do some cool things, but he hadn't thought about applying it that way.

Oriana shook her head. "Not without damaging the mind."

Griffin pressed his lips together. "What about the Court of Enchantment? Is there an enchantment a spell, anything that can bring back memories?"

Devlin thought about it. There were a few different ways to erase memories, but he'd never thought about being able to recover them.

"I'd have to look into it. My specialty is enchanting items, like what I do to the trees to keep us safe. Like the gauntlets Alice wears."

"Hmm." He finally looked away from Alice. "Can you enchant her so that the Jabberwock can't pierce her skin?"

Devlin shook his head. "She's mortal, fae enchantments might kill her. I've done what I can, the cloak, the gauntlet. I could have made more had Cerise not had my workshop raided."

"You're awfully invested in keeping her alive." Oriana laughed. "I thought you were supposed to just bring Alice to Cerise."

He nodded, but didn't explain any further. Alice let out a strangled cry and then settled down.

"I think she's dreaming." Devlin sighed. "She never seems to sleep sound."

Griffin frowned. "She was like that as a child too."

"How do you know that?" Oriana raised a brow. "You weren't around when she was here as a child and I doubt you've spent time in the mortal realm."

Griffin's brows knitted together. "I don't know."

Devlin glanced at Cerise and then back to Griffin. "You said you came into Cerise's services after she saved your life?"

He nodded. "Seven years ago. I woke up with her watching over me. No memory of where I came from, or how I got injured."

A crazy idea crossed Devlin's mind and from the look on Oriana's face he had a feeling she had the same thought. Devlin went to ask his question when Fehin landed near them and squawked. Alice jumped with a gasp and then cringed. "World moving."

Oriana lay a hand on her back. "Take a deep breath. It was just Fehin."

Alice nodded and took a few steady breaths. Devlin saw her body shaking from where he sat. "Maybe we can have a healer take a look at you when we get there."

"Probably not a bad idea," Oriana agreed and helped Alice up. "Help me get her on Fehin?"

Alice tried to push her away. "I'm fine. I can get up on my own."

Devlin rolled his eyes as Fehin bowed his head to allow Alice to try and climb up on him. After a few attempts trying to pull herself up Alice let out a huff. Griffin went over to her and offered her a foot up.

"Thanks," she muttered before getting up there.

Devlin let Oriana get up before him. He looked down at Griffin. "We'll see you at the Red Tree Forest soon."

Griffin gave him a sharp nod and then Devlin nudged Fehin to take to the sky. The wind swept over them as the bird flew to the Red Leaf Forest. More than once Devlin saw Alice nod off in the front, each time making his gut clench. Most mortals would have died in Fairy by now, but she was fighting things off at every turn, including the poison. Griffin may have given her the antidote, but it was Alice's stubbornness that was going to get her through the rest of it.

Hopefully it'd be enough to get her through the battle with the Jabberwock.

They flew until Fehin could go no further. And after that, they walked until Alice was about to collapse.

Oriana tucked Alice in under the shade of a tree. "She's exhausted and we still have a day to go."

Devlin nodded. "She'll make it. She's too stubborn not to."

"Do you think Griffin has gone back to Cerise to update her?" Oriana took out her canteen draining it of the last bit of water.

"I don't think it matters. We're going to the Court of Hearts as soon as we get proper transportation from the Court of Creation. So if he updates her, then so be it." Devlin shook his head. "The more and more I think about this, the more I realize it's a bad idea. We're leading her to her death."

Oriana stayed silent and Devlin let out a long sigh as the breeze kicked up around them. "I know we're hoping that she defeats the Jabberwock and takes Cerise down, but there's so much we didn't count on."

Oriana nodded. "We just have to focus on what we can control. We can help Alice out as much as we can with her battle. We're equipping her with the skills and items that she will need, but it's up to her to wield them properly. The fact that the needle missed her gauntlet tells me that Alice had no idea that they could have blocked it. And that is a gap in her training. We've been focusing on swords, but we need to work on defense. The gauntlets and the cloak could save her from the Jabberwock's claws and teeth."

Devlin glanced at the sleeping mortal. "And if...when she defeats the Jabberwock, then what? Law says that if she tames it or defeats it, she becomes the Lady of Hearts."

Oriana laughed. "That law doesn't apply to mortals. It'll depend on what happens with Cerise afterwards. If we're to believe the prophecy, she'll also be defeated by Alice. Probably before she faces the Jabberwock, since she's supposed to die by that." She frowned. "Unless we're understanding it wrong."

Devlin raised a brow. "What do you mean?" He thought through the prophecies that they'd been given.

"The mortal woman who steps through the mirror, drinks the tea, and eats the cookies will bring the Red Queen to her knees. She shall defeat the beast with creation's sword, and she shall be no more," he muttered.

Oriana sighed. "She shall defeat the beast with creation's sword. Maybe it's not the Jabberwock. Maybe it's something else. And maybe 'she shall be no more' refers to the beast."

"You think the beast is Cerise?" Devlin frowned. "I hadn't thought about it that way. The Jabberwock has always been considered the beast."

"And then there's what Cibil said as well: 'Forsaken is the mortal, no longer of her world. Forgiven is the Red of Hearts, her sins cleansed in blood. Cursed is the Court of Creation, for the ruler has been lost. And dead are the wanderers, for they found what lurks beyond. The one you sought is no longer your blood.'"

Devlin shook his head. "None of that makes sense. Alice isn't forsaken, we're still with her, guiding her. Who the hell would forgive

Cerise and with whose blood? Well, we know where the Court of Creations ruler is. And the wanderers?"

Oriana swallowed. "I think that might be my parents. They went beyond."

"There are other fae who went beyond the mountains." Devlin tried to comfort her, but he knew she was probably right. He tried to find more to say but she patted his knee. "I think I know what the last line means."

"Brendyn." Devlin sighed. "I don't know how, but I think Griffin is Brendyn. There's something about him and the way he's fighting to protect Alice, even though he serves Cerise."

Oriana nodded. "I've been thinking about it. Seven years ago, Cerise would have done anything to save Brendyn so that Alice would come back. I think she tied his heart to Griffin's. I don't know if he's truly Brendyn or not. Cerise's powers would have been weak then and she may not have had the power to pull off something like that properly..."

"Something went wrong." Devlin caught on to her train of thought. "What do we tell Alice?"

Oriana shook her head. "Nothing right now. Absolutely nothing until we know for sure."

Allie woke up before Devlin and Orianna, the two fae were still fast asleep on the ground despite it almost being evening. She sat on a rock and sipped her water trying to decide if what she had heard was a dream or not.

Brendyn's heart was tied to Griffin. If that was true there was no way to get her brother back, but he also wasn't truly dead. She frowned at the thought. What had Cerise done? Could it be undone so her brother could pass on?

She reached into her bag for a piece of jerky, but touched something soft. She cried out and jerked her hand away from whatever she touched.

Laughter came from her bag. And she looked down to see Kit's grin growing in the dark of the bag. She took a deep breath trying to calm her hammering heart. Kit crawled out of the bag and flicked his tail. "Hello Alice."

"Kit, what the hell?"

He stretched his paws out in front of him and arched his back. "I was just waiting for you to wake up. Where might you be off to now?"

"Are you going to turn around and tell the queen?" Allie asked, raising a brow. "Because she's already sent someone to stalk us."

Kit laughed and rubbed up against her. "No, dear Alice, I'm here to make sure you're on the right course. It seems to me like you're heading towards the Court of Hearts. Which means you are indeed heading the right direction."

"What do you want Kit?" Allie looked up where the stars were starting to twinkle in the purple of the fading sun.

Kit curled up next to her. "I want to wish you luck. On breaking the curse on the stone, defeating the Jabberwock and bringing Cerise to her knees. I think if anyone can do it. You can. And I think you're realizing that you're not Allie anymore, that you're turning back into Alice. *The* Alice."

She thought about that. In the cave with the Spinner, all doubts about what she had to do flooded from her mind. She had to get the sword and defeat the Jabberwock. She'd started to believe in the impossible.

Then she was taken out by poison. But she assumed living through that was part of facing the impossible.

"You know I'm right, Alice." He drew out her name.

Allie nodded. "I do, which means I know it's time."

"You were called upon to save Fairy Alice, and now you know the way."

Her stomach churned. Sacrifices must be made in order for her to save Fairy and to save her friend. She glanced at Kit. "And then what?"

"And then the fae tell the tale of the mortal who saved us all." Kit grinned and his body started to fade from the tail forward. "Don't forsake your friends Alice. They will pull you through."

His grin was the last thing to disappear. Alice looked over at Oriana and Devlin. Friends. Her friends had been in Fairy all along. Not the mortal world. She was always destined to come back here.

"Once upon a time, there was a girl named Alice," She muttered. "And she followed a white rabbit down a rabbit hole and found an entire new world."

"And in that world, she discovered the girl in the red dress, who welcomed her with open arms. The two fell in love, but Alice was mortal." Oriana stated and looked over at her. "And mortals couldn't stay in Fairy."

Alice raised a brow. "Until she returned to change the Red Queen's heart."

"Do you think you can change her heart, Alice?" Oriana asked her, sitting up. "Do you think you can save Cerise?"

Alice pressed her lips together. "I think with the right actions and the right words, I might be able to."

Oriana looked at her. "I hope you can."

Alice glanced over at Devlin who was still sleeping. "Are we flying or walking tonight?"

"Flying, once Devlin wakes up." Oriana stood and untied the Sword of Creation from her back. "This is yours."

Alice wrapped her hand around the hilt and held the scabbard with her other hand. She pulled the blade out with a swift movement and examined it. The black blade caught to rising moonlight, and blue swirls appeared that she hadn't seen while it was in the cave. The same swirls that were engraved in the hilt. "It's beautiful." She put the scabbard down and tested the sword with a few swipes.

The weight of it felt natural in her grip as she moved through the forms, almost as if the sword was meant for her. She smiled as she ended a form and looked at Oriana. "Shame we'll have to return it." She picked up the scabbard and sheathed the sword.

"You don't want to mess with The Spinner, Alice."

Alice shook her head. "No, I don't. I like my head where it is and I rather my hair doesn't get turned into thread."

"Remember, mortal hair is no good for that." Oriana nudged her. "So you're safe there."

Alice snorted. "That's right, so how about I rather not die from being poisoned?"

"Yeah, that's a good idea."

Alice sat down on the rock again and sighed. "Even that was exhausting."

"You're going to heal up," she promised.

"I hope so, because if I can't move quick enough than the Jabberwock is going to eat me in one bite."

"I don't think his mouth is that big." Oriana started laughing. "Maybe a couple bites."

Alice shook her head. "Do you still have that drawing?"

Oriana nodded and pulled it out of her bag, handing it to Alice. She unrolled it and stared at it. "So in the human world, there's a myth about dragons." Alice said.

"Myth? Dragons used fly through Fairy." She smiled. "Wonderful creatures."

Alice pointed to the long neck of the Jabberwock. "In the stories, the weak point is almost always the underbelly of the creature. This drawing shows that there are no scales under the Jabberwock's neck, I'm willing to bet that the stomach is the same."

"So you think that will be its weak spot?"

Alice nodded. "Yes. So all I need to do is get under it and skewer it on my sword."

"Alice," Oriana warned. "The beast weighs a ton. All it would have to do is drop down and squash you."

She nodded. "I didn't say I had a plan on how to do it, but that's what I need to do." She looked at the stubby legs of the beast and pressed her lips together. "They don't exactly teach this in the mortal world."

Oriana snorted. "I'm sorry to say that defeating the Jabberwock isn't something they teach in Fairy either."

"You don't even have myths of how the Court of Hearts tamed it?"

"If we do, they are kept within the walls of that court. That's not a secret that they would want out."

Alice sighed. "Yeah, I guess that would make sense."

The bushes behind them rustled and Alice turned around, drawing her sword. Her heart pounded as a shadow appeared in front of them, cast in the darkness of the trees.

But she would have known that shadow anywhere. "That's a Fachan." She swallowed. "I ran into one at the Court of Enchantment."

Oriana pulled her sword out. "They move quick."

She remembered. The one-legged creature had been able to hop around without balance issues. It's one giant eyeball blinked at them as it jumped forward. Oriana went to strike, but it dodged to the side, heading for Alice.

Its feathery face opened up to a massive mouth with jagged teeth. Alice stepped back, but took a firm stance waiting for it to come at her. She lunged forward thrusting with her sword, only stopping when she heard the squish of the eye being stabbed through. She pulled the sword out and Oriana came up and sliced the thing in half.

The body fell to the ground in two pieces. The fingers on the hand twitched a few times before completely falling still.

Alice held her gag back. "Still gross. And I still don't understand how something with one leg is so balanced." She shuddered. "I also thought Devlin's enchantments were supposed to keep those things away."

"He fell asleep before he could cast the enchantment. He's also exhausted." She sighed. "We should wake him up so we can get going. I don't want to wait to see if any other creatures pop up tonight."

Alice nodded and went to Devlin. "Hey, it's time to get up."

He moaned and rolled onto his side. "Too tired."

"We were just attacked, Devlin, it's time to get up and move." Alice nudged him with her foot. "One eyeball creep came. Let's go."

He opened an eye. "Look, just give me a little bit longer?" He closed it and was back to sleep.

Alice glanced over her shoulder at Oriana. "Well?"

"I guess let him sleep," she muttered, but she looked concerned.

"Is he okay?" Alice asked. "Do fae get sick? Did he get poisoned?"

"No, I think he's just exhausted. Come on, let's work on your defense while he sleeps."

Alice gave the sleeping Devlin. "Yeah, okay."

Cerise looked over the words of the prophecy. She'd written it down to study the wording of it to make sure she was right. She just needed to avoid the part about her. Let the Jabberwock kill Alice before she had the chance to kill her.

She tapped the table and sighed. She'd gotten a bird from Griffin with a message. He had located Alice and was bringing her in willingly. They had to travel from the mountain to here and Alice had been poisoned.

That's all the message had said. Nothing about why they had been at the mountains, but at least he'd managed to find her. Bringing her here by force might have been the better choice, but it didn't matter.

Because Alice would be there, and soon she'd face the Jabberwock. Dead. That's what the mortal deserved.

"My Queen." Ace walked in. "I received a message from March. He's located Dor, but he can't get to him."

She took a deep breath and looked up from the scroll. "What do you mean he can't get to him?" She looked up at her captain of the guard. "He's a tiny fae; trap him in a cup."

"He wrote saying that Dor is held up in the Court of Enchantment and that the lord there isn't allowing visitors."

Cerise raised a brow. "Oh really? Is that why they haven't answered our message?" She growled. "Because they aren't allowing visitors?" The rage sounded in her voice. "Send a soldier there. Tell them we're declaring war."

"Cerise," Ace started and she glared at him. "My queen," he corrected. "I know you want to take over the courts, but declaring war when dealing with a prophecy is not the right course of action."

"I can't wait for Alice to die. The Court of Enchantment is purposely going against me. They need to be taken care of first. Send the soldier and prepare your army," she growled and swiped the scroll off the table in rage. "We start with the Court of Enchantment and then move to the Court of Time."

Ace hesitated for a moment, but then bowed. "As you wish." He walked out muttering something, but she didn't have time to worry about that. The Court of Enchantment was plotting against her and if she didn't move quickly, they would move first. She would not allow them to take over her kingdom.

She went and snatched the scroll off the floor and looked at the words again, except now they were all scattered on the scroll as if her throwing it had shaken them up. Magic. There was no other explanation. But it wasn't her magic... She glanced over her shoulder to the door where Ace had just left.

No, he rarely used his magic unless he had to. He had something against the gifts he'd been giving though his blood line. So whose magic?

She stared at the words, waiting for them to right themselves, but they didn't. She rolled the scroll up and stormed through the hallways until she reached Lavin's room. Throwing the door open she tossed the scroll to the seer. "What is the meaning of this?"

Lavin wasn't sitting in the crouch like he normally was. His back was turned to Cerise, his gaze out the window.

"Answer me," Cerise demanded.

"I don't have to look at it to know." He muttered. "Something is changing the course of fate and that prophecy may no longer be true." He put his hand against the glass of the window. "There's something out there, something that has shifted. I can hear my sibling calling for me on the wind."

Cerise stalked up to him and grabbed his wrist, turning him to face her. His eyes flashed red, but he didn't pull away, didn't hiss at her. Nothing like his normal mannerisms. "You will tell me what the new prophecy is."

"It doesn't work like that, my queen." He gently pried her hand off his wrist. "If it did, I'd have one for you, but as it sits anything that has to do with Alice is a blur. Unreadable. Which makes things uncertain." He turned back to the window. "I do not like uncertain, my queen."

Neither did she. She wanted her answers now. "Will Alice still fall to the Jabberwock?"

He glanced at her. "I don't know."

Devlin had finally woken and they'd taken to the sky. Alice held tight to Fehin's feathers as they landed in the Forest of Red Leaves. Her heartbeat faster at the idea of the Court of Creation. What if they denied her access this time? Or help?

Fehin's feet landed without a sound, and he leaned forward to let everyone get off. Devlin helped Alice off. She looked around and sighed.

There was no sign of the gate, nothing that even said they were near the entrance of the Court of Creation. She frowned as she started walking towards the direction she thought she went last time. When Griffin had attacked her and she fled.

Devlin and Oriana followed her, but she knew they were keeping their distance in case the court didn't want them there.

She paused and closed her eyes. She imagined the dark gates that had been surrounded by the shadows. The swirling pattern of the black iron had curled in intricate swirls. The top of the gates were arched together. Maybe if she could conjure the image of them, they would appear.

"Wow." Oriana's voice made Alice open her eyes. There were the gates right in front of her.

Alice smiled. "I can't believe that worked." She reached for the gate but it swung open before she could touch it. "I guess we're going in." She stepped in with Devlin and Oriana at her back. She glanced over to make sure the two didn't disappear when the gates closed, leaving them in the endless strawberry fields.

"Not how I imagined this court would look," Oriana said.

"I imagined a lot more people." Devlin followed up. "And fewer berries."

Alice held a finger up. "Just wait," she muttered. "Another gate will come up in a moment."

As if on cue the silver gate shimmered in existence. The silver metal of it weaved and waved as if it was alive. Oriana gasped. "Liquid silver?"

Alice shrugged. "I don't know, but it's beautiful." She took a step forward and like before the gate swung open. "Boy, am I glad you guys are allowed in this time." She laughed as she stepped foot on the cobblestone road. The white and gray stones led the way into the city, bordered on each side by houses. Alice took the time to admire the wood and the craftsmanship of the houses. Skill shown in the way the walls met, the windows were surrounded by carvings of branches and trees.

"This place is beautiful," Oriana breathed as they walked through the roads. Alice nodded. "It really is."

She gently touched the shoulder of a passing woman. "Excuse me, could you tell me where I can find Marrow?"

The woman smiled at her. "You'll find her in the palace with the other councilors. They are having a meeting." Her smile faded. "There has been rumors of war coming and with our Lord missing, the councilors are in charge."

"Thank you." Alice bowed her head. "Have a good night."

The woman thanked her and continued down the road. The three of them walked down the road until it ended in a wide circle. A few people were still there mulling around, pushing carts out, and some chatting.

"The market place," Devlin whispered in her ear. "The life of the city."

She glanced back at him. "It looks different from your city."

"Each court is a bit different." Oriana nodded. "There's a lot of music and dancing in my court. You'd love it."

Alice sighed. "One day, when this is all over I'll have to come and spend time in each court. Without a threat hanging over my head." She looked around the roads that shot off of the circle marketplace. Only one had no houses or businesses lining it and the cobblestone seemed to be made of the same liquid silver as the gate.

"I'm assuming we head that way." Alice took a few steps towards it. Feeling a pull in that direction.

"When you were here before you didn't pay attention to where you were going?" Devlin sighed. "Such a mortal."

"Marrow pulled me through the city too fast to see where we were going. My hood also obstructed my view." Alice rolled her eyes. "So I didn't really get a chance to site see."

Oriana laughed. "I think that's fair." She linked her arm with Alice and pulled her down the road. With each step they took, the pull in Alice's chest became stronger.

The road curved over a hill allowing them a look at the castle for the Court of Creation. The three spires of the castle moved towards the sky, wrapped in vines that blew in the wind.

A massive wall surrounded the castle creating a courtyard between gates, but a stark contrast of the greens on the spires, the gates were black, moving with thorns. Alice's heart leapt. "This isn't the building that Marrow took me to. I would have remembered this."

"Let's keep going." Oriana nudged her. "We've come this far. All we're asking for is help. The worst they can say is no."

Alice nodded, but the only thing keeping her going at this point was the pull in her chest. All the walking and traveling had zapped her energy, and she had to focus to keep her feet moving forward as they walked.

Pick up the foot, put the foot down.

She repeated the words in her head, forcing her feet to continue. Her limbs became heavy and she stumbled to her knees. Devlin came up next to her. "Alice?"

"Just feeling weak again," she muttered, trying to push off the feeling. "I'll be okay. Help me up."

Devlin pulled her to her feet and she stumbled again. "We can't just stop in the middle of the road and camp." Devlin picked her up. "We have to keep moving."

Alice nodded. "I'm fine...just let me..." the world flipped upside down before it went completely dark.

"There's still poison in her system." Marrows looked at Devlin. "The antidote cleared what it could, but it must not have been enough."

Soldiers had come to greet the three of them not long after Alice had passed out in his arms. They'd taken her directly to the healer, and they'd yet to see her.

"She was doing fine yesterday. Weak, yes, but she was up and practicing with her sword. The fever was gone." Oriana paced the study where they'd been waiting. "We don't have time for this. She has to heal, we have to head to the Court of Hearts."

Marrow crossed her arms. "She has to heal first or the Jabberwock will just have to look at her and she'll die."

Devlin sighed. "Let's get some rest and let Alice rest. I'm sure the healer here knows what they are doing."

Marrow nodded. "I would like to speak to you two about alliances before you go."

"Alliances?" Devlin raised a brow. "The Court of Creations has hidden in the shadows for years and has survived every conflict because of how secure the magic is around the city. What has you scared enough that you want alliances?"

Marrow looked over her shoulder and then jerked her head. "Please, come talk with me elsewhere about this."

Devlin nodded and he and Oriana followed Marrow out of the hall and down to a room with a large oak door with black handles. "This is the King's meeting room, obviously he's not here...but it's the safest place to talk. We don't need any more rumors flying around the city about war."

She pulled open the doors and the three of them walked in. A table sat in the middle of the room, round, made out of the stump of a giant tree. Five chairs surrounded the table, and the room was lit from the stain glass window that looked over the city.

Oriana walked up to the window and studied the image. Swirling colors moved from the center. One side of the window was man and the other side fae. "This was when our worlds were separated."

Marrow stepped up next to her. "That's exactly what it shows, today. Who knows what it'll be tomorrow." She guided Oriana back to the table, but Devlin continued to stare at the window. One of the mortals looked suspiciously like Alice. Short hair, black clothing...and just something about the way she was looking back at the portal.

"Don't put too much thought into it Lord Devlin." Marrow's voice broke his focus on the image. "The window is enchanted to show us things from the past and the present. I believe it was your great grandmother who made it."

Devlin turned around and sat next to Oriana at the table. "That was a long time ago then."

Marrow nodded. "It was. I hear she was a wonderful woman."

Devlin smiled. "I've only heard stories. Now, what have you heard that has your council so nervous?"

"Your father sent a bird to us. As you know we typically do not reply or meet with any of the other courts, but this one has struck a chord with us. He has received a declaration of war from Cerise."

Devlin growled. "What?" Why hadn't his dad sent him a bird about it? Of course, what could Devlin had done? He had a duty to make sure that Alice stayed safe, but he didn't trust his dad to not bend to Cerise's will.

Oriana let out a string of curses. "Has he responded to her?"

"I don't know, his letter didn't sound like they had, but if my spies are correct, Cerise has an army big enough to wipe out the Court of Enchantments."

Devlin did quick math in his head. That would make Cerise's army massive. "So you're not allying with us for your sake, but ours."

"Believe it or not, the Court of Creation has a duty to protect the other courts and make sure that Fairy stays balance. It's one of the reasons we hide, because if we don't exist than the rest of Fairy falls."

Oriana frowned. "That's why you're the only one that can be ran by a council."

"Yes, and until our king returns, that's how it will remain. If he returns." She sighed. "But we offer an alliance to both of your courts." She looked up at Devlin. "I will send your father a letter detailing it, but I know that you are the one who is in your right mind."

Devlin shrugged. "My father's been through a lot, but yes. I typically do the political dealings. It would just be a formal thing that you send him a letter."

Oriana sighed. "And I'm acting ruler right now because my parents ventured to the other side of the mountains."

"We are all hoping it doesn't come to this, but if it does, we have your back. If Alice can manage to defeat Cerise as she's prophecies to, then we won't have to worry."

A knock came at the door. "Marrow?" A woman opened the door. "Alice is awake."

Devlin tried not to jump out of his seat. "How is she?"

"She's..." the woman hesitated for a minute. "She's going to be okay, we've started finishing the healing process. Her fever has come back though and I'm afraid she's a bit delusional."

Oriana stood. "May we see her?"

The woman glanced at Marrow. Devlin looked to the fae. "Please."

"Let them see her. Maybe some friendly faces will help bring her out of her delirium." Marrow stood. "I will have dinner delivered to you in the infirmary."

"Thank you, Marrow. We truly appreciate all the help."

She bowed her head and led them out of the room. "Someone will show you to your rooms when you are done visiting Alice. You all need rest, and I know you are eager to get to the Court of Hearts."

"We won't be leaving until Alice is ready." Oriana stated. "We don't want her weakened when we get there."

"Of course." Marrow nodded.

"Right this way please." The woman said, leading Oriana and Devlin down a different corridor.

They followed her into another wing of the castle and up a flight of stairs to yet another wooden door.

"Alice doesn't know where she is and she keeps asking for her brother. If her brother is here in Fairy, I think it might calm her if he comes here."

Well that would be a loaded situation right there, Devlin thought. "Her brother died seven years ago."

She sighed. "Alright then, hopefully you two can help her." She opened the door. Alice lay on a bed, her hair sticking to her face with sweet. Her eyes were closed, her chest heaved with every breath she took.

It was almost like when the Spinner's poison first took ahold of her. A young fae woman was kneeling by the bed, wiping Alice's forehead and whispering to her.

Devlin couldn't hear the words, but Alice nodded her head slightly. The fae looked up and the grim look on her face brightened a little at the sight of Devlin and Oriana. "You must be Alice's brother."

Devlin choked back a laugh. "No, but I am her friend. I'm Devlin and this is Oriana."

The woman stood. "I'm Leigh, I've been put in charge of Alice's healing."

"A bit young." Oriana pressed her lips together.

"But I have experience with the Spinner's poison and magic." Leigh's smile tightened. "Whoever gave her the antidote delayed the effects and allowed for Alice to live this long."

Alice made a noise of pain and Devlin's heart skipped a beat as he rushed for her side, taking her hand.

"We're giving her more of the antidote in hopes to finish killing the poison. Mortal bodies weren't built to handle fae poisons." Leigh wiped her hands on the white apron she wore, almost like a nervous habit.

Oriana sighed. "I'll have to go talk to Griffin then. We're not going to be ready to travel any time soon."

"I won't release her until the poison is completely out of her system." Leigh nodded.

Devlin put a hand on Alice's cheek. "I don't want her traveling like this anyway. Please Oriana if you could let Griffin know, because I doubt he's welcomed into this court."

Alice's eyes opened and she met Devlin's gaze. "Where's Brendyn?"

Devlin sighed. "Alice...Brendyn is gone. Remember?"

She closed her eyes. "But I can feel him near."

"In Fairy, those who die are never really gone," Leigh said. "Maybe he's visiting you in your dreams."

Alice cringed. "Where's Griffin?"

Devlin frowned. "He's not here. He'll meet us when you're healed and ready to travel."

Alice didn't answer him, her breathing evening out as she fell asleep. Leigh motion Devlin away from Alice. "Let her sleep."

Alice's hands gripped the sheets and her brows pinched. Leigh changed the rag out on Alice's head.

Devlin stepped back from the bed and sighed. "Please, let us know if anything changes."

"Of course." Leigh didn't look at them as they left.

Oriana stomped through the Red Leaf Forest, looking for Griffin. She hadn't found him right outside the gate like she'd been hoping. Sending a bird probably would have been the wiser choice, but she'd felt like she needed to deliver these words in person.

He probably would have thought they fled if they sent a bird.

A rustle to her left had her spinning on her heels and her sword drawn. Griffin stepped out, his hand on his heart. "Alice. Where's Alice?"

Oriana caught him as he fell. Laying him on the ground she examined him for wounds where his hand was clenched. Nothing was there. "Alice is safe, there was still poison in her, so she's with a healer in the Court of Creation."

His hand shook has he grabbed hers. "Tell her. You have to tell her about me. I know you know. Tell her."

Oriana squeezed his hand. "You're not completely Griffin. Brendyn?" She asked, her voice low.

He nodded. "I'm remembering. I'm remembering what she did. Griffin, he was on the brink of death. I can't stay attached to him forever. He has to remember. He has to go home."

Oriana nodded. "If I tell Alice, it'll break her heart."

"She's stronger than you think," he said. "Freeze time, reverse time. Do whatever you have to, to let my heart go."

She frowned. "I don't know if my magic is capable of that."

"You have to believe that it is. Believe the impossible." Another movement of branches came from behind Oriana and she spun with her sword.

A man stood there, his cloak blending in almost perfectly with the trees and brush surrounding him. Woven branches were embroidered into cloak over his heart. His eyes reflected the light. "Hello, Lady of Time." He had his own sword out. "I suggest that you drop your weapon."

Griffin jumped to his feet, seemingly done with whatever struggle he had been in the mist of. "Go away, Bèarn"

Oriana tensed. The Bèarn were supposed to be dead. All of them from the war. Her parents had gone to the other side of the Dark Mountains to see if there had been any survivors. She hadn't heard back and seeing this man confirmed the fears that she'd spoke to Devlin about.

"I simply want the Lady of Time to deliver a message to the Red Queen." He took a step forward, his sword pointed at Oriana's heart. "You tell her that we are growing strong and we are not afraid of her kingdom or the horrors they put us through."

Oriana nodded. "I'll be heading to the Court of Hearts as soon as my friend heals."

"Your friend? Alice?" He grinned. "Cibil has told me all about her. I can't wait until she visits our side of the mountain, so she can see the horrors that Fairy truly holds for mortals."

Oriana shook her head. "Alice will be going back to her home when this is all over." Why would the seer tell a Bèarn about Alice? Why would one seek out the seer? Did they not have seers in their own land?

"Are you so sure that this isn't Alice's home now?" He put his sword away. "Do not forget to deliver my message, Lady of Time."

Oriana stared at him. "And what if I don't?"

"Then you might find yourself more enemies from beyond the mountain." He bowed his head and disappeared in a swirl of wind and dust.

She looked at Griffin. "Well, we need to get back to the Court of Creation." She turned. "And I need to speak to Devlin and Alice."

"Just one problem," Griffin said, his voice tight.

Oriana raised a brow. "Which is?"

"I am not welcomed there, so the gate will not return unless I leave you." He crossed his arms. "Do you remember where the gate was before?"

Oriana glanced around her. "I think I can find my way back. The question is. Are you going to be okay?"

"Promise me when this is over, you will separate the hearts that are in me?"

Oriana pressed her lips together. "I can promise you that I will try. My magic doesn't lie with hearts like Cerise's does, but I will see what we can do about it." She placed a hand on his chest. "Until then, try to remember where you come from so that you might be able to go home once you fulfill this deal with Cerise." Power hummed through her hand when she placed it over his heart. She tilted her head to the side. "Interesting."

He put a hand over hers. "What is?"

"There's a magic around your heart, but it's not Cerise's. It's her mother's, but I feel no malice from it. It's..." She tried to find the words as the energy flowed around her fingertips. "Protective." She frowned at the idea that Cerise's mother was capable of something.

Griffin looked just as confused. "We will think on that later. Go back to Alice and when she's healed, you'll find me here. We will all go to the Court of Hearts together."

Oriana pulled her hand away and nodded. "Of course. As we planned."

"As we planned."

⁂

Alice stared at the ceiling when she woke that night. She assumed it was night at least, but with no windows in her room, she couldn't really tell. But everything was quiet around her. Her muscles ached and her mind was foggy, trying to pull up memories of Brendyn and Griffin at the same time.

A water basin with several wash clothes draped over the edge sat on the floor. Alice slowly sat up, her whole body shaking with the effort. It was like she'd gone backwards in her healing instead of forward.

"Stay down, please," a soft voice whispered. A fae ran to Alice's side. Her braided red hair hung over her shoulder, and her black clothes had a white apron over it. "You're still weak and there's still some poison left in your body. If you move too much, you'll speed the spread of it again."

Alice lay back down. "Water? Please," she asked, trying to process what the fae had said. "Who are you?"

"I'm Leigh," she smiled. "You're my charge. Let me get you some water." She helped Alice sit up with pillows behind her. She walked off leaving Alice there for a moment.

Alice took a deep breath, trying to push the pain out of her body when she exhaled. "Where's my sword?" She peaked under her blanket. "Where are my clothes?"

Leigh laughed as she came back with a glass of water. "Your clothes are being washed and your sword is safely tucked away."

She helped Alice drink from the cup. Alice closed her eyes. "So what now? I just waste away as the poison takes me?"

"No, between magic and then antidote, you'll be back up in a couple days. I won't let you die on my watch, Alice. You're too important to Fairy."

But if she had been some nameless mortal, would she have been condemned to death? Of course, if she had been some nameless mortal she wouldn't have been in this situation. She never would have been welcomed in Fairy. "Thank you for taking care of me."

"Of course, now please, rest some more." Leigh put a hand on Alice's and warmth spread through her. The heat chased away the aches in her muscles and started to ease her back into sleep.

"I don't want to sleep." Alice muttered. "The dreams get worse each...time..." She couldn't help her eyes drifting shut as the dream realm welcomed her in.

"It's okay Alice," Brendyn's voice cooed to her. "You're safe now. Let your body rest."

She wouldn't look at him, her eyes clenched shut. If she opened them, he'd turn into a monster. A creature of the fae. Because that's what always happened when her dreams started this way. She couldn't face him. Not like that.

"Open your eyes, Alice." Griffin's voice startled her into opening her eyes. She met his dark gaze and growled.

"Why are you in my dreams?"

He smiled and it pulled on the scar across his face. "I don't know. This is your dream, not mine."

"Nothing is what it seems in Fairy. If you're here, there's a reason. I don't have dreams like this at home."

"You're right. I wanted to show you what you'll be fighting. What the Jabberwock is capable of."

She shook her head. "I don't want to see." Her heart picked up speed and Griffin waved a hand. They stood in the middle of an arena, much like the ones she'd seen in history books about Rome. The stadium seating rose high above them. Cerise...no, not Cerise, her mother, stood at the front of in a raised thrown. Her blood-red dress swirled down her body, caught in the wind. Her hair tousled away from her face, leaving her wicked smile clear.

Alice blinked and she swore the queen flickered to Cerise and then back again. "Bring him in," she yelled. "Let the filthy fae meet his doom."

Guards in red armor dragged a chained fae forward. Not any fae, but Griffin. Alice turned to look at the present Griffin, but he was gone now. Leaving her alone to watch.

"Griffin Nymphaea, you are being charged with harboring a mortal in your home. Keeping them from facing justice in the Court of Hearts."

Griffin looked up at her, his dark gaze reflecting the red of the queen. "A mortal you wanted dead. He has no crimes."

"He wandered into our land. That is crime enough," she growled. "Bring out the Jabberwock."

Griffin shook his head. "No, please my queen."

"Now you want to call me your queen, when before you refused. Beg for your life, Griffin. It won't help."

Alice put a hand over her mouth as a gate opened and the Jabber-wock stalked out. With its neck extended upwards, the beast was at least three times Griffin's height. The wingspan stretched out, making the wings look at lot larger than they had in the drawing.

Alice's stomach churned as the beast opened its mouth, venom dripping from the sharp teeth there. It took a step towards Griffin, the guards scattered and Griffin pulled his two swords off his back to face the creature.

The Jabberwock threw its head back to strike...

Alice woke with a jump and a shout. Her heart pounding in her chest, sweat dripping down her face. She tried to catch her breath as she looked around the empty room. No Leigh in sight, no Devlin or Oriana, no Griffin.

She took a few deep breaths. She needed fresh air. She needed to get out of this room.

She stood, finding that her body was much less sore than the last time she woke. She found a robe hanging on the bedroom door and wrapped herself in it before padding out of the room and into the hall.

Still empty.

Part of her wondered if this was another dream and something was going to come out of the walls to scare her. What she found instead was a hall that seemed to branch two parts of the castle. Windows bordered each side of it, allowing a view over the city. Alice turned and watched out the window for a few.

The sun was rising, the light starting to touch the slanted tiled roofs of the houses in the city. The rays made the city glitter in the morning. Further down the way water sparkled leading through the outskirts. Alice imagined running her hand through the running water, trying to find her peace.

"You really shouldn't be out of bed." Leigh stepped up next to her. "You worried me."

Alice glanced at her and then back out to the city. "I'm sorry. I had a nightmare and couldn't lie in bed anymore."

Leigh felt her head and smiled. "Your fever broke. That's a good sign. Let's get some food in you and then we can call Devlin in to see you. He's been pestering me since I sent him away the other night."

Alice frowned. "The other night? How long have I been sick for?"

"Three nights." Leigh hesitated. "I know you are eager to continue your travels, but I couldn't allow you while the poison had such a hold on you."

Alice nodded. "No, I would have been useless and probably gotten myself killed. Thank you. I don't remember much of it."

"Your fever was high and you were delirious most of the time." Leigh put a hand on Alice's elbow and started leading her back to her room.

Alice sat in her room sipping the broth that Leigh had brought her up from the kitchen. The door opened and Devlin stepped in. "Alice." Relief flooded his face as he ran to the bed. He pulled up a chair that Leigh had put there earlier. "Thank the gods you're okay."

Alice offered him a smile. "I'm good now. Leigh assures me that the poison is gone now. All of it."

He let out a long sigh. "We were so worried about you. Had we known the poison was still in your system, we wouldn't have pushed you so hard. We would have taken that last day easy...we would have."

She put a finger to his lips. "Hush, it's fine. Honestly I don't think I would have survived if we hadn't pushed." She studied the dark circles under his eyes. "You haven't slept much, have you?"

He shook his head. "No, Oriana left to meet with Griffin to tell him about our change of plans and hasn't been back. You've been so sick that you were asking for your brother."

"I was dreaming about him," she said honestly. "Almost every time I closed my eyes he was there." She shuddered. "And they were never good dreams."

He sighed. "I'm sorry, but now that you're healed we can continue our travels towards the Court of Hearts."

"Not until Oriana returns." Alice shook her head. She didn't want to continue on without both of them. And if Griffin did something to Oriana, then their deal was broken, but that didn't mean that Cerise didn't get to her. "Has Marrow sent anyone to look for her?"

"Yes." Devlin sighed. "Hopefully she'll return soon."

Alice nodded. "Have we sent a bird to Griffin?"

"You think he'd answer us?" Devlin raised a brow.

"I think he will if we remind him that not hurting anyone in our party was part of the deal." Alice crossed her arms and put down her bowl of broth.

"I'm more concerned that Griffin took her back to Cerise. There's been a declaration of war made from Cerise to the Court of Enchantment. She could forcefully take over the Court of Time if Oriana was in her custody."

Alice frowned. "She's not playing by her normal tactics then."

"You can't judge her movements on a children's game you played with her. These aren't little pieces on a board, this is real court politics." Devlin growled.

"You don't think I know that? I have nothing else to judge her moves on. I don't know your histories and ways, but I am taking this seriously." She slowly stood. "If I wasn't, I'd have marched back home the moment I thought I had a chance. I may have not been here for seven years, but I'm not going to abandon my friends to face whatever monster Cerise has turned into."

Devlin met her gaze. "I'm sorry Alice, I didn't mean to upset you."

"We've come this far and you think that I'm not taking this serious, that it's not real to me." She shook her head. "I have been poisoned, attacked, hunted, and I've been taught to fight, about a creature that can kill me with a scratch, and a bit about the world. This place is as real as my home."

"I wish it was your home, Alice. I wish you never left," he muttered. "I need some fresh air." He turned and left her room, leaving her standing there, confused.

Leigh walked in and raised a brow. "Devlin is under a lot of stress. He's been out every night looking for Oriana."

Alice sat down on her bed before the healer could yell at her for being out of the bed. "She's my friend too, and I'm worried."

Leigh sat next to her and patted her knee. "I know, and you're healing." She hesitated for a moment. "And you'll be on your way to the Court of Hearts as soon as Oriana returns."

Alice nodded. "Yes." Dread filled her and her stomach felt heavy. "I dreamed about the Jabberwock and Griffin."

"Dreams mean a lot in Fairy, Griffin probably meant for you to see the Jabberwock." She stood. "I have some other duties to attend to. You're well enough to take small walks, but please don't overdo it."

Alice nodded. "I'll try not to."

Leigh gave her a stern look and then shook her head, laughing as walked out.

Oriana was lost. That was the only explanation for why she was walking around in circles. She hadn't seen any sign of the gate and she'd been gone for two nights. Which meant either Devlin had forgotten about her, or couldn't find her.

The entire time that she'd been wandering around the Red Leaf Forest, she'd been thinking about the power that she felt around Griffin's heart and about the glimpse of Brendyn that she'd seen when she'd first run into him.

If the power was meant to protect Griffin, then undoing it could kill him, but that would also set Brendyn's heart free.

Could she sacrifice someone like that? She rubbed her eyes as she passed a stump she'd seen four times already since the sun had rose. She sat on it and let out a long sigh. Where on earth was that stupid gate?

"Oriana?" Devlin's voice called through the trees. "Oriana?" It came again and she jumped to her feet.

"Devlin!" She cupped her hands around mouth and called again. "Over here!"

Devlin pushed through some branches aside and threw his arms around Oriana. She hugged him and laughed. "I'm so glad you found me, I was starting to worry that I was hopelessly lost."

Devlin sighed and pulled away. "We were worried that Griffin gave you to Cerise and that we were going to have to go to the Court of Hearts without you."

"Alice?" She asked.

"Much better. She should be ready to travel tomorrow. Marrow has agreed to give us an escort to the Court of Hearts, as a show of our pending alliances."

Oriana let out a long breath. "Hopefully Cerise doesn't see that as a threat."

"No, that's what we're hoping for. She'll know that she is outnumbered in soldiers, that we'd have the advantage."

That was a possibility, but Cerise could react rashly to it. "Let's go then. I'd like a hot bath and a good meal before we travel again."

Devlin grinned. "There's a small feast tonight, in Alice's honor. I'm glad you'll be back for it. Did you find Griffin?"

She nodded. "There's something about the magic around his heart. We were right about him being tied to Brendyn."

"What about the magic that's surrounding it?" Devlin stopped and looked at her.

"It's a protective magic and I don't know what will happen if we undo it." She sighed and dread filled her. "When I found him he was begging me to undo the spell, use my time magic or freeze it because Brendyn was remembering everything." She rubbed her eyes. "I don't know what to do Devlin. I could take the life of another to send Brendyn free."

Devlin put a hand on her shoulder. "One problem at a time."

"Move forward," she agreed. "There's nothing I can do about Griffin now, but we can go back to the Court of Creation and celebrate Alice being alive and well."

Devlin smiled at her. "That's the spirit."

CHAPTER 19

The carriage bumped and shook as the horses drew it over the land. Alice stared at Griffin who sat across from her. Oriana sat to his left and Devlin sat next to Alice.

"This ride will go a lot faster than walking," Griffin stated. "But we'll still have time to stop and work on your sword skills on our way."

Alice nodded and looked out the window. They'd left the Red Leaf Forest behind a couple hours ago while the sun was rising. "Did Oriana really get lost in the forest?" The question had been on her mind since Oriana had returned. Her mood had shifted when she joined them for dinner like something was weighing on her mind.

Her smiles hadn't been as wide, and Alice had caught her staring off into space more than once.

"I did." Oriana shrugged and Griffin laughed. "I'd walked in circles a few nights until Devlin found me. Embarrassing for sure."

"I had no idea that she was lost in the forest." Griffin shrugged. "I just knew that the gate wouldn't show up if I was with her."

Alice leaned back in the seat and nodded. "I had this dream..." She shook her head. "Never mind, it's not the time to talk about it. What's our plan when we get to the Court of Hearts?"

Griffin regarded her for a moment, and Alice looked away to avoid his gaze. "I will take you to the queen, and then she will do whatever it is she plans on. And I will only have to serve her three more years."

Alice raised a brow. "Assuming she sticks to her deal."

"Or assuming she doesn't die. If she dies, he's released from her deal," Oriana added. "And maybe her magic."

Something flickered in Griffin's eyes and Alice frowned. "What happens then?"

Devlin cleared his throat. "We'll cross that bridge when we come to it."

"If we come to it," Oriana added. "The important thing to focus on here is that we are going to be walking into enemy territory with no idea what to expect, except for what the prophecy has given us."

Alice squirmed in her seat. "I don't like being beheld to words of prophecy."

Griffin smirked. "Spoken like a fae."

"Still fully mortal," she shot back.

No one argued. Alice closed her eyes. "I dreamed about the Jabberwock. It was much bigger in my dream than it looks in the drawing."

"It's huge," Griffin confirmed. "Quicker than you'd expect as well."

Oriana and Devlin looked at him. "You faced it?"

"And he died, or almost died," Alice stated. "I saw part of it in my dreams. Which makes me wonder, Griffin, how are you still alive?"

Griffin shifted in his seat. "The Jabberwock tried to kill me, yes. He caught me across the face, which is where the scar comes from, but that's all I remember. I know someone came to my aid, and that someone paid dearly for the price." He rubbed his chest, his brows pinching in confusion. "The punishment was..."

The carriage crashed to the side, throwing everyone against the wall of it. The drivers cried out as the horses panicked.

Griffin shoved the door opposite the ground opened and jumped out. Oriana scrambled after him. Devlin gave Alice a boost up.

The impact had shaken her, but she managed to get out and on her feet with Devlin behind her.

Guards in red armor surrounded the carriage, every spear the guards carried were pointed at the four of them.

Griffin held his hands up. "We are on our way to the Red Queen now, there was no need to attack the carriage."

The soldiers parted and Cerise walked through them, her red dress swaying in the wind. The corset kept the fabric tight against her chest and a crown of rubies sat on her head. "We thought you were the Court of Creation, that is their carriage after all."

Alice swallowed at seeing Cerise dressed like her mother. She truly looked like a queen as she stood there among the guards.

Alice stepped forward. "We're not in your lands yet, there was no reason for you to attack even if it was the Court of Creations carriage."

"Ah, Alice, finding your voice among my people I see." She walked towards her. "You're the one I am looking for."

Alice met her gaze. "These are not your people. Oriana is the Lady of the Court of Time and Devlin the Lord of the Court of Enchantment. I would assume that you would respect them as equals."

Cerise's eyes flashed red. "Hold your tongue mortal."

"Where is the girl who believed that the Courts were supposed to work together? That these two were your friends and to be your allies. Why fall into your mother's trap of war and bloodshed?"

"That girl is gone. Alice, you can't soften my heart like you did when we were children. I have a court to run, soon all of Fairy will be mine to run. My soldiers are already marching on the Court of Enchantment. Once you're dead, Fairy will give up hope that you will stop me."

Alice put her hand on the hilt of her sword. "Then have your guards kill me."

Oriana and Devlin stepped in front of her, but Alice saw hesitation play across Cerise's face. Tension made the air heavy around them as the soldiers waited for their command.

"No," the Red Queen finally said. "You are to be made an example of. Death by the Jabberwock." Her lip lifted in a sneer. "Just like your brother."

Alice felt like Cerise had punched her. "What? No, Brendyn died when he fell. When we tried to go home." Her voice shook even though she tried to control it. Cerise had to be lying. To catch her off guard.

"Alice and Griffin will ride with me back, Oriana and Devlin… put them in chains. I'll deal with them when we get back."

The world suddenly froze around them, only Alice, Devlin, and Oriana were moving. Alice looked at Oriana. "Run. Don't let her take you."

"We can't leave you."

"You have to, because you have to protect your people. This is the new path of fate. Go, please?" Alice begged. Sweat dripped down Oriana's face and her body shook. "I know you can't hold it much longer Oriana. Please. Freeze me and go. Run."

Devlin glanced at Oriana and then nodded. "We're more help to her free than we will be in Cerise's jail."

Oriana nodded and a moment later Alice felt magic wash over her and the world stood perfectly still.

Oriana stumbled as her and Devlin ran from the group. Her magic tried to pull her back to the area, but she forced herself to keep moving forward. "I won't be able to hold it for much longer." She gasped and Devlin put a hand on her elbow to steady her.

"It's okay. You've done enough." He promised and lowered her to a rock. "Fehin is on his way."

As if on cue the giant bird landed in front of them with a whoosh. Devlin smiled. "See?"

Oriana let out a strangled laugh and glanced over her shoulder. "We left Alice."

"I told you, we're going to be more help free than we will captive. We both knew that her fate was to end up at the Court of Hearts." He helped her on to Fehin. "What good are we going to do if we're in the dungeon?"

Oriana held on to Fehin's feathers. "What good are we if we're on the run."

"Cerise got what she wants, she has Alice, alone." Devlin pulled himself up and wrapped his arms around Oriana. "She'll keep her attention on Alice."

She hoped so. "But what do we do now?"

"For now, we fly back to the Court of Creation and regroup." He nudged Fehin in the side gently and the bird took off.

There was no talking as they flew through the air back towards the Red Leaf Forest. Oriana jerked the moment she felt her magic snap away from the group and back to her. Like a rubber band that had stretched too far and broken, it hit her hard. She put her head against the soft feathers of Fehin's neck and tried to convince herself that Devlin was right, that leaving Alice there had been the correct thing to do.

And that they hadn't just abandoned a mortal, their friend, to die alone.

***

Cerise stumbled as the magic surrounding her broke. Alice and Griffin both stumbled as well, Griffin put a hand on Alice's elbow to steady her and Cerise knew the two of them had also been caught in Oriana's magic.

It had to be Oriana, it felt like hers when it wrapped around them and she was the only one with the power to make everything freeze. And now, Oriana and Devlin were both missing.

Cerise grabbed Alice by the front of her cloak. "Where did they go?"

"I have no idea." Alice's eyes widened. "I thought they'd stay with me until the end." The honesty in her voice shocked Cerise and she let go, then started laughing. "Oh you foolish girl. Mortals have no friends and no allies here. Fae will always save themselves when they have the chance, no matter the cost."

Alice pressed her lips together like she wanted to argue. Cerise tilted her head to the side. "Don't tell me you truly thought Oriana and Devlin cared for you. This Fairy Alice, everyone is out for their own skin. They left you because they didn't want to be taken by me, because that would mean I won. Griffin, take her into the carriage."

Griffin grabbed Alice's arm and dragged the woman to the carriage. Cerise looked at Ace. "Those cowards."

"I'm not sure if they are cowards or if they have another plan. This is a carriage from the Court of Creations, which means they were welcomed into the city."

Cerise looked at the carriage that her men had overturned to stop it. The white wood was wrapped in green vines, Ace was right. "It means nothing. Alice simply wormed her way in and the court wants to stop me. They've made it clear that they won't ally with me already. But now we have Alice, we've declared war on the Court of Enchantment. And Alice's so-called friends ran away, leaving her with me. Tomorrow we announce a public fight with the Jabberwock."

Ace bowed his head. "As you wish my queen. Would you like me to ride in the carriage with you?"

"No. I would like to speak to Alice and Griffin alone while we travel." She walked to the carriage. "Keep on your horse next to us though, in case there are problems."

"Of course, my queen." He bowed his head again and went to his own horse. Cerise took a moment to run her hand down the nose of the white horse that was attached to the carriage. Dressed in red the horse looked magnificent. It nudged her hand and she smiled before moving to the other horse. Her finger danced over the black hair of the horse, its red mane fell over its neck, a stark contrast to the rest of the body. He was bred from the royal stables. His eyes flickered with shades of red as he nudged her hand for more attention.

For a moment she felt at peace, despite the fact that she had Alice in the carriage waiting for her or that she was about to condemn one of the only friends she ever had to death.

She took a deep breath and got into the carriage. Griffin was sitting next to Alice who had her arms crossed. Her sword lay across her lap, but the hilt was toward Griffin. Cerise tilted her head to the side as she studied the swirling pattern on the hilt. "That's a beautiful weapon, Alice."

Alice lay her hand on top of it. "Thank you, it cost me a lot to get it."

Cerise raised a brow. "You're a mortal, you have no fairy money."

"I didn't say it cost me money," she snapped back and then looked out the window of the carriage as it jerked into motion.

Cerise glanced at Griffin. "You fulfilled our deal. You brought her to me."

Griffin nodded. "Like I told you in my letter, we were delayed. I had to make a deal with her, or she would have hid in the Court of Creation forever."

Something tugged in her gut, telling her that he was lying. But Griffin was loyal, he wouldn't betray her. He was bound by their deal. She met his gaze. "What took you so long in the Court of Creation?"

Alice answered. "I almost died of poison, so I had to take some time to recover. Sorry I wanted to be at my best before I faced your beast."

"Griffin?" Cerise asked for a confirmation. Her question was aimed at him, not at the mortal.

"She speaks the truth. She was poisoned in her endeavors to get the sword. She was poisoned, and because of my deal with you, I saved her life giving her the antidote. But when we were traveling, she fell ill again and the Court of Creation took her in and lent her their healer."

Alice raised a brow. "Satisfied? Can't believe the words of a mortal?"

"I can't believe the words of an old friend who broke a promise." Cerise snapped back. "And whatever Oriana and Devlin taught you, I hope they taught you well, because when we get back to my court, you're going to face the Jabberwock."

If there was one thing Alice was learning about Fairy, it was traveling by carriage was worse than traveling by horse. She felt every little bump and shake of it and by the time they stopped for the night, she was motion sick.

Cerise's words also ate at her. Would Devlin and Oriana come back for her or would they abandon her completely?

She was the one who told them to go. She sent them away. Because she didn't want to see what Cerise would do to them if they stayed. She didn't want her friends to suffer.

"You'll have a small meal, and then you will stay in the carriage guarded by Griffin and March." Cerise broke the hour long silence that had settled over them.

Alice had expected her to ask more questions, to probe deeper into what happened when she'd sent Griffin after her, but the Red Queen had remained silent.

"You should be grateful that you aren't in chains, Alice. Take what freedom I am willing to give you." Cerise got out of the carriage and Alice looked at Griffin.

He shrugged a shoulder. "I'm not sure why her plans changed, but I agree with her, take advantage of not being in chains, because

I'm sure when we get to palace, you will be." He got out as well, leaving Alice alone in silence.

She closed her eyes and took a few breaths before getting out of the carriage. She strapped her sword back on her as she followed Griffin to a campfire. Several of the guards had gathered around as an older gentleman dished food from a pot on the fire.

"How long have they been set up for?"

"They travel lighter and faster than we do. They were here an hour before as scouts. They got the camp set up and the food started."

Alice looked around and laughed. "Fancier that sleeping on the forest floor with dried fruits and bread to eat."

"Don't say that until you've tasted the food." Griffin smirked, but it disappeared the moment Cerise approached them.

"Get her a bowl and then get her back to the carriage. The soldiers are already starting to whisper about her being here and what powers she might hold."

Alice smirked. "I'm mortal. I have no powers." She pulled her cloak over her sword hoping Cerise wouldn't take it.

Cerise noticed though. "Don't worry Alice, I'll let you keep your precious sword so that you'll have it when you face the Jabberwock. With my soldiers around Griffin watching you, you won't be able to use it to escape."

"I'm not planning on escaping, Cerise. I'm planning on seeing this through."

Cerise laughed. "The mortal willing to give her life for what? The glory that the fae will bestow upon you? If you die, nothing changes."

"I'm told it'll save Fairy and bring your kingdom to its knees." Alice met Cerise's gaze. "And maybe that will humble you a little bit and remind you of who you used to be and the dreams you had for Fairy."

Cerise spun away from her. "Do not speak to me like you still know me, Alice."

"I know that girl is still in you. I know that she would be ashamed of what you've become and what you're doing."

Cerise stormed away from them. Griffin put a hand on Alice's shoulder. "Your friend is gone, Alice. All that's left is a shell of cruelty."

Alice didn't want to believe that. She saw hesitation in Cerise's eyes when she spoke about the Jabberwock, the way Cerise had loved on the horses before she'd gotten in the carriage, that girl Alice knew had to still be in there.

"She needs to have a change of heart. That's all." Alice smiled. "And I think I know how to do that."

Griffin shook his head and nudged her forward. "Let's get you a bowl of chow."

Alice walked with him, and the older man handed them both a bowl. "Mortals in Fairy." He shook his head, his short hair flickering back and forth with the movement. Alice swore the silver flowed in each strand. "Never thought I'd see a day that a normal mortal would make it this far."

Alice shrugged. "I had help." She looked down at the chunky glop in her bowl. "Um, thanks."

"Don't go turning your nose up at it, because you only get bread in the dungeon." He muttered and turned to serve the next Fae.

Alice grimaced. "That's a hell of a last meal," she muttered, and then walked back to the carriage.

Griffin snorted. "At least you're getting one." He opened the carriage door. "In you go."

Alice raised a brow. "You didn't when you faced the Jabberwock?"

"I didn't. I got a nasty lashing and blast of magic before I went on the field." He muttered and then shook his head. "But that time is long over. I hope you get some rest, Alice." He shut the door.

Alice scooped her spoon into the bowl to pick up whatever the meal was. Something that resembled a potato and rice filled the spoon and she shoved it into her mouth, cringing a little.

It wasn't horrible, but she'd rather have the jerky and cheese and be sitting around the fire with Devlin and Oriana. She forced herself to finish the stew and then lay down the best she could on the carriage seat. Tomorrow night she was going to die and there was nothing she could do to change that fate.

CHAPTER 20

The palace was a welcome sight for Cerise. Traveling through the woods and between courts was exhausting, dirty, and boring. There was part of her that wanted to point out everything about the Court of Hearts to Alice. Things like the way the houses were all tinted with red, that if she listened closely there was an echoing of drums like a heartbeat, that the roses were only red.

But one look at Alice's face told Cerise that Alice had other things on her mind. Then she reminded herself that Alice was a traitor and would be a victim of the Jabberwock. She met Alice's gaze, but the woman turned away from her to look out the window.

Alice raised a brow at what she saw going by. "Shame I won't get a chance to explore the city, it looks beautiful."

Cerise shifted in her seat. "I wouldn't let a mortal just wander around my city. Not like Devlin and Oriana."

"I never got a chance to explore the Court of Time, really." Alice shrugged a shoulder. "I was too busy avoiding you and worrying about who was going to betray me to you."

Cerise scoffed. "No one owes you loyalty."

"I never said they did. But Oriana and Devlin proved that I could trust them through this."

"Until they left you." Cerise shook her head. "Oriana froze us with her magic and then disappeared. Cowards, the both of them."

Alice looked away. "They got me this far."

"You're right, they led you to your death. Your fate is sealed, it's been foretold." Cerise shrugged. "They could have taken you back home. Let you live, instead they put their own selfish needs ahead of your life."

Griffin tightened his fists and Cerise raised a brow. "Do you have something to say?"

"No my queen." He shook his head. "I don't."

She didn't believe him, but let it go. Her control on him was slipping and if she didn't find a reason or a moment to take his heart, she'd lose him completely when his four years were up. She locked her jaw at that thought.

The carriage jerked to a stop and footmen opened the door, letting Cerise out. Griffin and Alice followed. Griffin wrapped his hand around Alice's wrist as if he felt she'd bolt.

No one in this Court would help her. They all knew that Cerise had been looking for the Alice.

Alice looked around and the hope Cerise had seen in her eyes faded. The castle towered over the village flags with anatomically correct hearts flew on each of the four towers. The fading sun reflected off the red and white fabric. Magic wrapped around them as they walked up the stairs, ripping any enchantments off of the visitors that might have been there.

Cerise smiled as her magic flowed over her. "Welcome to the Court of Hearts, Alice, where I will rule as queen over all of Fairy, not just my court."

"You forget that the prophecy says that you will fall." Alice turned to face Cerise on the stairs.

The prophecy had changed though, shattered according to Lavin there was no real prophecy. Alice didn't need to know that.

"Griffin, take her to the west wing, fifth door. There're no windows for her to escape from there and the door locks from the outside."

Griffin nodded and dragged Alice up the stairs. Cerise followed, picking up her dress as she climbed the stairs. Alice was finally in her grasp. "Ace?"

"Yes, my queen?" Ace came up behind her.

"Send word to the other kingdoms that we have Alice, and that tomorrow night Alice will face the Jabberwock. I want them to know that all hope is gone now."

"Of course." He rushed past her up the stairs. Cerise walked into the castle and veered to the right to go to her wing. A hot bath was well deserved at this point and as she soaked in her victory, she wanted to imagine the future that was to come. All hail the Queen of Hearts.

Alice slammed her hand against the door as Griffin tried to shut it. "Hold on. I have a favor to ask."

He raised a brow. "What favor? We're in her palace, nothing goes on here that she doesn't know about."

Alice nodded. "I know, but it's not really betraying her, and it won't break your deal." She prayed that this would work.

"What do you need, Alice?"

For a moment she swore she saw part of Brendyn peeking out in Griffin's dark eyes. "There's a red stone that I need. It holds a fae captive and part of my deal is to free him."

Griffin raised a brow. "And how is a mortal going to free a fae from a magical stone?"

"Haven't gotten that far in my thought process, but the first step is to get the stone." Alice shrugged. "From there I have an entire day to figure it out."

Griffin nodded. "I'll see what I can do."

"And Griffin." She caught him again before he could shut the door. "If I could free you now, I would."

He gave her a soft smile. "I'm in debt to her for only four more years, after that I can find my own path. Thank you, Alice. Rest, but practice your forms and remember the power of objects in the fae world." He closed the door and she stood there staring at it.

She had plenty of objects given to her by the fae now. Her cloak, which she didn't know if it would withstand the teeth or the claws of the Jabberwock, but she hoped she didn't have to find out. The gauntlets which were enchanted to make it harder for fae to see her, but she'd often wondered if that enchantment had worn off.

She turned to look at the room. A large four-poster bed sat in the middle of it, draped in red of course. The crimson sheets were tucked in tight with a blanket folded at the foot of the bed. Pillows covered the top part of the mattress. A chair sat next to it, plain looking compared to the bed. Made of dark wood with no intricate designs, so normal looking it could have been from the mortal world. Alice let out a long sigh, after traveling for so long, sleeping in a bed sounded wonderful.

The thing damn near called for her. She walked towards it, taking her cloak and sword off, laying them on a chair before she kicked her boots off and climbed into the bed. She didn't bother with the blanket, because as her head hit the pillow she fell asleep.

So you've made your way to the Court of Hearts. Elken's voice said. Alice opened her eyes to find that she was lying in a field of flowers, the clouds floated above her in the blue sky. This dream felt much more peaceful than the ones that she'd had while traveling to the Court of Hearts.

"I'm currently waiting for my battle against the Jabberwock." Alice sighed, not looking next to her. She knew that's where Elken lay, but she didn't want to face him right now. She wanted to enjoy the sun on her skin and imagine that she wasn't going to be facing a terrible beast.

"Rest is good, and I'll let you be, but I wanted to tell you Alice, I was serious about our deal. You free me and the kingdom is yours."

Alice laughed. "I'm Mortal, those kinds of rules don't apply to me. But I do plan on freeing you because I think the Court of Creation needs their king back."

"And what will you do if you defeat the Jabberwock?" He asked.

Alice looked at him and studied the shifting colors of his eyes. "Go home, I guess. Figure out what to do with my mortal life."

He smiled at her. "Maybe this is home, Alice."

"Mortals don't belong in Fairy. We all know that." She turned back to look at the sky. "I'll miss my friends." Suddenly she felt like a child again. "But mortals belong in the human world." Her heart ached at that thought. She missed her parents, but she had nothing at home. Not really. She was always considered the weird one, the crazy one. The one who was still traumatized by the death of her brother.

Would staying in Fairy really be that bad?

"Don't think too hard on it Alice." Elken said. "Because if you do, you might find that's not what you want and fate isn't done with you yet."

Alice stayed silent and closed her eyes, basking in the warmth of the sun.

When Alice opened her eyes again she was staring at the red fabric. Without a window there was no telling how long she'd slept. The bedroom door flung open and a couple women came in. They were dressed in pastel pinks with blood-red aprons. "It's time for you to get up and bath." The first one said while the second one pulled Alice out of her bed.

Alice batted her away. "I can stand by myself thank you."

"You need to be bathed and dressed before you can have tea with the queen." The second one touched the ends of Alice's short hair. "You're filthy."

Alice wasn't going to argue, the lady was right. "I could use a good bath," she agreed. "But I wasn't aware that I was having tea with the queen."

"She insists that your last meal be with her."

There was something strangely morbid about that. Tea with Cerise was how her adventures in Fairy started, and tea with Cerise was how she was going to end it.

***

Washed, dressed in red, and irritated, Alice followed the two women into a large room. A fire roared at the left side while Cerise sat in a red wingback chair with a tea cup in her hand. Her guard stood at her back while Griffin stood behind the other chair.

Alice moved forward the red fabric clinging to her body almost like a second skin. She had insisted that she bring her cloak and her sword, though the cloak was slung over her arm. Her boots thumped against the floor as she made her way to the other chair. "Cerise."

"You will address her as my queen." The guard behind her said and Alice looked up at him and then to Cerise.

"She's not my queen. I'm mortal." She sat in the chair and Cerise leaned forward to put her tea cup on the table. She delicately picked up the tea pot and poured tea in the empty cup.

"It's alright Ace, Alice is unfamiliar with our ways, remember?" Cerise smiled. "Please, Alice, enjoy a cup of tea, before I have you taken to the arena."

Alice leaned forward and took the cup from her. "When I knew you, you weren't concerned with titles."

"Those days are over, Alice. Like I told you. I am to be queen over all of Fairy and that can't happen until you are dead and I don't have to worry about you ruining my plans." Cerise picked her tea cup back up and leaned back in her chair.

Alice swirled the tea in her cup. "Shame. Now that I'm an adult in the human world, I could come and go as I please." Alice glanced up at Cerise. "We could have tea parties and run around the city together."

"You didn't return until Devlin and Oriana lured you here again." Cerise stared into her cup.

Alice nodded. "The last time that I returned home, I tried to explain to my parents where I went, what the world was like, and that I still had hope my brother was alive. To them, I sounded like I was in psychosis or that I had created these illusions to deal with the trauma of being in a horrific accident with my brother." Alice frowned as memories of her mother sitting her down to explain what their next steps were. That she had to let go of the fantasies in her head if she wanted to be considered normal and move past her brother's death.

"You could have stayed here instead of returning home." Cerise pointed out. "We could have kept you safe here."

Alice raised a brow. "Your mother hated mortals, and I wouldn't have survived in the forest of Fairy as a mortal child. My parents put me in a hospital to help me. They put me through therapies and medications, and treatments to help me forget Fairy."

"And you forgot and never returned." Cerise shook her head. "And here we are now."

Alice let out a growl of frustration, wishing Cerise could see what was in her heart, what her truth was. Be like the Spinner who could sense intentions instead of a brick wall. "I never forgot about you or Fairy. I have drawings and writings all over my room at home about this world, about my time here. You are being childish, Cerise. Starting a war, sending me to the Jabberwock, all because I didn't return? Because I was incapable of coming back until now?"

"Because you are a mortal and you are a danger to Fairy and my rule over it." Cerise stood, her tea cup falling on the ground, forgotten. The shattering of porcelain was almost deafening. Alice met Cerise's gaze and frowned. "You never wanted to rule, Fairy. Your mother did. You're trying to walk in her footsteps, why? When did your heart get so corrupted that you're willing to kill innocent people?" She glanced at Griffin behind her and then back to Cerise. "That you were willing to use your powers to bind hearts?"

"That's not my magic," she whispered and sat down. "It's my mother's."

Alice raised a brow. "Your mother tied my brother's heart to Griffin's?"

Griffin jerked behind Alice. "Do not bring me into this."

"Griffin faced the Jabberwock because he was harboring your brother."

Alice's heart fell. "He survived the fall."

"Barely," Cerise sighed. "I found him and Griffin's house was the closest place. Griffin helped nurse him back to health."

Alice looked back at the hunter behind her. "You saved him."

"And then continued to hide him. Your brother was injured to the point that he couldn't have returned home and leave the help of Griffin's healer. My mother found out and Griffin paid the price. He faced the Jabberwock."

Griffin made a pained noise and Alice looked behind her. "What happened?"

"Your brother managed to get in the ring and..." Griffin turned pale, his eyes flashing to the hazel color of her brother's. "Alice...run." Griffin fell to his knees. "Run Alice. Don't do this."

"Your brother was bit by the Jabberwock." Cerise said standing. "My mother chose to punish them both by doing this to them." She waved at Griffin. "And then Griffin was to serve me and my mother as our hunter. No memory of who he was, tied to the heart of a human."

Alice swallowed. "That's horrible. Your mother is dead, Cerise. You could undo this spell. You could stop the suffering of those two." Her brother. Grief tore through her at the thought of not being there when he survived the fall, leaving him in Fairy. Visiting and not knowing that he had survived and faced such a terrible fate.

Cerise looked up at Alice. "I don't think you understand the strength of my mother's magic."

Dread filled Alice. "What did she do to you?"

Cerise turned away. "Take her back to her room."

"Cerise, wait."

Cerise stood up and threw her hand out. Magic wrapped around Alice, burning filled her lungs, squeezing. "I am your queen," she snarled. "Not Cerise, not your friend, your queen."

Alice gasped around the magic, clawing at her chest to try and get a breath in. Her head spun and her vision started fading. As the world went black, Alice swore that Cerise's eyes tightened in pain. Her friend had to still be in there.

When Alice woke, she found herself once again staring at the red fabric of the four-poster bed. Her lungs burned with every breath she took, but she could at least breathe. She sat up and put a hand to her head.

"Oh Alice," Kit purred, peeking his head up from his spot on her bed. "What did you do to anger her so much?"

Alice rubbed her eyes. "I asked her what her mother did. What are you doing here?"

"So you've noticed, that Cerise is more like her mother than she was before." Kit's fluffy tail flicked back and forth. "It would be best for a lot of us if her mother's magic was to fade."

Alice leaned forward. "You didn't answer my question, Kit. What are you doing here?"

"Well, Alice, if you must know." Kit stood and stretched, under him was a red jewel, about the size of Alice's palm. He batted it over to her and she picked it up. "My brother had me on an errand, said you needed this thing for some reason."

Alice frowned and picked the stone up. Power radiated from it, but a power she knew. It was the same magic she felt pull at her when she was at the Court of Creation. Her heart pounded as she realized what she was holding. Her mind focused on Kit's words. "Your brother?"

Kit nodded and scratched his ear. "Yes, Griffin."

"You never mentioned you had a brother."

Kit grinned, showing his pointy cat fangs. "No one asked. Griffin and I weren't close, I'm ashamed to say I wasn't there when he faced the Jabberwock." Kit's smile faded. "If I was and I was in my fae form, maybe things would have been different."

Alice sighed. "Now that I know what happened, I wish I was also around." Kit nudged her hand.

"Let's not dwell on the past though. There's a future in your hand." Kit rolled over and stretched out.

She looked down at the jewel in her hand. "I have no idea how to break the spell on this. I'm mortal."

Kit snorted. "If mortals had magic, what would you assume you'd have to do?"

"I don't know." Alice glanced at him. "Can't you just tell me?"

Kit let out a weird meow. "I wish I could Alice, but that's not how this works. Now, if you want to free him before your battle I suggest you think about the myths and stories you grew up on, because the human stories are based in our reality."

Alice pressed her lips together and sighed. "Blood, because for some reason it's always blood."

She put the stone down and drew her sword, and froze. Kit sat and stared up at her. "What's wrong Alice?"

"In the stories, they always slice their arms, but I need my arm for my fight."

She swore the cat rolled his eyes. "Try the finger?"

Alice glanced at the size of the jewel and then nodded. "I guess that will work as long as it doesn't have to be soaked in blood."

She slid her thumb across the blade and watched the blood well up in the cut. She wiped the blood on the jewel and waited.

Nothing happened. Alice sighed. "I don't know any magic words." She looked at Kit, who was focused on the stone.

A crack started crawling over the front of the stone and Alice stepped back, gripping her sword. The jewel shattered and there on the bed was Elken. He tossed his hair back showing off his pointed ears. His doublet was covered with swirls of black and white dancing together.

Alice stared at him as he smiled at her.

"Thank you, Alice." He stood and picked Kit up. "And you Kit."

Alice stared at him and then put her sword away. "Now what?" was the only thing she could think to say.

He laughed. "Now, you go and slay the Jabberwock. I'll see you at the end." He promised and him and Kit disappeared in a swirl of shadows.

Alice took a deep breath trying to recover from her shock of setting free the King of Creation when there was a knock on the door.

"Alice," Griffin's voice came from behind the closed door. "It's time."

She grabbed her cloak off the chair and put it on. "Believe in the impossible, Alice, and you can do anything. I just summoned the King of Creation from a jewel with my blood. I survived traveling all over Fairy to make it to the Court of Hearts. I am a mortal in the fae world. All of that is impossible. Yet here I am."

Griffin opened the door and offered her a small, sad smile. "Are you done with your affirmations?"

Alice nodded. "Yeah, I guess I am." She paused. "Is Brendyn really a part of you?"

Griffin nodded. "He is, until the magic breaks and then his heart, his soul, will be set free and go beyond the veil, truly."

"Does he know I love him? And that I didn't want to leave him behind."

Griffin smiled, truly this time. "He does, Alice, and he loves you very much. We're both rooting for you."

Alice stepped into the hall and Griffin shut the door at her back. "Then let's go kill the Jabberwock."

Griffin led her down the hall and down a flight of stairs. At the bottom waited guards dressed in black armor with red stripes across the front looking like claw marks. Marks of the Jabberwock she realized.

One stepped forward, his dark hair was pinned back in braids. His brown gaze met Alice's. "You are to come with us. The Queen's hunter is to watch by her side."

Alice moved away from Griffin and the man who had stepped forward grabbed her wrists pulling her toward the rest of the group. She tried not to stumble as the fae pulled her along and to the outside of the palace and down the stairs.

A black carriage with the same red marks sat at the bottom. The two horses to draw the carriage were also black. Alice swallowed.

"We'll bring your body back in the same carriage. It's easier to just use the mourning one to start with." The fae said as he shoved her into it and then slammed the door.

Alice tried to breathe as panic clutched her heart. Her hand wrapped around the sword and she prayed to any deity from the mortal realm or the fae world that would listen to her.

CHAPTER 21

Alice could hear the crowd from the tunnel she was in. Two of the Jabberwock guards stood by her, each with their hand wrapped around the top of her arm. As if she was going to run away.

There was no running from this though. The tunnel was closed off behind them as soon as they entered and the bars ahead of her led to the arena where she was going to face the beast.

She couldn't tell from the noise if the crowd wanted to see her dead or if they were cheering for her. Why would Fairy cheer for a mortal woman? The bars faded away, she assumed by magic, and the two guards guided her forward. Her heartbeat steady in her chest as she tried to walk with confidence. Tried to believe in the impossible. Seers could be wrong. She could survive this, but if she did, would Cerise be brought to her knees? Would Fairy be saved if Alice didn't die by the Jabberwock?

It was too late to try and change fate more, because after a few feet more, Alice stood looking up at Cerise on her throne, Griffin to her left and Ace to her right.

"Alice," Cerise's voice echoed over the crowd, amplified by her magic. The crowd hushed at the sound of Cerise's voice.

Alice looked around at the crowd. Different color of cloaks and clothes surrounded her, there was no telling who was from which court or if they were all from the Court of Hearts. She spotted no friends among the faces that stared back at her.

"You are here to face the Jabberwock because you dare come into the fae realm as a mortal, you conspired against me, trying to throw me from my throne."

Alice started to protest but the guard shook her as Cerise continued.

"The Seers foretell you falling to the Jabberwock, so let's see what fate has to deal you, Alice from the Mortal world." Cerise motioned and the guard moved away from her, leaving her in the middle of the arena.

The dirt was solid under her feet as she tried to make sure she was grounded. She turned around to watch the guards go back to the tunnel and the bars return.

The tall white walls around her led up to the crowd which she paid no more attention because above her in the blue sky came a screech that had her covering her ears.

A shadow of wings fell over her as the Jabberwock swooped in from the sky. She dodged to the side, rolling on the ground to avoid the claws of the beast when it landed.

She looked up at the maw of the Jabberwock as it opened it letting out another scream. Its teeth glinted in the light and drool dripped from the mouth, landing with a hiss on the ground. A nasty reminder that it was poison.

Alice drew her sword and spread her feet into the stance that she'd been practicing her entire time in Fairy. The Jabberwock reared its long neck back, displaying its scaleless underbelly.

She had been right. Now all she needed to do was get close enough to stab her sword through it. She launched herself forward, but the tail came around from her left. She jumped over it, landing on her feet, but it came back quicker, and swiped her down.

The spikes didn't touch her. That time. She jumped to her feet as the Jabberwock swiped down at her with its front claw.

Alice moved out of the way, but she knew she wasn't quick enough, and pulled her cloak up just as the claw tried to catch her side.

It skidded across the fabric creating a noise like fingernails on chalk board. Alice flinched at the noise, but dropped the cloak back down and moved away from the Jabberwock.

The crowd booed her and she tried to ignore them. Hundreds of people had come to see her die today, disappointed in the fact that she had managed to not be mauled by the Jabberwock's claws.

The beast took a step toward her, reaching out with its neck and snapping at her. She jumped away and swung downwards at the head, only for her sword to ricochet off the scales there.

The back part of the Jabberwock's from arm hit Alice, sending her flying across the ground. Her head pounded as she slowly got up.

Griffin wasn't kidding, this creature was fast and Alice was too slow. She needed to figure out how to get under it. She took a deep breath and ran toward it. It swiped down with its claw, but she slid under its upper body to its belly to avoid the claw. She positioned herself for a strike and thrust...

Claws wrapped around her and pulled her out from under. Had it not been for her cloak, the tips of the claws would have pieced her back.

The Jabberwock tossed her to the side, her sword flew from her hand as she hit the ground again. She pushed herself up on all fours, trying to remember how to breathe. The sword glinted in the sunlight on the other side of the Jabberwock.

Alice let out a curse as she stood. Her muscles protested and she knew she wouldn't be able to take any more throws from the beast, as it was, she could taste copper in her mouth. Every breath seemed to be harder than the last.

She had to get to her sword. She started circling around the

Jabberwock as it watched her. Half way there, it struck. Its mouth poised to strike her neck.

Alice held up her arm in an attempt to stop it. Its teeth clamped down on the gauntlet that Devlin had given her. A flash of green magic ignited at the impact.

The creature drew back with a screech of pain, rearing away from Alice. Her wrist burned and she struggled to get the gauntlet off quick enough as the poison ate through it. Alice dropped her arm and shot toward the sword, but the tail swiped her again, dragging her away from the sword.

Alice clambered to try and get over the edge of it, but failed, the tail running over her, a spike barely missing her.

The entire world seemed to slow down and then freeze. A shiver went up Alice's spine and she knew what had happened. She looked to her left and saw Oriana standing on the wall her hands held out.

"I can't hold everyone long enough. Get your sword and go. Do what you must, Alice," Oriana called. "Save our land."

Devlin stood behind Oriana his head held high. "Fight, my friend, we're with you."

Alice ran and swiped her sword up off the ground, just as Oriana's magic failed and the world started moving again.

She knew why the seer predicted her death. Alice ran toward the Jabberwock with all of her speed and slid under it again. It swiped at her again and snagged the cloak. Alice tore it off and continued her path. Its back foot stepped on her, trapping her against the hard dirt. The claws bit into her sides and she felt the poison eating at her already.

Believe in the impossible.

She cried out and slammed her blade into the belly of the Jabberwock. Warm sticky blood poured onto Alice from the wound.

The Jabberwock cried out and shot into the air away from Alice.

She lay on the ground panting. The pain in her body forced her vision to tunnel, the poison started to numb her sides. But she was alive. She used her sword to help her stand and looked up at Cerise.

Cerise held a hand to her mouth and Alice couldn't tell if it was in shock at what had happened to her or the Jabberwock, but she had to admit it was nice to not see the smug look on Cerise's face anymore.

Wind pounded down against the Alice as the Jabberwock beat its wings and started to come back for a landing. She managed to move away before its hind feet could trap her again.

Damn she thought she'd gotten it and it had gone off to die somewhere. But here it was...merely wobbling on its feet.

At least it looked as woozy as Alice felt. Alice took a deep breath and forced herself to focus on the creature. Adrenaline pumped through her as the creature took two shaky steps toward her.

Alice braced herself, rushing the creature would do no good right now. She doubted it would be stupid enough to let her do the same thing twice. It struck out at her again, but the whole body lurched forward and stumbled. Alice crouched down and drove the sword into the soft flesh at the base of the neck and the top of the chest.

Her heart pounded as the Jabberwock froze. She pulled the sword out and the beast stumbled to the side. Falling. The ground shook at her feet as the wings settled over the dead beast.

She looked at the glazed over eyes and waited for them to clear, but nothing happened. The Jabberwock didn't stir. Didn't breathe or cry out. It was dead.

Alice looked up at Cerise. "It's over." And then she cried out as she fell to the ground, her body burning from the inside out. She swore her blood boiled as she lay there in the arena in a pool of her and the Jabberwock's blood.

Someone cried out, but she couldn't pinpoint the voice. Her eyes tried to close, but she willed them to open when she heard footsteps at her side.

Red clad knees fell into her sight and Alice struggled to turn her head to see who they belonged to.

She met the pink eyes of the fae child she once knew. The girl in the red dress looked down at her, tears in her eyes.

"No, not like this." Cerise cupped Alice's face. "No, please, don't leave me."

Alice frowned and lifted a bloodied hand to Cerise's face, laying it against her cheek. "And the sins shall be forgiven with blood. You're free, Cerise." Alice ran her hand over the rose necklace at Cerise's throat. "Let your mother's magic go."

Alice's hand fell to the ground and Cerise let out a sob. How could she have been so foolish? How could she let this happen? She'd been so blinded by the power that her mother had left her. All she wanted was to rule Fairy and then maybe she'd be good enough for someone. For Alice. For her people.

And now the mortal lay dead in a pool of blood. Cerise put Alice's head in her lap and stroked her blood matted hair. "Please, come back to me," she begged.

"My queen?" Ace asked. "You need to leave." He held his hand out to her. "It shows weakness to the people for you to cry over the death of a mortal."

Cerise looked up at him and down at Alice. "I've made a terrible mistake."

"Even if you have, you must get up and leave." Ace pulled her up. "I'm worried the people might riot."

Cerise looked up at the silent crowd and then to the corpse of the Jabberwock. She nodded and took his hand. She turned away from the corpses and walked toward the tunnel.

"Hmm." A voice made her stop and she turned around to find Elken standing over Alice. Her first instinct was to tell him to get away from her, but he bent over her.

"What are you doing?" Cerise demanded, her voice shaking from the tears. She tried to take a step toward him, but Ace held her back.

The man looked at her. "Alice has fulfilled the prophecy, she's slain the Jabberwock, and brought the Red Queen to her knees, but I made her a deal, and I can't have her dead." He picked Alice up and looked at Cerise. "I will see you at the meeting of the Courts, because we all know war is coming. And not from the Court of Hearts, but from across the dark mountains." He disappeared with Alice and Cerise swore her heart shattered.

Ace pulled her toward the tunnel and the bars disappeared. "I will have the guards disperse the crowds, until then you will stay here with Griffin. You are not to leave this tunnel until I know it's safe."

Cerise nodded, feeling like a child, and having no words or energy to argue. She looked at Griffin. "It's time to let go of the magic." She looked at him. "Brendyn, I'm so sorry." She touched the blood on her cheek then wiped it over Griffin's heart. "You're free, both of you. I release you from our deal, Griffin." Her voice shook. The magic around Griffin shattered and he gasped, falling to his knee.

He looked up at her, his dark eyes swirling with the shadows of the Court of Creation. "Now, release my brother."

Cerise frowned. "I don't know who your brother is. If my mother has cursed him, it should be released."

Kit wandered from the shadow, his grin bright against the darkness of the tunnel. "I don't know; I rather like being a cat." He purred and rubbed against Cerise's leg. "I would make a good palace cat."

Cerise looked down at Kit and then up at Griffin. "Brothers?"

Griffin nodded. "Brothers. Now, free him."

She nodded and bent down, running her magic through him, breaking the powers the kept him in his cat form. Kit didn't change back to his fae form, he smiled at the two and disappeared.

Cerise closed her eyes. "Seven years of terror, of evil."

"You will have to work to undo it." This time the voice belonged to Devlin and him and Oriana walked down the tunnel. "To make amends to your people, to the other courts, to Alice." Devlin's voice was a hiss. "You will have to go to the mortal world and tell her parents she's dead. Deliver her body."

Cerise shook her head. "Another fae took her body."

Oriana's eyes widened. "Who?"

"I don't know him. He said he'd see me at the meeting of the Courts though."

Devlin looked at Oriana and then to Griffin. "No." The three of them said together.

"Who was it?" Cerise demanded. "Who took her body?"

Griffin met her gaze. "The King of Creation."

Everything hurt. From her pinky toe to the tips of her ears. Alice thought death wasn't supposed to hurt. But she swore someone stepped on her ribs...wait, the Jabberwock did that. She forced her eyes to open and stared up at Elken.

"A dream?" She asked.

He smiled down at her and shook his head. "No, Alice. Not a dream."

"I should be dead." She cringed as she tried to move. "The poison..."

"Has been taken from you," he said. "But you are still healing, those injuries will take time, even with my best healers. Even for a fae."

Alice stared at him. "I'm mortal. I should be dead." She swallowed. "Cerise...Cerise was holding me when I died."

He held his hand out. "Come with me."

She took a deep breath and took his hand. He helped her gently to the other side of the room. They walked by a wardrobe, a desk, and a vanity. By the time they'd gotten to the covered object on the other side of the room, her breath was labored, and she swore she was going to pass out.

But the moment Elken took the cloth off the mirror, her breath caught in her chest. Her heart skipped a beat, because what looked back at her, was her reflection, but something had changed.

She raised her hand to touch the tips of her pointed ears, her eyes swirled with colors instead of the brown that normally stared back her. Her hair also shifted between colors, from her brown to the gray of old age and every hue between. "This is impossible."

"This is Fairy, Alice, and when you're the King of Creation, nothing is impossible."

Alice turned to him. "You changed me to a fae?"

"To save your life, besides, like you said, mortals can't be queens, but now...you are." He bowed. "The Queen of the Court of Creation."

ABOUT THE AUTHOR

A.L. Kessler is best known for her paranormal "Here Witchy Witchy" series. A self-proclaimed coffee addict, she resides in Colorado Springs with her family and menagerie of animals. Although she writes mostly urban fantasy books, all of her books have a hint of magic. When she's not writing her next book, she loves to read and visit with friends and family.

To learn more about her, check out her website: http://www.amylkessler.com or follow her on Facebook: https://www.facebook.com/alkesslerauthor